Praise for

Finding Jake

"I devoured *Finding Jake*. The tension is almost unbearable in this thriller-cum-character study as layer after layer of a father's soul are revealed as reflected in the character of his missing son. Utterly engrossing." —Alice LaPlante, *New York Times* bestselling author of *Turn of Mind* and *Circle of Wives*

"*Finding Jake* is truly compelling. I read it in one sitting, tearing through the pages right to the unexpected ending—which stayed with me for days." —Paula Daly, author of *Keep Your Friends Close*

"A compelling read; disturbingly relevant in contemporary America." —*Kirkus Reviews*

"Reardon deftly builds suspense by setting his dual story lines on a collision course toward a shattering—and surprising—conclusion." —*Publishers Weekly*

"Reardon . . . beautifully captures the parental second-guessing that is magnified in times of crisis . . . [and] does an excellent job maintaining suspense throughout the book. The reader is afraid to know what she thinks she knows. Ultimately, what is revealed about Jake is unavoidable and unpredictably heartbreaking." —*Booklist*

"*Finding Jake* is compelling psychological suspense—but also so much more. A journey into the depths of a parent's worst nightmare, it is at turns heartbreaking, surprising, devastating, hopeful. . . . I'll be thinking about this one for a long time to come." —Alison Gaylin, *USA Today* bestselling author of *Stay With Me*

" 'Every mother's nightmare' is a phrase that comes up a lot in domestic suspense stories, but nightmares are hardly restricted to mothers. Bryan Reardon's first novel, *Finding Jake*, tells the harrowing tale of a deadly school shooting from a father's perspective, a twist that makes the story sadder and lonelier because, unlike mothers, fathers don't often have access to quality support systems. The suspense is killing, but it's nothing compared with this father's anguish as he tries to find his son—the real boy, not the one he thought he knew." —*New York Times Book Review*

"Readers will love this brilliantly paced book, which tries to answer all these fundamental, atavistic human questions of primal bereavement in tense, emotionally-wrenching narrative form that will leave readers questioning their own lives and the lives of those they think they know only too well." —Examiner.com

FINDING JAKE

FINDING JAKE

BRYAN REARDON

WILLIAM MORROW

An Imprint of HarperCollins*Publishers*

P.S.™ is a trademark of HarperCollins Publishers.

FINDING JAKE. Copyright © 2015 by Bryan Reardon. All rights reserved. Printed in the United States of America. No part of this book may be used or reproduced in any manner whatsoever without written permission except in the case of brief quotations embodied in critical articles and reviews. For information address HarperCollins Publishers, 195 Broadway, New York, NY 10007.

HarperCollins books may be purchased for educational, business, or sales promotional use. For information please e-mail the Special Markets Department at SPsales@ harpercollins.com.

A hardcover edition of this book was published in 2015 by William Morrow, an imprint of HarperCollins Publishers.

FIRST WILLIAM MORROW PAPERBACK EDITION PUBLISHED 2015.

Designed by Lisa Stokes

Library of Congress Cataloging-in-Publication Data has been applied for.

ISBN 978-0-06-233951-5

15 16 17 18 19   OV/RRD   10 9 8 7 6 5 4 3 2 1

With limitless love comes limitless worry . . .
To Lily and Ben, of course.

FINDING JAKE

PROLOGUE

My name is Simon Connolly. You may have heard of my son, Jake. Most people have, but they don't know him. Not really.

As for me, they don't know me, either. I'm not even sure why I'm still here. I can barely stand up, let alone venture beyond the front door. If I let such a simple effort beat me, I'm not sure what's left.

As I step outside, the sun warms the too-tight skin of my face. Although the air is gentle, inviting, the season has not changed. It remains the bleakest winter imaginable and the toes of my New Balance push dried leaves across the pavement. Each sound stirring memories too fresh to accept.

So much has happened that I struggle to envision the next day, the next hour even. But going to the mailbox draws my focus to a pinpoint intensity and gives me purpose. Neither necessity nor curiosity provides the motivation. On the contrary, my driving force is a last desperate attempt to embrace banality. Get the mail, I tell myself, like before.

I never could have imagined that an oversize purple envelope, resting in that box, could contain such a bright glimmer of hope. I don't even notice it until I am back inside; but, when I do see it, when my eyes focus and I read the name written on the front in young, bubbly script, my heart stutters. It is addressed to my son.

Maybe someone out there knows him better than I thought.

CHAPTER 1

JAKE: EIGHT MONTHS BEFORE HIS BIRTH

It all started with a fateful decision and the most wonderful news of my life, not necessarily in that order. On a gray day in late February, the kind of day that makes everyone wish Christmas lights still hung from their neighbors' tree branches, my wife called me at my office.

"I took it," she said.

I knew that by "it" she meant a pregnancy test. In the movies, the wife always calls saying I have to tell you something, brace yourself. In reality, my wife and I had been married for five years, and engaged for three before that. I'm not saying that I was so in tune with her womanly cycle that I knew she was late before she did. What I am saying is that there is much less surprise when it comes to married couples' privates than the movies like to admit.

"And," I said.

"Don't sound so excited." She laughed.

I cleared my throat and tried again in my effortless deadpan. "I feel like my heart is going to jump out of my chest."

"Cliché." She laughed even harder.

Only one person, my wife, knew I wanted to be a writer. An English minor in college, she felt compelled to critique me on occasion, but she was always unflaggingly supportive of this hidden dream of mine. She'd buy me "How to" writing books and fancy fountain-type pens for Valentine's Day.

"Caught again."

"Look, not by phone. Let's go get some lunch."

"Sure." I really just wanted to know if I was going to be a dad, but the suggestion of lunch pretty much clued me in on what I expected to be good news. "Where?"

"Fancy. How about Blue Coast? Noon?"

"I'll meet you at the restaurant. Love you."

"I love you, too, Simon. And I'm pregnant." She hung up.

I wanted to call her right back, to laugh and talk too loudly about the news, but I knew that wasn't how this had to work. My wife had an agenda. Not in a bad way, just a very deliberate way. This monumental news must be celebrated with a lavish meal and discussed in hushed tones while surrounded by opulence. This was not meant in a showy manner, more like an artist applying color to a canvas. She was painting our memory and I was all for it.

Blue Coast was about as hip a restaurant as Wilmington, Delaware, could support. Although it would be lost in the midrange mediocrity of a city like New York or Chicago, it tried its hardest and rose above the mom-and-pop Italian places and the vanilla chain restaurants that most of Delaware favored. Instead, Blue Coast had that not-quite-Wilmington look with its minimalist architecture and deep, rich, but subtle colors. Soft but modern alternative music piped through the hidden speakers and men and women in business suits sat at two-tops, some leaning forward and whispering intimately about love or money, others leaning back and scoping out the room to see who was who and who wasn't.

I met my wife there. She was already sitting at a table, her long, runner's legs crossed and her dexterous fingers tapping along on her BlackBerry. I stopped at the host stand and just watched her for a second. Dressed in a form-fitting suit jacket she'd bought in NYC and had tailored by a woman who lived in a trailer with her three young kids, she fit right in at the restaurant. The crease above her right eyebrow hinted at some struggle at work.

She was a lawyer for one of the three nationally prominent law offices in the city. Due to the corporate tax laws of Delaware, its chancery court was one of the most powerful in the U.S. judiciary system; therefore, the big boys set up shop here. She did not practice corporate law. Instead, she was a civil defense expert and the office's youngest local partner.

We met when she was still in law school. At that time, she was interning for the state's prominent U.S. senator and I was working for the county executive. I was his go-to guy, at least in my head, and was very busy that day. The Democratic presidential candidate was coming in to stump for votes. Not for himself, but for the candidate for Delaware's other U.S. Senate seat. The race was closer than anyone expected considering the Republican incumbent was well liked and hadn't been caught with his pants down, neither literally nor figuratively.

I was helping find volunteers to work the event and her name came up. I had never met her but one of the other guys there said she was the "best." At what, I didn't ask. Had I known what she looked like, I might have, because when she showed up that day all bets were off. She walked into the office in these form-fitting black pants and a T-shirt that kept offering the most suggestive peeks at her perfect abdomen. Her blond hair, shoulder length and sleekly straight, was pushed behind one tiny, cute ear. If I had called it cute that day, she would have written me off as a frat boy idiot. What caught my eye, though, was a perfectly shiny silver ball pierced through the cartilage halfway up the side of her ear.

"Who's that?" I had asked a buddy of mine.

"She's that intern from *the* senator's office. Goes to Villanova."

"Wow."

She claims that she heard me say that. I think that little tidbit became legend as she told and retold our love story over the years. Either way, our eyes met, as cheesy as it sounds, hers icy blue and mine dark as midnight. I followed her around the entire day. It got so bad that the presidential staff blacklisted me from further events because I pretty much ignored my duties and just shadowed her. By the end of the day she was in my web, or maybe it was the other way around.

Standing at the entrance to Wilmington's hippest lunch bistro, a tempest of contradictions swirled in my mind. There she sat, looking as amazingly beautiful as she did that first day we met. It was as if the cloying progress of time had no effect. At the same time, so much had changed. She, the fresh-faced new girl, the *intern*, was now a partner at a big-time law firm; me, the impressively young and successful leader of the day, was now the less impressively young and less successful bureaucrat who had stayed in the same position like my feet were encased in government-issued quick-dry cement.

Rachel looked up at that moment, seeing me and smiling. With a little wave, I walked across the restaurant. Along the way, I recognized people at a few of the tables.

"Hey, Connolly," a guy in a suit said. His name was Bob Weston. Although he worked for a bank, I'd met with him and his boss a few times about county tax issues.

"What's up, buddy?" I said, grabbing the hand he offered and patting him on the back while we shook. He craned his head. Most people have to, considering I'm six feet four inches tall. "You playing ball tonight?"

"I'll be there," I said.

"Me, too. Whadaya think of that new pitcher the Phils signed?"

I tried to give him a short answer, something about the fact that a single pitcher wasn't going to help them return to the glory of 1993. I glanced over my shoulder while I spoke, but Rachel was flipping through her calendar. Still, I hated keeping her waiting, so I closed up the conversation faster than I would normally and moved on. I nodded to a few other acquaintances and smiled when Rachel looked up again.

"Hey there," she said.

I'm not going to say she was glowing (cliché!), although some kind of warm energy seemed to radiate from Rachel's eyes when she met mine. I could tell she had been thinking, a lot. Something about the curve of her eyebrow made me smile. I pulled her to her feet and gave her a squeeze. Normally, on a workday, that would be all the PDA we would dare, but not today. I kissed her full-on, not a peck. When I pulled back, her cheeks flushed.

"Wow."

"I love you," I said. "You look so beautiful."

We sat down. I held on to her hand.

"How are you feeling?" I asked.

She grinned. "Same."

"Oh."

Rachel's head cocked to one side as she assessed my reaction. I thought I might have messed up. Maybe my inflection hadn't appropriately lifted or maybe my eyebrows betrayed me. Her grin became a smile, the one she gave me when I didn't exactly know what I had done but I knew it was good.

"What?" I asked.

"You just look happy."

And I was.

The first half hour of lunch consisted of banter over the best names for our child.

"Ben?" Rachel offered.

I shook my head. "Every time I hear you call him, I'll know you're picturing Ben Affleck without his shirt on. How about Simon? Then we could call him Junior."

"Cliché."

I laughed. "Do you want to find out if it's a boy or a girl?"

"I think so," she said. "Why not? It would give us time to do things right."

"You mean gender stereotyping?"

"Stop it." She smacked me on the forearm, lightly, lovingly, while she smiled.

As we spoke, I sensed something bigger behind her words. I've always been too observant of nuances. I knew it was best to ignore it, not to press her, but I've never been able to resist.

"What are you thinking about?"

"What do you think about day care?"

I blinked, two or three times, sensing a loaded question. I attempted to tread lightly. "It's great . . . for others?"

"Seriously."

Uh-oh. "What do you think?"

"Come on, Simon. We talked about this."

We had, I guess, in passing, maybe over drinks when we were twenty-four. I wondered if it was a husband thing, trying in vain to remember conversations deemed time wasters to *he* but paramount to *she*.

"Yeah, I mean, that's kind of . . ." I stopped myself, my senses tingling. I was about to say *up to you* at the end of that, but I had a sudden feeling that was not my best option. Instead, I finished with: ". . . what I was thinking."

"What were you thinking?"

"About day care." Then that little guy in my brain charged with digging up the hard-to-find stuff earned his room and board. "Like your nephew and niece. I mean, those kids are awesome. I think we should just cheat off them."

My wife's reaction calmed my nerves. I'd hit dead center in the sweet spot of marital communications, I could tell. I was so proud, until she continued.

"And my brother . . ."

Honestly, I didn't hear anything she said after that. Rachel's brother, soon-to-be Uncle Marky, was legend. A college football standout with shoulders wider than my, well, anything of mine, represented everything right about men of the new millennium. A successful midmanager in the corporate world with an MBA from Duke, he surprised everyone when he decided to stay home with his kids. His wife, a college associate professor, worked full-time. Mark went on to raise impeccably perfect little angels, a boy and a girl, while starting his own successful consulting firm.

"He's amazing," I said when I noticed the expectant silence. "Really."

"Financially," she said, which didn't make sense to me, probably because I missed something. "That's what I'm saying. What do you think?"

"About what?"

She frowned. "About staying home with the kids."

"Huh?"

I'm not a dull person. By dull, I mean I am not slow witted. I knew where she was going. Nor was my obfuscation meant to be humorous or disrespectful. Nor was I utterly surprised. My response represented a deep-rooted defense mechanism. In other words, I was scared out of my Dockers.

CHAPTER 2

DAY ONE: FIVE MINUTES AFTER THE SHOOTING

Jake's room is a mess. I asked him to clean it Sunday but he insisted it would have to wait. He ran off to a buddy's house and did not return until after dinner. I forgot to nag him; ergo, his room is still a mess.

Without thinking about it, I start to clean. My schedule is light today. Checking my phone for messages, I halfheartedly pluck dirty clothes off the floor. No new messages means a fade-away jumper from the top of the key. Swish, Jake's Lax shorts disappear inside the blue nylon hamper by the door. I lean down, grabbing hold of a textbook, and shake my head. Jake is always forgetting stuff, leaving homework or books at home, not taking his phone with him, leaving the cap off the toothpaste. All part of what makes him Jake.

Turning to place the book on his desk, I notice the cover: *Psychology 101*. Having been a psych major, nostalgia urges me, an otherwise nonsnoopy parent, to open the hardbound cover and leaf through the pages. I move toward the window for light and notice a torn-out spiral notebook page full of Jake's handwritten notes folded up inside. I pull it out but do not unfold the sheet. I face the age-old parental dilemma—to look or not. Giving myself a second to consider, I look out the window.

Although we own two acres, our house sits fairly close to the street. Two large, dark-leafed maples engulf the front yard, obscuring the view for most of the year. Opening the shades, which Jake always closes, I glance outside, my fingertip toying with the frayed edge of the paper.

The day is warm for November, making it easy to forget that Thanksgiving is only two and a half weeks away. Half of the maples' leaves have turned a steely brown and fallen. Half of that half I raked and dumped in the woods out back the week before last. A fresh layer of the dead foliage blankets the yard. I add that to my mental to-do list.

Maybe I should have noticed something amiss. I feel no ominous dread hanging over me or the house, or even Jake's messy room. That's what everyone always says, that they wake up the day of some tragedy and feel it coming. Not me. I am blindsided.

The first hint shows itself while I look out the window. The neighbor across the street and down two houses is the resident stay-at-home-mom-extraordinaire. I have referred to her as the mayor since Jake was about two years old, mostly because next to her, I felt like I raised my kids like we lived in a den in the woods somewhere. Standing at Jake's window, I see her car careen down the long driveway. She takes the ninety-degree turn onto the street without slowing, her maroon van with its bike rack on the roof literally tipping up on two wheels. The tires scream and she is gone, jetting out of sight down the tree-lined way.

At that instant, my cell phone dings, announcing a text. I startle, half tossing the psychology text onto Jake's desk and racing to our bedroom. I'm not sure why I react the way I do. I certainly have no idea what the message says, but something about the way the neighbor raced down the street fuels my pace as I rush out of the room.

My phone rests on the nightstand beside our bed. Putting the notebook page down, I scoop the phone up and read:

Shots have been fired at the high school. Calmly report to St. Michael's across Route 5.

I'm moving before I process what I read. The terse statement gives direction: report to St. Michael's. In times of utter chaos, the human mind responds to orders. It provides an avenue for action while our thoughts flash like a lightning storm.

At a run, I swipe my keys off the counter in the kitchen and I am out the back door. Crossing through the tight space between the front of my Ford pickup and the wall of the garage, my shin slams into our old bike rack. I don't feel it, nor does it slow me down. I am in the front seat, driving out of the neighborhood, careening through a stop sign, before I've processed anything but this direction.

It is not until I see other cars, driving as recklessly as my own, that I begin to understand. There has been a shooting at my kids' school. My kids, Laney and Jake, are at the school. My kids are in danger. I am not afraid. I am not worried. I am protective, animalistic in my instincts. I will do anything to keep my children out of danger. I will die to protect them. This is not bravado. It is simple fact.

CHAPTER 3

JAKE: AGE SEVENTEEN MONTHS, FIVE DAYS

I was a male lion. Scratching at my neck, I expected to run my hands through a silken mane, long and luxurious. When I yawned, I imagined the world could see my impressive canines. I would roar, call out across the Serengeti, exclaim my dominance, but it might wake Jake up.

That was how I felt being a stay-at-home dad of a seventeen-month-old. From the day at Blue Coast when I agreed to shift my career and take care of a baby, my baby, that is, I lost myself. At first, I reveled in the idea of never having to wear a suit again. That joy, however, was surprisingly fleeting. I never realized how much I'd miss seeing the cast of characters that make up an office. I also did not realize how much I identified with my job, or how much my job identified me. I had started to pick up small writing assignments, but it was not the same. That may sound dramatic, but a stay-at-home dad can trend toward sounding that way.

At the same time, I had missed nothing of my son's life. I sat on the floor with him when he first sat up. I remembered that day so well, watching his little muscles tense and that now-familiar expression of stubborn intent cross his perfect little face. Even better, that bright smile of accomplishment that radiated once he made it up. When Rachel came home, I never told her about it. Instead, when he sat up an hour later, she got so excited.

"Simon," she had squealed. "Jakey just sat up for the first time."

I entered the room and made a big show of it.

"Oh my God," I had said. "Are you sure? Did you help him? That's amazing."

I did, technically speaking, lie to my wife, but it made her so happy thinking she'd been there for the big moment. Plus, it wasn't like Jake was old enough to catch me yet.

Shaking the memory out of my head, I decided to check on Jake. He slept in his car seat in the living room. Shoeless, I padded across the kitchen and onto the hardwood of the foyer. A hand on the wall, I peeked around the corner. He was exactly where I'd left him, still snugly buckled in after our short drive. He fell asleep only in the car. At least that is what I had decided. So I drove him for about five minutes at nap time. Once asleep, I headed home, easing the seat out of its frame and gingerly carrying him inside. He had been asleep for about half an hour, although those minutes passed like seconds.

He stirred, his little hands jolting up like a maestro conducting an orchestra. That used to freak me out so I asked the doctor about it. He said it was some kind of startle reflex all kids have. That was good enough for me.

I stared for a moment longer. Although each minute Jake slept floated like a little island oasis, I lingered, smiling. He had his mom's hair, straight, wispy, and streaked with subtle auburns and haystack yellows. Luckily, he had her eyes, too. When awake and open, they shined with such a unique blue that I found myself locked on to them at times, lost in their tiny perfection. His coloring, though, was all his dad's. I liked to call it black Irish.

The moment passed and I backed out of the foyer. In the den, I left the television on but muted. *Big Cat Diary* was on. I'd seen the episode at least four times but I settled down, Indian style, on the earth-tone shag carpet and watched.

The sound of Jake waking up, a soft warble usually accompanied by the most adorable scrunched-up expression, lifted me off the carpet. I have no idea how long I sat there transfixed by the screen. If nap time translated into pure gold, I would have wondered why I squandered it just sitting there, but I was too tired to really think about it. Instead, I answered to Jake's soft call and freed him from his seat. He clung to my neck as I walked him back out to the den. I placed him down. He immediately toddled to the corner by the ragged olive green couch my wife and I had owned since our first apartment.

"Ball," he said.

Jake picked up a tiny, soft football. He threw it at my head and squealed. When I picked it up, he raced (maybe "raced" is a bit strong, more like stumbled) at me, launching his tiny body, a perfect shoulder tackle. I fell back, exaggerating, and he screamed, then we laughed together until he got the hiccups. That never stopped Jake. He launched himself again and again, screaming and laughing and hiccupping louder each time. At one point, I swept him up in a huge hug. He squirmed out and went back to the game.

This went on for about twenty minutes, each successive tackle less exaggerated. By the end, I'll admit that I barely flinched when he landed in my lap. My eyes went up to the screen. Another episode of *Big Cat Diary* had started. I watched it, still muted, while Jake crawled all over me. Rolling onto my side, I felt exhausted, a yawn letting loose as I scratched my neck. Let the women hunt. Right?

"What time will you be home?" I asked Rachel later that evening.

I could hear her shuffling paper on the other end of the line. I reminisced. Shuffling paper had been so great. I missed it horribly.

"Regular time," she answered.

It was about four o'clock. Slipping a light jacket on my son, I held his hand as we walked out into the garage. I stowed the stroller in the truck when not in use. As I fished it out, Jake wandered onto the wide area of the driveway. He toddled back and pulled a small basketball out of a bin in the corner while I yanked at the lever that supposedly opened the confounding stroller.

"Don't pick that up," I called out when I saw that the ball had been replaced by a small rock. "Not in the mouth."

Jake smiled, as if my words gave him an excellent idea. He brought the pudgy little hand holding the rock up to his lips. His mouth stayed closed as he looked me in the eye.

"No," I said.

Someone laughed, startling me. All of a sudden the woman from across the street and down two houses, Karen Brown, appeared in my driveway.

"Jakey, that is going to taste awful, sweetie."

Jake lowered the rock. I glanced at him and then at the neighbor. I never would have dreamed of phrasing it that artfully. "Oh, hey."

"Hi," she said.

Karen Brown had sharp, birdlike features and wore her black, straight hair pulled back in a bedazzled hairband. Her clothes clashed with my running attire. She wore an expensive pair of perfectly fitting jeans and a warm-looking, tailored blue blazer. Her socks were thick and woolly. This was obvious because she wore Birkenstock sandals over them.

"That's a good boy." I wasn't sure if she was talking to me or Jake.

Jake turned his attention to Bo, Karen's boy, her first and what she openly admitted to being her last child. He was a year older than Jake. Regardless, when Jake stomped toward him, Bo backed away. Karen, ignoring her son's obvious discomfort, walked over to me. I didn't say anything as Jake chased Bo into the yard, but I didn't take my eyes off my son, either.

"How are you and Rachel settling in?" she asked.

We had moved into the house about a month before, leaving behind our modernized twin in downtown Wilmington, the starter home we bought a year after getting married. With its exposed brick walls and impossibly narrow kitchen, it remained a beacon of our pre-kids life. I had to look away from Karen because my mind took me back to that time. I could almost see Rachel and I fixing a post-party-in-Philly snack, the mundane act of food preparation transforming into a sensuous dance, our bodies swaying smoothly in the tight space, the food left half finished and clothes left in a haphazard trail leading to wherever we felt like culminating the night.

The spontaneity of such moments seemed so distant, replaced by the reality of child rearing. Although Rachel had thought it was an awful idea to move with a sixteen-month-old, I pushed it, unable to fathom raising kids in the city. We needed to live in a better school district. She had protested, saying something about Jake not starting public school for three years, but I locked on and would not let go. Jake had to go to a good school in a safe community. My tenacity somehow led to that moment, me standing in the driveway reminiscing about the torrid days of old while returning my gaze to the slightly confused eyes of a stay-at-home mom.

"Pretty well," I answered.

"Great. Don't you just love the neighborhood? Sue, who used to live in your house, did you meet her? Well, she misses it terribly."

"I met her at our closing. Didn't she move down Route Five, closer to the high school?"

"Yeah," Karen said. "But she's really unhappy. Says the neighbors don't even talk. We are so lucky."

I wasn't sure what to say to that. I, for one, could go days (maybe weeks) without talking to the neighbors. Not that I disliked them. There were days I could go without talking to anyone, a new trait that expressed itself since I'd left the office. Conversations at work, whether about the job or not, had been simple. In the suburbs, though, the same exchanges left me either confused or apologetic.

Rachel said it was due to the fact that I had no ability to talk about women's issues. I figured the answer couldn't be so simple, because talking to the men came no easier. She could still be right. The truth was that I didn't walk either path anymore, not fully. I certainly was not a woman, yet sometimes I didn't feel too much like a man, either.

As expected, the other women did not seem to share this condition. They prattled on about this and that, much as I had in the office, without seeming to stumble. Their conversations hung like riddles, so obvious to the tellers yet so utterly befuddling to me.

"I bet it's nice being closer to the school, though," I finally added, talking about Sue's move.

Karen looked over my head, as if my words hung floating in a little comic bubble. With a shrug, she made eye contact again. "Are you all unpacked?"

Jake picked up a stick. He didn't swing it at Bo, but Bo screamed and ran toward his mother. My son must have thought that was funny because he gave chase, again.

"Jake."

I used my fatherly tone. Karen startled and Jake froze.

"Whoa," she said, laughing uncomfortably, Bo clinging to her leg.

My brain hurt. I wondered if that *whoa* had been directed at Jake, at his stick, or at my fatherly tone.

"Sorry about that," I said. "He's a little feisty today."

"No problem. So, are you all done decorating?"

Later on, after I went inside, I wondered if she wanted me to invite her in. I'm sure that's what a normal mom would do. At the time, I felt oddly uneasy and just answered her.

"Rachel is moving along. The house is a little country for her, but she's trying to modern it up."

Karen chortled. "If you don't like country, why'd you buy this house?"

The house was a twenty-seven-year-old colonial with light green siding and black shutters. Rooms blocked off the layout, unlike the open areas common in newer houses. Her question, however, seemed pointless to me.

"The schools," I said.

"Oh," she answered, once again staring at that comic bubble over my head.

Rachel arrived home at six fifteen that night. Jake and I stood in the den, dressed and ready to go to Rachel's sister's for dinner.

"Getting home early, huh?"

I didn't mean to sound snide, but her tardiness left me stressed. Really, it wasn't that she was late. I just wanted her to call and let me know. I had used up all my ideas for how to entertain Jake. I could have put a show on but I didn't want Rachel to come home and see him plopped in front of the tube.

"Sorry. I got caught by someone as I was walking out. I just couldn't get them to shut up."

I didn't say anything.

"What?" she asked.

"Nothing."

"What?"

"You could have called."

"I said sorry, Simon. I mean it. I feel awful."

I remembered how that kind of stuff happened all the time at the office. Unfortunately, it had been a long day and I was tired. We packed up the car and drove to her sister's house mostly in silence. I decided I should tell her about Jake's day. That eased the mood and by the time we arrived, everything flowed again.

Once there, Rachel slipped into the kitchen with her sister and I sat down on the couch next to Uncle Marky. His youngest, eight-year-old Connor, looked like Gulliver next to my Jake's Lilliputian. I slipped to the edge of my seat, sure every move Connor made would crush my son's skull or break his arm. I thought Mark sensed my discomfort. He smiled.

"How's it going?" he asked.

"Okay."

"I mean, staying home. It's tough, huh?"

I looked at him, debating. I sensed his desire to connect with me on a common ground. At the same time, I hesitated. For some reason, I felt guarded. Sometimes, I just didn't want to admit it was tough.

"No, it's good," I said. "I was teaching Jake how to crossover today."

Mark laughed. "A regular Allen Iverson."

"You got that right."

I could see Mark wanted more. For an instant, I actually thought about opening up. This man had endured my life already. Mark could be an invaluable resource. At that moment, I simply was not up for it.

"Dude," he said, "I get it. When the kids were little, I never wanted to talk about it, either. People would come up to me and say, *Hey, so-and-so is a stay-at-home dad, too. You two should hang out.* I never took them up on the offer."

"Why not?" I asked, some of my guardedness fading.

"I honestly have no idea."

Hearing him say that was so liberating. "I get it. Sometimes, when I talk, I feel like all that comes out is the tough stuff about staying home. But it's not all bad. It's just really different."

"Exactly." With an effortless turn of the head, he called out to his son, Connor. "Don't touch that."

I laughed. "Eyes in the back of the head."

He nodded.

For a moment in time, I felt totally understood.

On the ride home, I told Rachel about my exchange with Karen that morning.

"Maybe Karen was offended by that school comment."

"Why?"

She laughed, but not in a mocking way. "We don't all think like you. Karen did not decide to live in her house, invest in her neighbors, buy into the *village* because of a simple, logical thought. To her, it's bigger than that, but more ethereal. It is about community, and safety, and belonging. It's about totally loving where she has decided to raise her children. By simplifying it like you do, it makes her think that none of the stuff that is so important to her matters even one bit to you."

"Huh?"

She laughed. "I'm just trying to help."

When we got home, I carried Jake, fast asleep, up to his room. He stirred but did not wake when I laid him gently down among his warm blankets and plush toys. I stood there, watching him for a moment, taking in the amazing fact of his existence. Rachel appeared at my side and grabbed my hand. We stood there for so long, like we were afraid to let that perfect moment pass.

Eventually, we tore ourselves away and padded to our bedroom. Rachel snuggled under the covers, the light on and a book on her raised knees. I got ready for bed, thinking about the night, about our conversation in the car, and finally the fight we'd had when Rachel got home from work. I decided I should apologize.

"Hey, sorry about giving you the business this evening."

"Which time?" she said, winking.

"When you got home from work."

I climbed into my side of the bed and she turned off her light. Neither of us moved. The silence seemed strange, not unpleasant, just not that common since we'd had Jake. I enjoyed it for a moment, then inched closer to my wife.

"How was work today?" I whispered.

She sighed. "Okay."

In a quiet tone, she told me a story about a secretary who couldn't get along with one of the new lawyers. I listened, and responded, and as she spoke, I put my arm around her. She nudged closer to me and I marveled at how graceful she was.

"How are you doing?" she asked after her tale ended.

"I'm okay. That is, when I'm not pissing off the neighbors."

She ran her hands through my hair. It felt good, reminiscent really.

"You're a great mom," I said from out of nowhere. The comment had not been planned out. It just appeared in my mind when I pictured her carrying Jake around before dinner that evening. He smiled at her when she kissed his cheeks. It had been such a real moment, beautiful and warm.

She moved again, this time her arms enfolding me. Her head rested on my chest. The warmth spread out from her, holding me tighter than her arms ever could. We kissed. Tentatively at first, as if it had been months. She whispered my name and I pulled her tighter to me, feeling her warmth spread even farther across my body as the stresses of life vanished.

I slipped the T-shirt she wore over her head. Our bare skin touched in that wonderful way, that surging instant that settles too quickly but leaves you wanting it over and over again.

"Mommydaddy."

Jake's call poured over Rachel like a cold shower. She pulled away, one becoming two again.

"Oh God," she said, guilt behind her words.

"I'll get him," I said.

"No, I want to. I just . . ."

Rachel got up and grabbed her T-shirt. I could see the flush of her cheeks receding as she covered herself and hurried out of the room. I leaned back, listening to her soothing voice as she comforted our son. To be honest, I felt torn. Part of me felt warm hearing just how great a mother Rachel was. Another part of me, a part I was not proud of, had a different thought. That part wished he hadn't woken up.

CHAPTER 4

Cars, all facing the same direction, jam the two-lane road leading to the school's entrance. Drivers lurch out of doors left open and run between the eerily still vehicles toward a bank of flashing lights, painting panicked faces in vibrant reds, yellows, and oranges.

I slam to a stop behind a white Ford Explorer, same year as my truck. The line of vehicles stretches for at least half a mile. Cars pile in behind mine as I jump out and race toward the school. Police have cordoned off the drive that runs up a steep hill to the entrance. A mob of parents, a vast majority being mothers, pack in, pressing against the yellow hazard tape. High-pitched questions merge, forming a shrill and frightening white noise that fills the air long before I arrive.

Without thinking, I run off the road and cut through the field that spreads toward the side of the school. Breaking into a sprint, I ignore the heated shouts telling me to stop. I have to get up there, to stop this madness. A drainage trench that leads to a storm-water retention basin runs parallel to the street. I leap over it. Before I take two more steps, a strong grip locks onto my bicep. Momentum swings me around and I face a large man in full body armor, SWAT emblazoned across his chest. He holds what looks like an automatic rifle in his other hand. I cannot see his face through the tinted visor attached to a black helmet.

"Down," he orders.

His voice is neither angry nor soft. I drop to the ground. An instant later, another officer, this one in a Delaware State Police uniform, appears. He lifts me off the ground and ushers me back across the gully.

"Sir, I understand you are worried about your child, but you have to be calm. We are asking all the parents to congregate inside St. Michael's, across the street. We will brief everyone once we have news."

A loud pop echoes down from above. The officer thrusts himself between me and the school, thinking it gunfire. I freeze, staring over his shoulder, my heart flailing against my chest. He must decide it is not, because his stance eases. From over his shoulder, I can see up to the school. A police officer comes out of the gym exit. Even from that distance I can see he is wearing surgical gloves. They are stained red with blood.

The officer pushes me and I move. A hook and ladder rolls up on the grassy shoulder and turns onto the drive. As it passes, I see the firefighters are wearing body armor over deep blue uniforms.

The noise becomes overwhelming. Hundreds of people shouting, talking, crying, and screaming. I cover one ear with a hand and stagger along beside the officer. The scene appears jagged and torn. Cruisers are parked at haphazard angles. People sway and move in jerky fits, and it's as if I can see some awful disease spreading through the mob. I am led through a throng of mothers; one reaches out for the officer's arm. He brushes her off, briskly, and takes me to the entrance of the church.

"Go inside. Sit down. Understand?"

I nod, but my attention focuses on a woman standing next to me.

She leans against the sign for the church. Her body language telegraphs an inappropriate calm. I feel physically uncomfortable looking at the slope of her back and the way her feet are crossed. Then I see her eyes. They are the eyes of a ghost, a shell of a human. Damp tracks run down both of her cheeks and I am left wondering, *What is she seeing that I am not?*

The church is now full. Minutes pass like hours. At first, no one speaks. We sit in the pews, shock spreading like a yawn. The woman next to me glances up at one point and quickly looks away. I do not know her. I watch as she scans the congregation (as it is). With a brisk wave, she moves, scurrying like someone bent at the waist to avoid the blades of a helicopter. She settles in beside another woman. They hug.

One other man waits. He stands in the corner by the door. I nod to him and he nods back. Minutes pass again.

After a while, the gossip starts. It is not everyone, only a few. I hear snippets of news, although I cannot fathom how any of them have heard anything.

"The science labs," I hear.

My mind races. Jake is in AP chemistry. He has lab almost every day. My stomach rolls when I realize it is about this time. I have to remind myself that these mothers cannot know anything yet. No officer has entered the church since I arrived.

I can take it no longer. I stand, stretching my legs as a pretense, but approach the other man. His name is Steve Yants. His son played Little League with Jake. I lean against the wall beside him. Neither of us speaks. What is there to say?

"Have you heard anything?" I finally ask.

He shakes his head.

"They said something about the science labs," I add.

He shrugs. "You know how they are."

I understand what he is saying. He's not talking about *moms*. He's talking about those parents who tend toward being know-it-alls, the ones who speak first (and most often). I chose not to mention that those same parents did tend to know things long before I did.

This makes me think of Karen. She had peeled out of her driveway before I received the text. I assumed the system had to progress through the distribution list, so some would hear before others. When I looked around the church, though, I couldn't find her anywhere.

I decide to go back to the pews. I try to find the words to use in exiting, but there is nothing. If I let myself speak, something totally inappropriate would come out, something like: *Good luck*. So I just walk away.

Once I sit, the door opens behind me. I turn to see Karen and three other women from my neighborhood walk into the church. Their heads are huddled together. Others notice their arrival. I debate getting up, going to them, and asking what they know. I don't. I want to, but my body feels so heavy. My surge of adrenaline is gone. I was unable to protect and I find myself ill-equipped for whatever it is we are now doing.

They proceed to the front of the church and merge with a larger pod of moms. Karen scans the rows of seats. She is looking for something. Her attention pauses on me. I am about to wave, but her expression is strange. She recoils maybe. Or is it all in my head? Whatever it might be, the moment passes. Her eyes continue to scan and I continue to feel permanently attached to the wooden bench.

"Are you okay?" the woman to my left asks. I think she might be the mom of a girl my daughter Laney knows.

"Yeah, sure," I begin to say, but notice she is staring at my hand. It rests on the shining veneer of the pew, although "rests" is a poor description. My hand, in fact, is twitching. I realize my thigh is as well.

The woman looks scared for me.

"Well," I stammer. "I mean, you know . . ."

"There's a paramedic by the door. Do you want me to call him over?"

"No, why?" I ask.

"You don't look—"

"I'm fine, really. Thanks."

I turn away from her, confused.

I realize I have not contacted Rachel. I struggle to remove the phone from the front pocket of my jeans. My fingers feel swollen as I dial, although they appear normal. By rote, I call her office. No one answers.

When I disconnect the call, the ringer sounds. Rachel's cell number shows up on the screen.

"Where are you!" she blurts out when I answer.

"Something awful has happened," I mutter.

"I know. The radio. Why didn't the school call me? When did you . . . Where are you? Where are the kids?"

"I'm waiting for them. I tried to get up to the school but they stopped me."

The line crackles. "Are they okay?"

"I'm sure they are."

"Simon, the radio is saying that at least thirteen kids have been shot."

My mind tricked me. I had blocked out the scene earlier, the police officer with the blood-stained hands. Swallowing hard, I close my eyes and lower my head. The sensation intensifies. At the same time, my pragmatic mind figures the odds. Thirteen out of two hundred or so kids. Less than one in ten.

"Simon? Are you there?"

"Yeah. I'm waiting for them."

"At St. Michael's?"

I nod, not considering the fact that she can't see me.

"I'm on my way," she says. The line goes dead.

I need to move. They expect me to sit in a pew and wait. Although the other parents, the moms, seem able to follow this direction, I cannot. I slide out of the church pew and pace. I walk from one end of the church to the other, following the outer walls of the building. By the time I reach the exit for a second time, pacing is no longer enough. I push the door open.

The sounds outside assault us all. Sirens scream and male voices bark out orders. I hear the idling engine of a hook and ladder and see it coming back down the school drive, leaving. I scan the police, looking for answers, but find nothing but chaos.

"Sir," someone says to my right. I turn to see a uniformed officer stepping up to me. He looks stern, unforgiving.

"What's happening? When—"

"Back inside, now," he orders.

I do not move. He grabs my arm. I turn to face him. As I do, I catch a glimpse of one of the moms in the back row of the church. She stares out at me with a face pale from fear and disbelief. I lock eyes with her, and the drive that fueled my action vanishes. I let the officer guide me back inside. He gives me a stern yet quiet talking-to, the words lost to my spinning consciousness. Instead, the looks of the other parents chide me and I realize that the sudden shock of the outside world, that demon I let inside by opening the door, caused them pain. I walk away from the officer and sit down. He shakes his head and returns to his post outside.

The first child arrives less than half an hour later and everything changes. Hope and prayer had buoyed the church up until the door opens and Scotty Truphant (he probably goes by Scott now, but I coached him in basketball when he was seven; he was Scotty then) walks in. A half dozen other kids enter, flanked by SWAT officers. They point their assault rifles at the ground. I notice this because I've already realized none of the kids are mine, so I have to look at something or I'll be up again, pacing.

By that time, the crowd in the church had swelled past capacity. Dads, mostly in business suits, stand with their wives. The parents of the kids, including Scotty's mom and dad, race up the aisle, engulfing their kids with abandon. Tears flow. Their sobbing hangs over the rest of us like ugly green jealousy. No one admits it. We all stare at the floor, waiting for the doors to open up again.

The officers usher the reunited loved ones out the back through the vestry. Soon, the front doors open again and more children are ushered in. I act happy for the parents in front of me when their daughter enters. But all I can think about is Laney and Jake.

I agonize as the crowd in the church thins. I should not feel jealous or bitter. In reality such emotions, those words, mean nothing in that moment. The storm of dread, the torture of time passing, it permeates my cells, turning me inside out molecule by molecule. I can act happy for those parents but that's just not real.

More reunions spring to life before my eyes and the pews empty. Hundreds diminish to tens. None of us, the remaining, makes eye contact. When the next child arrives, I stop watching the door. At this instant my parental intuition fires. I know something awful has happened.

Rachel bursts into the church. I blink, because Laney appears with her, attached to her side. I stand and race to my daughter . . . and to my wife. I embrace them both, engulfing Laney, finally able to protect. From what, I am still unsure.

I stare into my daughter's eyes, so thankful that she is okay, trying to convince myself that she is standing right before me, that this is not some kind of illusion. My heart races and I feel the blood throbbing through my body. Half of my nightmare dissipates. Laney is okay.

I look to Rachel. In her crisp lawyer's suit, she is a beacon of confidence. I am now in awe of her ability to find Laney. Then I look in her eyes and I see the truth of it.

"Where's Jake?" I ask.

Laney looks up at me with an expression I have seen before but never understood. Rachel pulls my daughter closer. She whispers something to her that I do not hear.

"I don't know," Laney says.

Rachel pulls back, looks at Laney. "It's okay. It's okay."

That is when I notice Laney is pale. I touch her forehead; her skin is clammy.

"She's in shock," I tell Rachel, who nods.

A paramedic approaches us. He reaches out, gently, moving as I imagine an angel might. His eyes meet mine. They are soft and understanding. Rachel moves a little, making space for this man who is a stranger, who now parts my family, and we are thankful for it. He places a blanket on Laney's shoulders.

"I'm just going to take you out back. Have you sit down for a little while before you leave."

"My mom," Laney sobs.

My throat tightens at the sound. My girl needs protection. I can hear it.

"Wait here," Rachel tells me. "Jake . . ."

They are gone and I am alone again. I shouldn't, but I count the families waiting. Fourteen.

A man in pleated polyester pants and an outdated tie walks through the door next. He looks vaguely familiar with his tinted glasses and thinning hair. I watch as the man walks up and sits down beside me.

"You're Simon Connolly?" The man extends a hand. "I'm Phil Hartman, the school guidance counselor."

I had talked to Phil before but never in person. I remember the first time his name came up, after Jake had been called to the office for something. I had laughed, telling Jake why the name was funny. I showed him an old *Saturday Night Live* best-of disc, the one with Phil Hartman playing Frankenstein. I learned later that Jake went to school the next day with the disc. He showed the entire class. He and Phil had not seen eye to eye since.

"Where's Jake?"

It comes out as a demand. I find myself pushing closer to Phil, my chest out. I almost step on his foot.

"It's okay," Phil assures, looking up at me, taking a step back. I know it isn't, though. "I just needed to speak with you. As a precaution, I've reached out to the elementary school. You might remember that all of the children were fingerprinted back then, in case of abduction."

My head spins. "Abduction?"

"I know. It was a long time ago," he says.

"What are you talking about?" I snap.

"Just a precaution. Anyway, I wondered if you would be willing to sign a release. Seems the local authorities never received Jake's card from the school. This will allow us to send it to them. Is that something you will do?"

"Sure," I say.

The release dangles from a clipboard. Phil holds it on his lap as I sign. When I look up, he is staring at me in an odd way. My eyes narrow and he looks away. I notice his hand trembling.

"Thanks," he mutters, getting up to leave.

"Is there any word on Jake? Do you know anything?"

He does not turn. "Not yet."

Phil walks out the front door, the first person to do that since I arrived. It seems too familiar to me, and the first suspicion creeps into my mind. Prints are used to identify bodies. Or to investigate crimes.

"No," I whisper.

One of the parents, a mom I do not know, cringes and moves farther down the pew, away from me. It seems I am a disease, and I am spreading.

CHAPTER 5

We were forty-five minutes north of Rachel's parents' beach house when Laney began to scream. Born with an ear-shattering, James Brown–like wail, no one could ignore our daughter when she let loose.

"What could it be?" I asked.

Rachel sounded exhausted. "Don't know. Maybe her diaper."

Before deciding to make the two-hour trip to the shore, we debated whether a four-month-old and a long drive mixed. At that moment, my ears believed not so much.

I pulled the car into a church parking lot directly off the highway. Rachel jumped out and checked Laney, but her diaper was fine. Once out of her car seat, our daughter quieted down. When we decided to start back up, everything seemed okay. Not one hundred yards down the highway, however, Laney began to scream again.

After ten minutes, Jake, his hands over his ears, had had enough.

"Maybe she hates the beach?"

A three-year-old's innocuous question rocked my world. Not born a beach person? Something about the ocean, the salty air, or maybe the calming sound of the surf bored deeply into my soul the first time Rachel took me to her parents' place. I felt more myself there than anywhere else. I think my reaction was one of the reasons she ended up marrying me.

In fact, I asked Rachel to marry me one night as we walked along the beach. Having dated for only ten months, the question popped out spontaneously (meaning no ring). As she looked out at the ocean and pointed out sparkling mermaids capping the distant waves, I dropped to a knee.

"Will you marry me?"

Rachel looked down, her eyes at once surprised and expectant. She took mere seconds to decide.

"Yes."

I think my head bobbed back. "Are you sure?"

She nodded.

"I mean, I don't want to pressure you."

She laughed. Somehow, she, too, read my thoughts. This was no second-guessing, it was simply my nature. At the time, Rachel had just celebrated her twenty-fourth birthday.

We laughed and held hands, walking the beach for another hour. We spoke, but our words held little importance. Instead, we settled into the new reality of being engaged.

Back at the house, we slipped into the bedroom Rachel shared with her sister-in-law who was drinking wine with the rest of the crew on the back porch. Rachel climbed into bed and I leaned in close. My stomach tied in knots.

"Are you sure?"

"I am," she answered, her eyes as bright as the full moon outside the bedroom window.

"Should we tell everyone?" I whispered.

"Tomorrow," she said.

"If you wake up and think this is crazy, I'll understand. Okay?"

She kissed me. "Good night Simon."

I smiled. "Good night, fiancée."

The next morning, we huddled. Rachel spoke first.

"Was that real?"

My ever-revving mind fixated on the dichotomy of my emotions. I felt too young for such an adult moment, but I felt too old to feel as giddy and as nervous as I did.

"I think so," I answered.

Just like that, Rachel and I decided to get married.

Thankfully, Jake, from day one, loved the beach as much as we did. He and I often rushed down early on Fridays while Rachel had to work. We'd reach the house and barely go inside before trekking the few blocks down to the sand. Playing, laughing, and wandering aimlessly along the near-deserted, off-season coast, at times our eyes would meet and even before he could speak, the mutual love was as clear as any sentence could be.

When I called Rachel those evenings, I would lie about the weather. "It was windy. The sand was blowing. Not nice at all."

Then I'd look around, hoping Jake was out of earshot.

So, hearing him even mention the possibility that Laney would not be a beach kid nearly caused my heart to stop. When I looked at Rachel, it seemed she felt the same thing. It just couldn't be.

Not five minutes later, the car quieted down. I dared a look back and Laney was fast asleep. Just as I was about to turn around, I noticed Jake held her tiny hand in his. My attention back on the road, I smiled and tapped Rachel's leg, thumbing for her to look back. When she did, I heard her coo of happiness.

"How cute," she whispered.

I nodded, feeling like I had the best family in the world.

. . .

I guess I forgot when Rachel mentioned it, but it ended up that her grandmother was visiting the beach as well. When we arrived at the house, Grammy M briskly strolled along the decking, a hand up to shade the sun, the other waving vigorously for a ninety-three-year-old.

"Hi there," she called.

Jake jumped out of the back door and raced to Grammy. Hitting the brakes a foot before reaching her, he stopped and put out his arms. Grammy hugged him and laughed. Rachel followed our son and I busied myself unlatching Laney's carrier from the base of the car seat. I tried not to jostle her, thinking she needed more sleep. As I eased her out of the door, Rachel reappeared. She grabbed the carrier and hurried back to show Grammy her newest great-grandchild.

"Don't wake her," I called after Rachel.

My wife glanced over her shoulder and shook her head. I know I nagged her about the kids, but I could sense something deeper. I stood on a ledge, dangerously teetering on questioning her mothering capabilities, the ultimate button push for a working mother. I deserved credit for seeing that, but lost it every time I couldn't loosen up on the reins. Was it such a big deal if Laney woke up?

With every ounce of control I could muster, I spun around and busied myself unloading our bags.

Inside, I ran into Rachel's dad. A tall man with broad shoulders and the most welcoming grin I'd ever come across, he grabbed a bag out of my hands. We looked at each other, eye to eye.

"Hi, G-Pa," I said, genuinely happy to see him.

"Hey there," he said. "Got any more in the trunk?"

"Nope, this is it."

He turned and I followed him back to the bedroom our family would share. At times, I could see Rachel in the way he walked. They both had an athlete's gait, as if ready to pounce on some fast-moving prey.

"How's the garden?" I asked.

"Great, great."

G-Pa was an avid amateur botanist. Never one to understand the draw of plant life, I was left with little more to add to the conversation. He looked at me and nodded.

"Gotta find the missus," he said, walking away.

I sighed. The ocean called.

An hour later, we were almost ready to head to the beach. Rachel remained inside getting Laney prepped for her first trip to the sand. Jake played out front on the street, hitting rocks with his yellow Wiffle ball bat. Enjoying himself, he made enough noise for me to miss Grammy M's approach.

"Hello, fella," she said.

"Oh, hey there, Grammy."

"How's everything going?" she asked.

I looked at her and sensed where the conversation was headed. She stood, her shoulders squared, ready to tell me something I had no interest in hearing. Her bushy gray eyebrows arched up and her milky, great-grandmother eyes appeared sharper than they had a right to be.

"Great. Real good."

"Have you been playing poker?"

Grammy played every Thursday evening with the ladies at the assisted living residence. I imagined her, often, wearing a green-tinted visor and taking the old maids for everything they had.

"Twice a month now," I said. "I have two groups going."

"You know," she said, licking her cracked lips, "poker's not a job."

My eyes closed. I felt like screaming. Luckily, Rachel saved me.

"You ready?" she called out.

I opened my eyes and watched her walk toward me, a little bundled-up Laney held close to her chest.

"Let's go!" Jake yelled.

Jake pressed ahead as I joined Rachel. In a hushed tone, I told her what Grammy had said.

She laughed. "She didn't mean anything."

"Probably not," I said, watching Jake. "But I'll admit that my stomach turns when people say stuff like that to me."

"Like what?"

"About work."

"Why? You work."

"I guess it's my button." I chortled. "I think Grammy just called me soft."

Rachel snorted, laughing so hard. "That's Grammy all right. Always going for the jugular."

Our conversation cut short when I had to catch up to Jake as he sprinted along the weathered plank bridge leading up the dune. At its crest, my son just ahead of me, I froze as briny, cool air washed across my face. There, ahead of us, the gray Atlantic Ocean rolled onto the sand, calm for that time of year. I turned just in time to see Laney as the wind pressed against her so-new face. She gulped, losing her breath for a second, and her eyes widened. As if scripted, the corners of her perfect little mouth curled up. She squealed, but no sound came out as her tiny hands grasped for the water still fifty yards away. I laughed. Rachel laughed. And Jake laughed. We fell into each other, a perfect family group hug as the Atlantic sang.

Once we returned to the grind of the real world, I realized how fleeting nirvana could be.

"Maybe you could work from home on Tuesdays?" I asked while on the phone with Rachel that first week back.

I stared out the window at the scene across the street and to the right—the weekly neighborhood playdate. Tiny humans jolting like pinballs against each other and the four decorative cherry trees in Karen's front yard. Bo, Karen's towheaded only son, sat under a bush. He might have been crying, I couldn't tell. I did not recognize many of the other neighborhood kids. That fact did not make me feel great.

"Daddy," Jake called from upstairs. "Laney's up."

The way he said her name made me smile. Almost a W at the beginning, but not quite.

"Great, buddy," I called back, holding a hand over the speaker. "I'll be right up."

"I have to go, Simon. Isabella needs me on a conference call with a client."

"What do you think I should do?"

I think I might have sounded desperate. Rachel, for her part, did not react.

"Why don't you just take him over?"

"Karen didn't invite me," I said.

"Lindsey did last week."

Lindsey was another mom from down the street. She had hosted the neighborhood playdate the prior week and had, through Rachel, asked me to bring Jake over. I had not, due to a prior engagement (grocery shopping) and an inexplicable yet numbing fear. A stay-at-home mom might not understand that. Watching them out the window, they seemed to live for Tuesdays. What I imagined was me sitting on an overstuffed couch, my pinky out as I sipped cappuccino and nodded interestedly along with so-and-so admitting how childbirth affected her woman pieces or how her husband made the funniest sound after orgasm.

"Look, I'll see what I can do," Rachel said. "But it won't be this month, that's for sure. I don't care if you go or not. It's just a playdate."

As I stared out the window, the sound of the children playing plucked at my nerves like Slash from Guns N' Roses. I could actually picture him with his poodle hair all crazy while he strummed the synapses inside my skull. Rachel's response left me wanting. I imagined, not for the first time, our roles reversed. I'd lean back in my roller chair, put my feet up on the desk, and say, "It's just a playdate."

"Easy for you to say."

"Just take a deep breath. It's no big deal."

I laughed, suddenly seeing the absurdity of a grown man being terrified of a playdate.

"Wow," I said. "I guess I'm moving about five spaces ahead. No playdate leads to Jake being left out, to Friday nights alone in his room listening to alternative music and reading crap like Silvia Plath."

"You crack me up," she said.

Even I could see how that was a total stretch. I thought about my own childhood. I remembered a good friend in the fourth grade who turned on me and told the rest of the class that I still watched cartoons. We really never talked again after that moment. Thinking back, I could list other examples. Life was built on putting those hard moments back together. My kids needed that stuff. Rationally, I knew that.

"You're right," I said, feeling strong in the moment, like I'd figured everything out. "Real men don't playdate."

Another laugh burst from Rachel, one of the real ones. The sound carried relief and nostalgia. I smiled.

"That's the Simon I love," she said.

I laughed back. "And don't you forget it."

Laney, five months old at the time, woke up like a little angel. From her first day on this planet, she appeared happy to have her eyes open, like she never wanted to miss anything. On the contrary, things like car seats and cribs cramped her sense of freedom. I picked her up and held her close to my chest, the warmth from her peanut of a body seeping through me, making everything a little better.

"Can I hold her?" Jake asked at my feet.

"Not yet, bud. I have to change her."

His eyebrows turned down and he stomped out of the room.

"Once I get her ready, you can. Then we'll go to the park. I'll bring your bike."

Although the weather could not have been better, I wrapped Laney in a snug baby suit, those all-in-one things that acted as socks, pants, and long-sleeved shirt simultaneously. It was pink, of course. Pretty much all her clothing came in pink or purple. She owned not a single hand-me-down from Jake. None of his clothes made it through me as primary caregiver. Not only had I ignored the existence of bibs, but I also just threw clothes in the washer and dryer (white, dark, whatever), and had no idea how bleach worked (or maybe I was just playing dumb). Either way, I tried harder for Laney. She deserved to look like her mom dressed her.

Carrying my daughter and carefully walking down the stairs, I felt better. I had almost forgotten my fear of the playdate. Then I saw Jake. He stood in front of the window, peering out. With no context, it could have been one of those great photos that some parents post on Facebook. The sun beamed in around him and the slight glare dappled the natural greens and browns outside.

With context, however, the vision told a different tale. He stared out at a bunch of kids playing. I felt sick to my stomach.

"You okay, buddy?" I whispered.

He didn't respond. Though I was not proud of it, those thoughts came back. I projected horrible emotion: rejection, loneliness, ostracism. Jake not answering magnified it to the point where it breathed and moved through the room like a specter. Laney squirmed in my arms. She felt it, too. That was what I decided.

I committed to attend the neighborhood playdate the next Tuesday. I would not allow my fears to make my son feel this way. I would protect him, and Laney, though I'd already sort of figured out she was better at this stuff than I ever could be.

Tuesday next arrived. Another mom, Regina Wold, originally from New Jersey and married to an accountant/sports enthusiast, hosted the playdate. Even the word *playdate* drove me near insane when I heard it. I had taken to whispering it like the older folk whispered the word "cancer."

That morning, I drank an extra cup of coffee, a vain attempt at delaying what I expected to be torture. Jake hovered around as if he, too, sensed the doom knocking on the door of our little world. Laney, however, remained oblivious. She cooed, already strapped into her car seat.

Taking Jake by the hand, I lifted Laney and walked to the garage. It was time. Not quite. Deftly, I unfolded the expensive stroller my parents had shipped to us, a gift in absentia from being there for her birth. They had been overseas visiting relatives and got home a day late.

Locking Laney into the front, I stepped aside. Jake jumped up onto the bar across the back wheels. He loved to ride there when we took walks. He had no idea, though, that this was no normal Connolly family stroll. I wondered if I'd ambushed my son, but honestly I had no idea whether he would like it or not. Maybe all this discomfort belonged solely to me.

The Wolds lived at the very tip of the cul-de-sac. Though I'd deemed Karen the mayor of the neighborhood, Regina held the crown. In a more confident, haughty way, she ruled. Her husband drove a sweet convertible Mercedes and she threw monthly parties at which she sold jewelry or something like that to the neighbors. For my part, I respected Regina. Although I would shy away from a confrontation, she tended toward the up-front and reasonable.

I am not sure I could have strolled any more slowly as we meandered down the walk. My stomach twisted and turned. *Too much coffee*, I thought.

"Daddy?"

I turned to Jake. "Yes?"

"Where are we going?"

I smiled. "This is Corey and Catherine's house. We are going to a playdate."

"Who's Corey and Catherine?" he asked.

"You know! Our neighbors?"

He looked at me like I had morphed into some strange fuzzy character at an amusement park, one that appeared ambiguously sinister.

In answer, I rang the doorbell. Regina answered.

"Silly, just walk in next time," she said.

I stuttered. *Why would I do that?* There was absolutely no way I would just walk into a house I had never entered before.

"Come on in," she added, shaking her head. She bent at the waist. "Hi there, Jakey. How are you?"

Jake hid behind my leg. I awkwardly attempted to coax him out while freeing Laney from the stroller. Regina chuckled warmly, then took Jake by the hand. Jake, stunned, went along with her, glancing back at me.

"The other kids are downstairs," she told him.

The two disappeared through what I assumed had to be the basement door. Laney wrapped around my neck, but when I looked at her face, she seemed thrilled. I eased into the kitchen, following the sound of voices.

A chorus erupted when I entered. "Hi, Simon."

Someone reached out for Laney, and without realizing it, I handed her off. Someone showed me to a chair. Someone poured me a cup of coffee (my fifth of the morning). It all happened so fast, like a huge embrace. I admit that it made me fidget, the warm welcome a double bind when added to my disquiet.

"Ms. Simons . . . ," someone said to my right. I turned, mishearing and thinking they were talking about me. They were, instead, talking about a teacher at the school. I glanced at Regina as she reappeared. I tried to figure out the age range of the group of children in the basement. Lindsey's daughter was in pre-K, so maybe under two to almost five years old or so. The moms seemed so comfortable and confident. I kept staring at the basement door. Some say men don't have the patience to raise children correctly. Golf takes patience and men love that. I see it differently. Men are just golden-maned leaders of the pride. We lie around a lot until something needs protecting. Then, it's best to just get out of the way.

I decided I needed to check on Jake. Being a homebody (I guess), I had not integrated Jake into large groups enough. I imagined bedlam in the basement. Jake tied to a train table, being sawed at by plastic woodworking tools. I glanced at Laney, not sure if I was comfortable leaving her there at the kitchen table while I checked on Jake.

Laney's eyes tracked with the conversation. I marveled at her ability to look fascinated. She smiled at the right time, cooed in agreement, even grunted in disdain. I tried to follow along, although my mind remained obsessed with the goings-on in the basement. I think some of the moms were talking about a cleanse diet.

"I drink a shake in the morning and then have a snack of whole foods."

Regina looked at me, so I nodded in agreement, although I didn't know what a whole food was. I figured it was not a whole bag of chips or anything like that.

"Would you like a slice of brain bread? Karen made it. Totally delish."

"No thanks." I shook my head. "I already had breakfast."

Lifting my cup, I noticed my hand shook. It had to be the caffeine. Laney looked like she might respond to something Karen said. *And what the hell was brain bread, anyway?*

"I'm going to check on Jake," I blurted out. "Is that okay?"

Conversation ground to a halt. Everyone stared at me, including my own daughter (at least that's how it felt).

Regina laughed. "I'm sure he's fine."

"Yeah," others chimed in.

"I'm just going to see. Is it all right if I leave Laney? She looks like she's having a ball."

Regina nodded, more to the others than to me. Tairyn, who held Laney, kissed my daughter's downy head, and all the other moms focused their attention on her. They talked about her clothes. Laney smiled (one of her first).

Ignored, I rose from the table. I glanced back when I opened the basement door. No one paid me any attention, so I slipped down.

The basement—I often wonder if I misunderstood the scene. To me, the place reeked of a nightmarish death trap. Kids littered the floor, along with jagged piles of toys, whirling dervishes of intermittent laughter and tears. I staggered back a step searching for Jake. I found him sitting in a corner, a Buzz Lightyear doll in his hand, staring unabashed at the other children. For their part, Jake's existence might have been a dust mote.

I eased down the rest of the stairs. A little towheaded girl, maybe four years old, walked up to me, her hands raised in the air, like she wanted me to pick her up. I stood before her, dumbfounded.

"In there," she said.

The girl pointed at a circular area cordoned off by a flexible toddler fence. I did not see any toys inside the space, but the little girl remained insistent.

"In there."

Awkwardly, I picked her up and placed her in the kiddy cage. I scanned the room, looking for Bo. He was playing memory with three other kids. For some reason, he wore a tiara. Jake noticed me and raced over.

"Can we leave?"

A chip of my heart crumbled away. "Not yet. Don't you want to play with everyone?"

Jake shook his head. I took in the room again. Although I knew my interpretation to be influenced by my own emotions, I saw every other kid playing together in one giant group. Rationally, this could not be true. I had recently placed the towheaded girl in a cage, but that was what I saw.

Why wouldn't Jake play with the others?

That moment injected the question into my subconscious, lodging it there for eternity. It may have peeked in before, tentatively testing the fertile ground of my introspective mind, but it gained purchase at that instant. Jake had never asked to have friends over. In preschool he kept to himself on the playground. What had I done? Years of self-doubt, guilt, and insecurity would follow.

Not soon enough, I found myself walking home, my children in tow. Entering through the garage, Jake hit the ground running, disappearing downstairs to his playroom. Laney turned her head, as if longing to return to Regina's house. I hugged her close and then looked through the games cabinet for memory, intent on teaching Jake the game.

Laney asked for the baby swing, or at least waved at it, so I secured her in the seat and picked up the phone. I called Rachel.

"How'd it go?" she asked.

"Okay."

She paused. "No, really?"

The floodgate opened. "Jake didn't play with anyone. Those kids have been playing together for, like, ten years."

"It hasn't been ten years," Rachel said.

"What?"

"Those kids haven't been playing for ten years."

"Jesus, Rachel." I rubbed at my eyes. "I know that."

"Were the kids being mean to him?" she asked.

"I don't think so. You know Jake. It's like a big group just overwhelms him."

"How were all the moms?" Her question sounded tentative, as if afraid of my response.

"They don't even want me there. They probably want to talk about bras and crap like that. Anyway, I don't know . . . I'm a guy!"

The rest I left unsaid. It presented itself like a hippo in my kitchen, though. *She should have stayed home with the kids.* I don't think Rachel picked up on it, thankfully, or the rest of the conversation would have progressed very differently.

"Where's Jake?" she asked.

"In the basement. Where else? I'm sure he's playing with that circuit board thing your dad got him."

"How's Laney?"

I laughed. "She did great."

"Shocker."

"I know, right?"

"I need to say this, Simon, so try not to get mad. I know you find this stuff hard, and I totally get it. You're trailblazing against the grain of cultural normalcy."

"Nice," I interrupted, not in a sarcastic way. The way she put it made me feel like Neil Armstrong, or at least like Captain Kirk.

"But, listen, it is not them. They want to make you feel comfortable. The other moms want you to feel like you can come to the playdate."

"So it's all me," I mused, maybe a little offended.

"Not at all. It's probably just as awkward for them. Just know that it's not malicious, or out of spite. They are not judging you. It's just different."

I laughed. "Because I have a penis?"

"Simon!" She acted offended, but I could tell she smiled.

"Sorry," I said. "Maybe I should go into the garage and do some carpentry. Or maybe I'll change the oil in the car."

"You don't even know how to do that."

"Would you rather me throw on some pearls and vacuum?"

We joked, but the topic flirted so close to reality that even I knew I should step back.

"Thanks for understanding," I said.

"I always try," she said. "I think I'll be home next week. I'll take the kids to the next playdate."

I tried not to cheer. "Okay."

"I love you, Simon. You're doing great."

"Love you, too."

She hung up and I smiled, the reaction of a man given a reprieve, a stay of execution.

CHAPTER 6

I am now alone. Not utterly alone, in the sense that no one else remains in the church, but all the parents have left. I had watched as an officer took the last of the thirteen out one by one. The first parent to be called out, a mom I do not know but have seen around school, appeared confused. Seconds after she disappeared behind a closed door, I heard her scream. Shocked, my head swiveled. I saw everyone else, as if their faces suddenly came into focus.

Evelyn Marks had sat on a pew behind and to the right of me. Her daughter, Leigh, had been in Jake's first-, second-, and third-grade classes. My mind forced a memory to the forefront, Evelyn and I sitting next to each other on a bench, watching our children navigate a bouncy house at Joey Franklin's eighth birthday party. The mother of Amanda Brown, one of Laney's friends, had stared at nothing, her face pallid. Julia George had looked around, her eyes wide and panicked. I coached her son James in soccer for three seasons.

Now, they are gone. I am the last. There is a phantasm of hope skirting the edge of my mind, teasing at the ominous mountain of dread I am holding at bay. I know for sure that the other parents' children are, at best, wounded, at worst, dead. This is a harsh thought, but it is true.

Unable to act, I am left to think. Questions snap into existence:

Could Jake have skipped school? Had he done that before? Did I really know where he went every second of every day?

Maybe Jake is hiding somewhere . . .

Is Jake . . . ?

A sliver of the shock tears away and I am left with a clear thought. More nervous than I have ever felt before, I fish out my iPhone. Going directly to recent calls, I hit Jake's number. His picture flashes on the screen, smiling and wearing a Notre Dame Fighting Irish base-ball hat backward.

Each ring tortures like metaphorical hot irons slipping between the fingernails of my emotion. My brain screams *NO* over and over again as I grip the phone like it is the ledge of a sheer and bottom-less cliff.

On the fifth ring, someone answers.

"Jake . . . buddy," I say, my voice cracking. *He's okay!*

I hear strange rustling, the phone rubbing against fabric. Muffled voices are just audible, like ghosts in the static.

"Jake!"

A much louder rustle, then the phone goes dead. I am frozen, the cool glass pressed hard against my ear as I try to breathe. I dial again, and again, and again. There is never an answer. Holding the phone away, my head folds downward and my temples throb.

Honestly, a daze clouds my consciousness. Reality slips into something less, and more. It becomes numbing absence and jolting awareness. I look up at the door, yet I cannot fathom the possibility that Jake is gone. He just answered his phone. That one time, he answered. It had to be him.

My phone rings. I fumble, my fingers thinking they belong to someone else. When I answer, I hear my wife's voice instead of Jake's. She is panicked.

"The police are here!"

"Tell them I just called him."

Her tone is tight, like an unexploded bomb.

"They're at our house."

"What do you mean?"

"The SWAT police are everywhere."

"Where are you? In the car?"

"He wants me to park," she says.

I listen to the disjointed sounds coming through the receiver. My wife talks to someone, I assume a police officer. The phone rubs up against fabric, the speaker coughs between the sound of muffled voices. I need her to get back on the line, tell me what is happening.

"Rachel." It comes out more of a shout.

I still hear her talking. Something about "entry." She is angry when she gets back on the line.

"They won't let me in, Simon." Her anger turns to obvious fear. "They're searching the house."

"What do you mean they're searching the house? Did you tell them about the call?"

"What call?"

"I called Jake's phone. He answered."

"You talked to him?!"

"No, he didn't talk. I just heard . . ."

I don't know what to say. I can't even ask myself why they might be searching our house.

Finally, Rachel speaks again. "Get over here."

"I can't leave. I'm waiting for Jake. I called his cell. He answered . . . or someone answered. I—"

I turn around. A police officer stands in the doorway of the church. He is looking at me. I turn away. He'll go away if I don't pay attention. My eyes close. Everything will go away if I don't look at it. It will all disappear, not like a dream, but like it isn't real. None of it is real. I am not real.

"Mr. Connolly?"

"What is it?" Rachel asks.

"Mr. Connolly."

"Nothing," I say.

"Who's that? What's going on? Simon?"

"Nothing," I repeat.

The officer is standing over me. "I need you to come with me, sir."

"Simon."

What does it all mean?

The officer leads me to one of the vestry's back rooms. White linen cloths drape a thick-legged, wooden table. A plastic bag filled with pounds of white wafers, perfect circles, rests on a counter in the back. Robes hang from pegs beside the door. I know I will remember every last detail of that room. Forever.

He pulls a chair out for me. I sit, and he sits across from me, placing a leather-bound spiral notebook on the table. The pen fits perfectly into the tubular wires. He slips it out and opens the pad. His eyes meet mine for the first time. I assume this is because I did not look him in the face before that moment.

"I need to ask you a few questions," the officer says.

Some leftover, primal instinct urges me to strike this man. My brain can't come up with a single reason why, but I have to restrain myself. I nod.

"Are you Jake Connolly's father?"

I nod, but he looks like he is waiting for more. "Yes."

"Did Jake attend school today?"

"Yes. Look, can you please tell me what's going on? Is he okay?"

The officer pauses, as if carefully choosing his words. This, for some reason, frightens me more than anything else that has happened so far. Finally, he answers.

"At this time, Jake's whereabouts remain unknown. All we know for sure is that his car was found in the student parking lot."

"What does that mean? He just answered his cell."

The officer checks his pad, tapping it as if he suddenly understands something. "Does your son know Doug Martin-Klein?"

Everything rushes over me, my entire life, Jake's entire life, everything that has happened, it all crashes on me like a tidal wave. I am drowning.

"Mr. Connolly?"

"Can I have some water?" I ask, my voice gravelly.

The officer looks me over. My primal instincts have vanished. He dissects me with his eyes. He picks at my guilt, my fear, and my failure. He understands it all, just as I suddenly did as well when he mentioned that name.

The officer walks out of the vestry. I am alone for some period of time, I do not know how long. The initial overwhelming blast of emotion fades. I am numb, but I am also aware again. When the officer returns with a woman in a wrinkled pants suit and a long, straight black ponytail, I am all too aware of what is going on.

"You think . . ."

I stop myself. As awful as it sounds, I need to be careful. I was about to say that they think Jake is somehow involved in all this. The reason I think this is simple—Doug Martin-Klein.

"Hello, Mr. Connolly, I am Detective Anderson. I wondered if I could ask you some questions?"

"Look, I'm going to find Jake."

I stand up. The first officer squares off, blocking me from moving toward the door.

"Please sit," Detective Anderson says. "We want to find Jake, too."

I am enraged now. Her tone implies our desire to find my son does not share a motive. "What does that mean?"

Detective Anderson blinks. My phone rings again. It is Rachel.

I answer without asking if that's okay. The detective waves her hand dismissively and looks at the officer.

"Rachel."

"They think Jake's involved in this," she says, her voice near hysterics.

I look at Detective Anderson but talk to Rachel. "Are you okay?"

"What the hell? Didn't you just hear me? They think Jake shot those kids!"

"I'm coming home," I say. My voice sounds soulless, even to me.

Rachel sobs, gasping for breath.

"I need to get home," I say.

Detective Anderson nods to the guy in uniform.

"Officer Gunn will drive you."

"I have a car," I say.

"We'll get that to you. We need to have a look inside it first. Is that okay?"

"Inside my car?"

She nods. "We just want to make sure we find Jake."

I don't believe what she says. At least, I don't believe her intent. Rachel's words buzz behind my eyes, making my thoughts pulse like lightning. They think Jake shot those kids. It does not make any sense. Except . . . Except for Doug Martin-Klein.

CHAPTER 7

JAKE: AGE SEVEN

Ten seven-year-olds screamed, hanging from the chain links like little apes. I let them. Some of the parents, and all of the other coaches, thought I was, at the least, disorganized. I liked the kids' spirit, though. No one could say my guys weren't having fun.

"Let's go, Jakey," I called out.

He stood outside the batter's box, his cleats digging at the rust-colored infield mix. His shoes appeared so small that I smiled. If he knew I thought he looked *cute*, Jake would have killed me. Shaking my head, I turned to the other boys, the members of our team, the Johnson Plumbers, or as we liked to call ourselves, the Mighty Green Machine.

"Who's up next?" They looked at me like I'd asked for the formula for rocket fuel. "Check the lineup. Remember?"

Ritchie and the other Jake, Jake T, hustled over. I turned back to the game. My Jake tightened one of his batting gloves and took up his stance. I found it amusing that all the kids owned two batting gloves, at least one bat, their own helmet, and at least one mitt.

Almost all of them stowed their equipment in a nylon baseball bag, including my son.

When we were kids, it was a little different. I remembered showing up for my Little League practices wearing Toughskins, a striped T-shirt, and hand-me-down sneakers, often from my sister. The coach showed up with a chewed cigar hanging from the corner of his mouth and four (or less) batting helmets (most missing sections of foam), two aluminum bats, and (hopefully) some catcher's gear. One kid came to the first game sporting a single batting glove. We all looked at him in awe and ignored the fact he struck out twice. He became our idol, or at least his batting glove did.

Jake hacked at the first ball, swinging so hard that he nearly fell over. I noticed his cheeks getting red.

"Don't be so hard on yourself," I whispered.

"What, Coach?" Ritchie barked out behind me.

I turned and smiled at him, noticing one of the other kids behind him.

"Carter, stop eating that," I said, walking over.

Carter, a kid with bristly hair and flat eyes, sat in the dirt, crisscross-applesauce (the new PC term for Indian-style I'd learned from Jake's preschool teacher). His pudgy hand, an inch from his open mouth, held a spilling mound of infield mix. His eyes met mine and he jammed it into his face. Most of the dirt puffed into a dust cloud surrounding his bulbous head but I could see dirt covering his tongue and teeth.

"Wow," I said.

"Carter hit me," Ben said.

"What?"

Ben was our power-hitting, best-catching, soon-to-be pitcher. I could not fathom Carter hitting Ben.

CRACK!

I spun around in time to see the baseball flying over the short-stop's head.

"Runrunrun," I called out, but Jake was already at first. He flew around the bases as the left and left-center fielders just looked at the ball rolling between them in the thick grass of the outfield.

"Get the ball!" their coach screamed.

Jake kept running. The Mighty Green Machine, sans Carter, sprang up and threw itself against the fence. The chains rattled as they cheered.

"JAKEJAKEJAKE!"

Finally, the left fielder retrieved the ball. By that time, Jake was headed to third.

"Whoa!" My hands went out in front of me, willing Jake to stop. I would have hated seeing him get thrown out after such a great hit. I forgot we were talking about seven-year-olds here. The throw from left careened past the third baseman, hitting the fence of our dugout.

Jake's (cute little) cleat hit the bag at third and he headed home. The catcher, looking very professional, threw his helmet down and squared off in front of the plate. Jake bore down on him as the third baseman raced after the ball. He picked it up in enough time to make the throw. It flew on a rope right to the catcher, but that massive glove failed the kid. The ball struck the leather and popped up. Jake slid into home, safe.

The team (sans Carter) stormed the field as Jake ambled back to the dugout. They jumped on him and around him, patting his back and knocking on his helmet. He smiled and laughed, but did not say anything.

In that moment, I felt such amazing pride in my son. Looking back, I could say that there were countless better reasons to be proud of him. I barely went a day without stopping and looking at him, seeing how great a kid he'd turned into. The truth was, though, that there's something about that moment watching your kid do something great, whether it's a spelling bee, a dance recital, or a baseball game. Leaning on the fence, I watched him handle his moment with a composed but good-natured reaction. I listened to the other kids talk to him in the dugout.

"Nice one," Ritchie said.

"Yeah," Ben said.

"Did you see that thing?" Ritchie said. "You killed it."

Jake nodded and smiled. He answered a couple of questions. Me, I tried to focus on the game, not wanting to show too much. I knew that if I made a big deal of it, it would embarrass him. So I waited and continued to eavesdrop.

"That kid on third tried to trip you," someone said.

"Nah," Jake answered. "I don't think so."

I thought Carter said something behind me, but when I looked back, he had just jammed more dirt in his mouth. For only a second I considered retrieving the ball for posterity but decided that would be passé. Instead, I turned to look at the team, expecting Jake to still be in the middle of the throng, but he sat alone on the bench, stowing his gear.

After the game, Jake and I loaded up the car and headed home. He buckled himself in and I looked at him through the rearview mirror.

"Nice hit," I said.

"Thanks."

"You tore the cover off it. That was our first home run. I'm really proud of you, bud."

"Ben hit one last week."

"No, he stopped at third, remember?"

Jake looked out the window, but I could see his smile.

"Your team was happy for you."

He nodded.

"How come you sat by yourself?"

I immediately regretted the question. Jake, however, did not miss a beat.

"I don't love crowds."

I laughed, amazed at such self-awareness coming out of a seven-year-old.

"Carter's a weirdo," he said after a while.

"What makes you say that?"

"He eats dirt. Plus, he hit Ben."

I still couldn't understand that. Ben was the alpha dog on the team. In my day, if a kid like Carter even looked funny at a kid like Ben, Carter would have been eating dirt in the old-school sense (not that he would have minded, I guess).

I sensed a teaching moment. Taking a deep breath, I thought about my words before I said them.

"I understand what you are saying, Jake, but it is important to be nice to everyone. I won't make you be friends with Carter. I've never made you be friends with anyone. But you should be nice. Look, it's probably hard for him being on the team. He hasn't hit the ball yet, and he can't catch . . ."

I knew immediately I should not have said that. Sometimes I spoke to Jake as if he was older than his actual age. When I glanced back, though, he didn't seem to react.

"All I'm saying is, just be nice to him."

"But he shouldn't have hit Ben," Jake said.

"That's true." I nodded thoughtfully. "But still. You should be nice."

What I wanted to add was that considering Carter appeared to be a total loon, you didn't want to be on his *list* when he went bat crazy. I knew enough to leave that part out.

Maybe a week after the game, I waited at the bus stop, surrounded by a dozen adults chattering in three distinct pods. I lingered on the fringe, watching Laney. She ran across the yard (Tairyn's), chasing Becca (Tairyn's daughter) and her little sister Jewel. The girls, all below school age, shrieked and giggled.

"Hi, Simon."

I turned my attention away from the girls and found that Tairyn had slipped in beside me.

"Hey there," I said.

"How's Rachel? I saw on Facebook that she's in London."

My wife's job had recently expanded to international business law. This sent her across the pond and back quite often.

"I think so," I said.

"You *think* she's in London?" Tairyn laughed.

From a purely impartial perspective, Tairyn happened to be beautiful. Her long, naturally blond hair looked like it belonged on a model. In fact, most of her looked that way, from her large blue eyes, her pouty mouth, her (as my college buddy would say) banging body. She dressed as if walking the streets of SoHo, in high Italian leather boots and perfectly disheveled layers of clothing that somehow flattered her figure. I wondered what might have led her to the same banal existence I'd blundered into.

"No, she is. She gets back . . ." I did not have to think about it. I knew the exact moment she would return, because the second she did, I would run screaming from the house, desperately needing some time away from the kids. Tairyn's arrival simply erased my memory.

"Friday," she finished for me. "You're a mess, Mr. Connolly."

I shook my head, attempting sheepishness. "I am."

"Anywho, Becca asked if Laney could come over tomorrow. Figure it might give you some time to yourself."

I froze, as asinine as that sounds. Rachel had coached me for this moment. Playdates had transformed as Laney aged. Like her mother, my daughter engaged everyone and always looked for the party. She made friends with every kid in the neighborhood, including those Jake had written off as mean or weird.

I had not adjusted well. I still preferred having the kids at home with me. Laney went to preschool until twelve thirty, so the two of us usually ran errands or stopped by the bookstore in the afternoon. Laney met Jake off the bus like a puppy left home alone all day. Jake tended to pick her up and hug her. The two got along great and spent most afternoons fighting imaginary, medieval armies in the basement, Jake the strong, silent knight and Laney (to my delight) the brilliant, effervescent, ax-wielding dwarf.

In the past, Tairyn, along with others, asked to have her over after school. I almost always said no. If Rachel happened to be traveling, then I always said no. In simple, easily understood words, Rachel explained that I had to change my ways. She said the next time someone requested our daughter, pause, breathe, and say yes.

I paused and took a breath, glancing over at Laney. She danced and carried on, totally immersed in the group, a bag of true happy.

"So different," I thought I said to myself.

"What?" Tairyn asked.

"Oh, nothing."

She looked at me, utterly confused. I just found it amazing how different my Laney was from Jake—yin and yang. I didn't really want to go into all that with Tairyn, though.

"Yes," I said.

"Yes what?" A surprised laugh punctuated her question.

"She can play tomorrow."

Tairyn appeared shocked, as if she expected me to decline. "Okay, then. Do you want to drop her off after you pick her up from school?"

My head cocked to the right. How did she know when I picked her up, or that she even went to preschool? Rachel said our neighborhood was a village. At times, I worried the townspeople might brandish pitchforks and chase me out.

"Excellent."

The bus rumbled into view. I smiled, fidgeted, and Tairyn eased up to Karen and complimented her Uggs. I stood, alone again, staring at the yellow behemoth as it inched closer. Laney grabbed my leg and did her little excited dance. She pushed ahead of the adults, anxiously waiting as the bus came to a stop. The doors opened and her dance intensified.

The other kids parted around Laney, barely giving her notice. One girl, Regina's daughter, patted her on the head. Then her brother appeared. She rushed to him and Jake picked her up off her feet. I sighed. Everything was right in the world, even if Laney had a playdate.

Jake sat at the counter, doing his homework. Laney sat beside him, drawing a picture with crayons and a number 2 pencil. I watched them, unloading the dishwasher as I did so. Laney, her brow slightly furrowed, glanced on occasion at her brother, emulating his grip on the pencil.

Suddenly, he looked up.

"Hey, Dad," he blurted out.

"Yes, son," I responded with mock gravity.

"I did what you told me."

"And what's that?" I asked.

"I was nice to this kid, because you told me."

At first, I did not understand. He stared at me while I thought, and I suddenly understood that if I didn't get this right, I would undermine some lesson I had thought important. That is when it dawned on me—baseball.

I lifted an eyebrow. "Like Carter."

He beamed. "Yup."

"Well, tell me about it."

Laney stopped drawing, listening intently as Jake began his story.

"Well, you see, this kid at school, Doug, always gets in trouble."

"What kind of trouble?" I interjected.

Rachel told me I needed to learn to listen without interjection, yet I thought asking pertinent questions displayed interest. Plus, Jake never minded.

"Like, he doesn't always act nice to the other kids. This one time, he pushed Katie B. into the water fountain."

"That's not good," I said.

He shook his head. "She was okay. And she is a little mean sometimes, too. But Doug should not have done that."

"But you let the teacher handle it?"

"I guess. But that's not what I'm talking about. See, the other kids really don't like Doug. He's . . . they call him weird. Well, today we had indoor recess."

"Why?"

"Too muddy from the rain."

"Oh."

"Well, I decided I would play checkers with Doug."

"That's nice of you," I said. "What did Max do?"

Max was Jake's best buddy in the second grade. For a moment, I wondered if I should ask that question, but I wanted to make sure that Max and Jake stayed friends. I liked that kid.

"He was okay, I think. He played with Kevin and Kent."

"Excellent. Like I said, though, I'm not telling you who to be friends with. I'm just saying that you never have to be mean to anyone, even if everyone else is."

"That's what I did," he insisted.

"I know. And I'm proud of you, buddy."

Laney leaned her head on his shoulder. "Me, too," she added in her adorable little voice.

Jake beamed, as did I. It was one of those rare moments that I assume most stay-at-home dads have. I basked in the fleeting glory, feeling like I might actually be okay at this.

CHAPTER 8

DAY ONE

The police cruiser banks a slow turn onto our street. I immediately see why. The calm, residential oasis that is our neighborhood has erupted. Layers of haunting activity radiate out from our home. Men in dark uniforms form the center as they scurry in and out of the front door like worker ants. Yellow caution tape cordons off a ragged, trapezoidal area. I cannot tell if it is a safety issue, or if it designates a crime scene.

Beyond the tape, dozens of vehicles, mostly white-and-black cruisers, form a jagged barrier. Six white news vans troll, some parked, some inching forward, looking for a crack in the defense. Women in awkwardly colorful outfits clash with the grass and trees lining our neighbors' houses. They speak into overly large microphones as giant cameras glow green. A man in a red golf shirt spots the car in which I sit. He looks around, his expression strangely blank, and locks in on us. I watch in a detached void. Everything takes on a surreal calm, an empty veneer over a scene that my psyche cannot survive intact.

The man in the golf shirt appears within a foot of the moving car. The brightness of the fabric grasps me like a monster's claws, pulling my soul away. I do not understand this, but I feel the tugging deep inside. Looking up at his face, I recognize him as a parent I've seen around school. Then the man sees me. His face transforms into a caricature of grotesque hatred.

"You killed my son!" A hand slaps the side of the car. "I'll—"

The rest is lost as he passes out of sight. I crane my neck and see another officer from outside subduing him. I realize I have the same shirt in my closet and my vision wavers. I slump over in the seat, bringing my head down between my knees.

"Are you okay, sir?" the officer asks from the front seat.

"Yeah," I mutter, not looking up.

The officer pauses. My vision clears but I do not lift my head. On the drive over, I have called Jake's number at least ten more times. Each time, the voice mail picks up after barely one ring. The rational side of my brain tells me that if Jake had his phone (God knew he forgot it often enough) he'd have called me or his mom by now. At the same time, he picked up earlier, or at least someone did. The rest of my brain knows that there is nothing at all rational about this situation.

The car door opens. A hand rests on my shoulder.

"Mr. Connolly," a man's voice says. "I'm Detective Rose. Your wife is waiting for you."

I don't recall getting out of the police car, nor do I remember walking over to where Rachel sits in the wrought-iron café chair on the patio behind our garage. Instead, I rise from the fog shrouding my being and find myself sitting beside her, my elbows on the mosaic surface of the small round table between the two chairs. Neither of us speaks for some time. This nook becomes an eerie eye of the storm.

"He's dead," Rachel whispers.

This makes me angry. My skin burns and beads of sweat burst on my forehead.

"You don't know that," I hiss back at her. "He answered his phone. I think he did."

"Did you talk to him? Did you *hear* him?"

She shakes her head. It is a motion that, in the past, frustrated me. It belies the true gravity of a situation by seeming overly accusatory. It is the type of nit-picking that only a married couple who survived child rearing can have and it fills me with guilt.

"I'm calling him."

She dials his number. I watch. With every ounce of my soul, I pray he will answer, that Rachel will be able to get my son on the phone. I watch for any sign on her face that would tell me he answered. When I see the tears, I know we've failed.

"I know," she says, dropping her phone, not looking at me.

I am unsure of what she means until I realize she is answering my original response. She is saying that she *knows* our son is dead. My teeth grind. I want to slap her. This is the first (and only) time I have felt this way. In fact, I have been known to be a judgmental prick when it comes to nongentlemanly behaviors. This reaction emboldens the guilt and my anger dissipates as quickly as it flared. I bend over and carefully pick Rachel's phone up off the asphalt.

"Why are they here?" I ask.

I know, at least in a cerebral manner, why they are here. I think the question comes from a deeper place. It is the first time that the thought—*What did I do*—enters my mind.

Rachel does not understand. The question clearly annoys her.

"I told you on the phone. They think he shot those kids."

"He didn't," I say.

It dawns on me that I have just done exactly what Rachel did to start the conversation. I state as fact something that is nothing more than a gut belief. Doubt is already creeping into the seams, but when I say that, I mean it. When I say it, I am 100 percent sure that Jake did not shoot anyone, but isn't that what every parent would think?

"That kid did it," she says.

I know she means Doug.

"I think—"

She cuts me off. "No, I mean I know he did it. I heard police talking. Someone fucking told them that Jake is a friend of that—"

"They aren't friends," I snap.

Rachel looks at me. Only she knows what she intends with that look, but I feel accused. She must blame me for Jake being *acquainted* with Doug. She traces it all the way back to that baseball game, in fact, and what she considers my misguided parental decisions. At least, that is what I feel in the moment. In reality, I doubt I ever told her the baseball story.

"Look, I just told him to be nice to everyone."

Rachel blinks, slowly. "What? What are you talking about?" She shakes her head. That's when I notice the tears. Rachel is not a crier. Usually, her tears come only when she is frustrated. Seeing them now awakens me from the circuitous path of my thoughts as they rattle through my skull.

Whether my wife and I have communication issues, or bigger issues, for that matter, is irrelevant. Thoughts vanish and instinct takes over. I go to my wife, hold her, and we cry, together, for a long time.

"Mr. and Mrs. Connolly."

An officer approaches us, his hands outstretched. He looks abashed. We both stare at him without saying anything. My throat is raw and the words are buried under the shock again.

"I can take you inside now. So you can get a few things."

"Get a few things?" Rachel asks. "What?"

Although not crying now, I can hear it just below the surface of her words. The officer can as well.

"Have you heard anything more about Jake? Has anyone seen him?" I demand.

The officer swallows and looks away. "Detective Rose will come over when he gets a chance. He can talk about all that with you. I'm just supposed to take you inside so you can get some things."

It dawns on me what he means.

"You won't be leaving soon, will you?"

He shakes his head. "I'm not at liberty to say. But you might want to call family, or reserve a room somewhere."

Rachel bounds to her feet. She looks ready to strangle the kid (because the officer can't be more than twenty-two years old). I grab her wrist and steady her. She staggers. Under any other circumstance, such a display of vulnerability would make her uncomfortable. Years of working in the male-dominated law profession has taught her to shun such frailties. Watching her now, I see the Rachel I met decades ago, before all that, the young woman so full of smiles and wide-eyed openness. I help steady her but feel weak myself. At the same time, I notice that the officer does not flinch. He has seen this tale before.

"Let's go inside before they say we can't," I whisper to her.

The officer leads us into our own home. I half-expect that they have ransacked the place, but everything looks eerily as it did that morning, except for the men and women wandering through our rooms, taking pictures and speaking in hushed tones. Attuned to the acoustics, I locate the center of activity, Jake's room upstairs. Instantly, I remember something.

"Where's Laney?" I blurt out.

"She's at the Bennetts'."

I guess I assumed Rachel would take care of her. She cannot see all this. But I hadn't even asked to be sure my daughter is okay. Rachel does not seem to notice this, though.

"You can go up to your room, but I have to come up with you," the officer says.

I nod but Rachel lunges up the stairs as if attempting to lose him. I let him follow her up and I bring up the rear. Our room is empty of activity and appears undisturbed. As I look at our bed, my current read still resting on the nightstand, my phone vibrates as it receives a text. I yank it out, my hope spiking.

What can you tell us about your son's involvement in the shooting?

Shocked, I check the ID but do not recognize it. I back into a corner and call the number, glancing around to see if the police notice (although not really sure why I do that). A man answers, his voice echoing as if he answered the phone in a basement.

"Simon Connolly. May I record this call?"

"What? Absolutely not! Who is this?"

"I'm Michael, author of *Blog You Later*. Can you tell me anything about your son's—"

I hang up. Not a second later, another text hits my phone. This one announces itself as the local news affiliate and requests an interview. I jam my phone in my pocket. It vibrates once more as I stare at my bed again. Something about the sound triggers a memory. Blood rushes to my head as I lunge forward, remembering the note I found that morning.

It lies on the carpet peeking out from under the bed. I pause, amazed that the police have not seen it. With a quick glance, I notice that the officer's attention remains on my wife. I kneel and scoop it up. As I stand, I unfold the paper and see sprawling lines of writing in Jake's hand. The top line reads:

THAT'S MESSED UP

I only have time to read that much. I quickly crunch the paper in my hand and jam it in my front pocket. My nerves tingle, sure that if the police see the paper it will be taken as evidence. I grab a carry-on my wife keeps stowed under the bed and focus on throwing underwear and socks into the bag, trying not to look at anything or anyone.

"What?" I hear my wife snap. "You're going to follow me into the bathroom?"

A door slams. My thoughts trip and stumble. I am packing to leave my house, which is in the process of being searched because the police think my son shot thirteen kids today.

Outside, Detective Rose finds us before we step down off the stoop. I take him in for the first time. A man in his fifties with military-cropped hair, either very short or gray at the temples, he wears a rumpled tan suit and brown Clark's shoes. His fingers are thick and scaly. I can't look away as he twirls a pen.

Seeing him triggers my need to act once again. I am being shuffled forward by circumstance. What I need to be doing is searching for Jake.

"I'm going to look for my son."

I move to step past him. He puts a hand up, stopping me. I pause.

"Would you mind if we sat down? I have a few things I want to go over with you."

I ignore his request. "Have you found out *anything* yet?"

Rachel does not react. It is almost as if the life, or at least the fight, drained out of her in the bathroom. She walks like the soulless as she follows Rose to the same café chairs we sat at earlier. The detective offers us the seats and he stands, flipping open a notebook. I remain standing as well.

"At this time, we are unsure of the whereabouts of your son." He is choosing his words carefully. "Was he alone when he drove to school?"

Rachel does not react. I am surprised.

"No. He drove our daughter this morning."

The detective writes something down.

"What? Do you know something?" I ask, annoyed.

"He was marked absent by his prime-time teacher," Rose answers. "Your daughter did tell one of our detectives that he dropped her off."

My anger could register on the Richter scale. "When did you talk to Laney?"

Rose's eyes squint. Suddenly, I am sure he is suspicious, not just of Jake, but of me. I realize now why Rachel has remained silent. We are suspects.

"I sent an officer over to the Bennett residence to ask her a few questions."

"Did you read her her rights?" I snap, without thinking. "Did she have a lawyer present?" I need to regain control.

The detective raises a hand. He looks to Rachel for help, but gets none. She is staring at Karen's house now, at least that's what it looks like. I feel my grip on the situation all but vanish.

"So you decided to question my fifteen-year-old daughter without telling me?!"

"I understand that you're under a lot of stress right now, Mr. Connolly. We are doing everything we can to locate the whereabouts of your son."

The word "whereabouts," used for the second time, cuts through me and I want to lash out. Just then, Rachel touches me lightly on the outside of my hand. I look at her but she is still staring off into space. Her touch, however, soothes my reaction, at least to Detective Rose.

"If you need to talk to Laney again, please make sure you let me know first," I say, calmly.

"I understand," Rose says.

"Look, I'm going to look for my son. Someone has to."

"It's best if you get your family somewhere safe. We're doing everything we can and will call you once we hear anything. I promise."

I shake my head. "I need to look for him."

"You can't, Mr. Connolly. The school is on lockdown. No one in or out. I'm sorry."

"But he might be somewhere else."

"We are following every lead. You have to trust us. Any interference could hinder us finding Jake."

This is the first time Rose uses my son's name. Strangely, it calms me. I agree to take the family to the hotel and get them settled. After that, I'm not sure.

"One other thing," the detective says. "Was your son friends with Doug Martin-Klein?"

Parked outside the Bennetts', I reach over to open my door.

"No," Rachel says.

I look at her. My mind remains in a dark haze. "What?"

"I'll go up."

Rachel gets out before I can protest. I watch her walk slowly along the walk to the Bennetts' front door. I see her strength in each step. I often feel she is the strong one in the couple. I roar and posture, but she's the business end of it all. That is, until someone needs protecting.

The note! The thought pops from out of nowhere. I fish it out of my pocket but look up in time to see Laney rush out of the Bennetts' house. She crashes into her mother, who holds her tightly for a moment. It looks as if Rachel attempts to whisk her back to the car, but Tairyn appears. A hand still in my pocket, I pause, trying to listen. I hear muffled, unintelligible words as I watch my wife's body language. She acts as a human shield, guarding her daughter from some invisible threat. I glance at Tairyn and notice what I take as a vapid frown, empty empathy.

The exchange lasts no more than two minutes but time weighs on my already-frayed nerves. I decide I will lower my window to hear what is being said just as Rachel turns and escorts my daughter back to the car. They move like apparitions, shades of my family. Rachel helps Laney into the backseat and sits down beside me. I pause, but she doesn't make eye contact.

"Drive," she whispers.

"I . . ."

When she finally turns, I see that all color has drained from her face.

"What happened?" I whisper, but I have the sense to take my foot off the brake and roll away from the Bennetts' house. "What did she say?"

"Nothing she actually meant," my wife says.

We drive to the Marriott downtown in silence. Wilmington is a commuter city. As we head in, all we see are people dressed for work. When we reach the hotel, it is more of the same.

I hold Laney's hand as we walk into the lobby. Not one step in, the giant television screen on the far wall assaults us. There, bigger than life, darker than the devil, appears Doug Martin-Klein's high school yearbook photo.

Rachel reacts first. She veers off, taking Laney in tow, and disappears into the women's room by the lobby's Starbucks. I am frozen in place, my very organs weighing me down as if they have all turned to concrete.

The television is muted, so Doug's picture is accompanied by the soft crooning of Alanis Morissette. The juxtaposition is more ironic than any of the lyrics of the song. I want to turn the volume up on the television. I need to hear what they are saying. At the same time, I need to get Laney and Rachel somewhere safe, so I peel off and approach check-in. Rachel appears as if from out of nowhere.

"We should get two adjoining rooms."

I consider discussing this decision, but think better of it.

"Where's Laney?"

"I'm right here, Dad," she says from beside her mother.

I blink. Somehow, the angle, or something, made it so I couldn't see her. But there she is. Her face looks drawn and her skin pale. Her eyes are ringed in black and red.

"Two adjoining rooms, please," I say.

When I have the keys, we walk to the elevators. Rachel leans into me.

"I'll take Laney to one room. You get the television on in the other. We need to know what's going on."

"We need to do something to find Jake," I protest.

I know I cannot just sit still, no matter what I told the detective. Rachel looks me in the eye when she speaks.

"I know. But do this for me first, so I know Laney's okay. Then go."

I nod, amazed at how well she understands.

Martin-Klein has been identified as at least one of the gunmen in today's tragic school shooting.

I hear this on national news. The affect remains as severe. I turn the channel to the local news. I recognize the reporter. We spoke once at a political fund-raiser three years before. Now, she stands outside a familiar house, one at which I had dropped Jake off more times than I would have liked.

What kind of kid was Doug?

My family needs me but all I want to do is go to that house, break down the door, force them to tell me what they know. Instead, I listen. The reporter speaks to a middle-aged woman in a black fleece vest and tan Uggs. I do not recognize her, although she looks my age. I'm half paying attention to her, because the reporter's use of the past tense jars me.

He was very quiet.

There is something predatory about the women, both the reporter and the woman to whom she speaks. Maybe I am the only person who sees it. The reporter leans forward, her mouth slightly open. I imagine that I can hear her breathing. She nods along with every statement, as if she knows.

The woman, probably the mother of some kid I know, has eyes wide open. She turns away from the reporter when she speaks, addressing the camera, all of us. She knows better. She saw this coming, and no one listened. Now is her moment.

The parents were quiet, too. Never really took part in the parties here, or the yard sales. Nothing, really. I never really spoke to them.

She uses the past tense about Doug's parents, too. My blood runs like shards of old, dead stone. His parents are not deceased, the tense usage is far more insidious; what their son has done is, in fact, a parent's death sentence.

Although many of the names of the victims are being withheld at this time, awaiting notification of the families, three names have been released. Amanda George, fifteen years old; Kandice Moore, seventeen years old . . .

I don't hear the third name. My horror latches on to Kandice Moore. My eyes close and I see her brownish hair pulled back into a tight bun, elfish wisps bouncing before her right eye. Big green eyes and a roundish face. Short, with an infectious smile. She had been Jake's date to homecoming. Now, she is dead.

That is not possible. It simply is not. Kandice Moore cannot be gone. An innocent little girl standing tiptoed upon the threshold of her life. No. Denial slams shut like the bars of a prison, pushing in on my soul, crushing.

I take out my phone and dial Jake's number again. It goes directly to voice mail.

"Jake." I do my best to keep my voice strong. "Please come home. It will be okay. I promise. Just come home. We can handle this. Please, buddy. Come back."

My entire body quivers as I end the call. Rachel's mother would say someone walked over my grave. Something about that thought sickens me. My mind slips to the possibilities, all the dreams I held inside, the decades of watching my son's life blossom. They parade in backward order, phantom grandkids, a mirage wedding ceremony, graduation from a college that was never determined. I am left wondering if my son has yet to even experience his first kiss. All dreams now, fading visages slowly engulfed by darkness.

CHAPTER 9

JAKE: AGE EIGHT

Jake sat in the backseat, his face blocked by the front of a book—
Football's Top 10 Lists. I stopped the car at the curb and I watched
him through the rearview mirror, amazed by how big he had gotten.
A thought occurred to me that I looked at a real person, not a *kid* or
a *baby*.

"You okay?" I asked.

"Huh?"

Jake put down his book, looking at me through his unruly, dark
bangs. His hair jutted and speared in random order atop his head.
He'd brushed it; I'd watched, but it didn't look that way. His face had
changed as well. Sharp angles replaced soft rounded cuteness. Even
the clothes he wore carried more weight, the Seattle Seahawks' logos
replacing made-up mottos like "Shooting to Win" or "All-star Kid."

"You okay?" I repeated.

"Yeah, why?"

"I mean, if you don't want to go . . ."

"To the party?"

We sat in front of the home of a kid in his class, Doug Martin-Klein. Other than the one day Jake came home saying he'd been nice to the boy, I hadn't heard mention of Doug since. In fact, I'd forgotten all about him, focusing on a handful of kids Jake spent time with at school, mostly playing football during recess.

"Yeah," I said.

Honestly, I felt slightly uncomfortable. I did not know Doug's parents at all. Neither attended any of the near-weekly birthday parties I'd taken Jake to in the last few years.

"Why wouldn't I?"

Jake looked perplexed. I smiled.

"Right?"

Together, Jake and I walked up to the door. He carried a perfectly wrapped (by Rachel) Nerf football in front of him like myrrh. I rang the bell. A very tall man in thick-framed glasses and a short-sleeved button-down answered. His bushy dark eyebrows did not move a millimeter as he spoke.

"Come in, come in."

He opened the door and held it. Jake walked through. I stepped to follow and the door jerked a little, as if he meant to close it.

"Hi, I'm Simon Connolly, Jake's dad."

"Nice to make your acquaintance. I am Doug's father, Dr. Francis Martin-Klein."

A boy Jake's age poked his head around the corner. His slatelike eyes, a little wide set for his narrow face, remained still as he smiled at my son. Slight of build, he swam in the maroon-and-orange-striped shirt he wore, the sleeves of which hung down to his knuckles. He had on dark, nonbranded sneakers and clutched a Ripley's coffee table book under his arm.

"Hello, Jake."

"Hey, Doug."

"Come on."

Jake followed Doug up a flight of stairs, I assumed to the kid's bedroom. I found it odd, considering this was a party. I looked at Dr. Francis Martin-Klein, who watched me as if he watched a couch or a chest of drawers.

"Um, are we early? I thought I got the time right, but I'm a mess." The doctor nodded. "Right on time."

He made no welcoming gestures, no nod toward the kitchen, no sweep of the arm. I cleared my throat. Considering my own burgeoning introversion, I never knew if the awkwardness came from me or from others.

Shifting my weight from one foot to the other, I noticed Doug's mother. She peeked around the corner from the kitchen. When the doctor turned to look at her, she vanished.

I cleared my throat. "Are other parents waiting around, or should I pick him up?"

I really hoped he would say I should stay. I had not grown accustomed to leaving Jake places unless I was familiar with the parents. He spent most of his time at one of two houses, both close friends of his.

"Okay," the doctor said, this time smiling.

I still did not move. Nor did he. I heard Jake laughing upstairs.

"We'll see you in two hours," he said.

I took a step back. Something in his tone or his choice of words hinted that leaving had been my idea. My head spun as I opened the door and walked out. When I turned to say good-bye, Dr. Martin-Klein was nowhere in sight.

Jake and Doug were squatted in the front yard as I drove toward the house. Something in the grass transfixed Jake, while Doug busied himself with an obvious focus upon something I could not see. As the car slowed, Jake looked up and saw me. With a wave, he turned and said something to Doug. Doug looked up without much reaction and watched as Jake ran to the car. My son jumped into the back and buckled his belt. An instant later, he held the book in front of his face again, a perfectly explainable déjà vu moment.

I waited, but Jake said nothing. The car rolled forward while I stole a glance in the mirror. I couldn't take it for long.

"How was the party?" I asked.

"Great." He kept reading (or at least looking at the pictures).

I paused, knowing I shouldn't pry. If I pried, I'd end up making something out of nothing. At the same time, the exchange with the doctor made it impossible to control myself.

"Who else was there?"

Jake's voice sounded matter-of-fact. "His parents, his cousin, his grandma."

My skull tingled. "Any other kids?"

"Nope."

"Wasn't it a birthday party?" I asked.

"I guess. This kid, Jeremiah, was supposed to be there but his parents canceled."

"What did you do?"

"We just played, mostly in his room."

"Played what?"

"I dunno. With some of these old-fashioned army men. They were his dad's, I guess. We started to build a fort in the woods behind his house, too. It's a pretty cool place to play guns."

Nothing added up. My grip on the steering wheel tightened and I took a deep breath.

"What were you doing just now, in the grass?"

Jake put the book down and found my eyes in the mirror. He looked guilty.

"Nothing."

"Tell me, please."

"Nothing, Dad."

"Just tell me."

"You'll be mad."

I sighed. "I won't, just tell me."

"Can I have an amnesty moment?"

I'd instituted "amnesty moments" when Jake was very young. Wanting him to always feel comfortable communicating with me, I said he could ask for one, tell me something, and I would not react. I would not get mad, nor would I ask any questions. At the time, I just wanted to make sure my kids felt comfortable telling me anything, even things that they knew might upset their parents.

"Definitely. Go ahead."

"Doug stepped on a toad. It was an accident."

My footing crumbled. In moments like that, I tried to think about what Rachel would do or say if she were in my shoes.

"Gross," Laney screamed from her car seat.

"I got his guts on my finger." Jake waggled it at his sister, who squealed. The sound ignited a deep, throbbing headache. I rubbed at an eye.

"Accident?" I asked, even though I was not supposed to.

"Stop," Laney screamed.

Jake laughed and pretended he was going to touch his sister.

"Stop," I snapped, harsher than I'd meant. Both Jake and Laney froze, the car becoming jarringly silent. "Accident?" I repeated.

Jake picked his book up. "That's what Doug said."

"Huh?"

"What, you don't believe me?" Jake asked. "I asked for an amnesty moment!"

I took a deep breath. "I totally believe you, buddy. You never lie."

"He lied about my Barbie," Laney said.

"Okay, sweetie."

I tried not to ask any more questions as we drove home. Pulling onto our street, I immediately heard the sound of kids playing, even through the closed windows of the car. About half a dozen kids were crammed into Karen's front yard. They played football with the abandon of those unafraid of tearing an ACL or straining a tired old back.

As we passed, I watched them. That familiar feeling of unease cropped up, filling me with a restless anxiety.

"Bo and the other kids are playing football. Why don't you head over? You've got nothing until dinnertime."

"Nah," Jake said.

"He promised to play knights with me, Daddy," Laney protested.

"Why not?" I asked. "You love football. You play every day at school."

"With my friends, yeah."

"What's wrong with Bo and Chase and them?"

"Nothing," he said. "I just don't want to play. Unless you *want* me to."

"It's up to you, buddy," was what I said. I didn't want him to, per se. I wanted him to want to. There was a big difference.

On Tuesday of that week, I took Jake and Laney to a park in town. The night before, it had rained. As we drove past the rolling hills surrounding our neighborhood, the greens shined with an unnatural brightness. The humidity broke with the storm and the air had a dry yet crisp touch. The perfect day to be outside in nature.

When we first arrived, the place was ours. Jake and Laney raced out onto the mulched playground, hitting everything in a quick circuit. While they climbed on a giant turtle, the late-morning sun dappling their laughing faces, I got the rare urge to take a picture. I knew that our family photo album suffered with me being the one home, but for that day at least, we would have a lasting memory.

"Guys, look over here," I said.

They turned and noticed my camera phone. Both made funny faces and I snapped the picture, laughing. It came out pretty good, so I decided to send it to Rachel's new phone. Something about looking at the picture, seeing the moment encapsulated in time, caused me to realize something. My kids' lives would be built on a foundation of moments just like that one. Although it could be tough being home with them, maybe even more so because of my gender, I realized a simple truth. I would miss very few moments of their childhood.

By the time I looked up again, three groups of kids had arrived, spreading out among the various slides and jungle gyms. Laney immediately cozied up to two girls about her age. Laughing, they played house under one of the wooden structures, selling mulch to the other children as they raced past.

For a moment, I couldn't find Jake. Finally, I saw him on a swing. He rocked slowly back and forth, watching everyone else play, a smile on his face. I could plainly see he was not bothered. For some reason, I was. I meandered over and sat on a swing beside him.

"What's up, buddy?"

"Nothing."

"You having fun?" I asked.

He nodded.

Shaking my head, I laughed. "Better than the playdate, right?"

It came out before I thought about it. When it did, it sounded way too familiar, too grown up to be saying to my son at his age. He laughed, though.

We sat next to each other for a little while. At one point, Laney came racing over.

"Is today Tuesday?" she asked, out of breath.

"Yes."

"I want to go to the playdate."

"Maybe next week."

She paused, looking me in the eyes. I could tell she considered arguing. Then one of her new friends called out and she raced back to her mulch store, content as always.

A minute later, my phone buzzed. Rachel replied to my text.

Looks like fun. Wish I could be there.

"Can we get going soon?" Jake asked.

"Sure, buddy," I said, still looking at my phone.

That night, after the kids went to bed, I still had the text on my mind. Finally, I brought it up as Rachel brushed her teeth.

"Should I not have sent you that picture today?"

"What?" she asked, spitting into the sink.

"The picture. Maybe I shouldn't have sent it to you at work."

She turned to look at me, her head tilted to the side. "Why not?"

"I know that it's hard sometimes for you. You know, being at work."

She shook her head. "Most people don't notice things like you do. I . . . I guess I was just a little jealous. I wished I was there at the park with you guys."

Although my mind slipped into a familiar rut, the one where I decided Rachel was regretting her decision to hold the full-time job and I failed to support my family, I push it back, knowing that avenue would lead to one heck of a fight.

"Should I not send you pictures then?"

"Simon! Of course I want pictures," she said. "What mother wouldn't?"

"Okay," I said.

I brushed my teeth. I wanted to talk more, to ask Rachel about her day, but my mind moved on to the next day's schedule. I ticked through the minutiae, which clothes the kids would wear, what we would do for lunch. At some point, Rachel must have climbed into bed. She was asleep by the time I got there.

CHAPTER 10

DAY ONE

Rachel slips from the adjoining hotel room while I am still staring at my phone. I have received fifty texts in the past three hours. All are either from family members or people in the media. Each feels like a shard of glass piercing my heart because not one is from Jake. Another text comes in as I put my phone back in my pocket. Paper crinkles as I jam it in and I remember the note.

"Oh shit," I whisper.

"What?" Rachel says.

I pull the notebook page out and show it to her. "I found it this morning and grabbed it while we were in the house. It's from Jake's book."

Rachel does not move. She looks pale. I open the paper and read. In the top margin above the normal classroom notes, I see a few lines written large enough for someone sitting next to Jake in class to read:

THAT'S MESSED UP! YOU NEED TO STOP. I JUST WANT
ALL THIS CRAP TO GO AWAY. AND GET RID OF THAT

THING. IF YOU LEAVE IT THERE, THAT'S IT. I'LL NEVER
TALK TO YOU AGAIN.

Rachel reads it as I do. When I look up, she seems guarded.

"What is he talking about?" I say.

She appears afraid to speak, as if any hope gleaned from this information might alight and fly away.

"It could mean anything," I whisper.

She holds out a hand. In it I see her car keys.

"Go look for him," she says.

I nod. Finally.

Once out of the hotel, I cross the parking lot to the car, Rachel's Audi. The key feels funny in my hand, shaped very differently from my Ford's. I pop it into the ignition and hit the gas. Her car wants to drive fast. The engine lives, breathing fire and raring to do zero to sixty in some absurd fraction of time. I let it, racing away from the hotel. The torrent of thoughts in my head silences. I am in motion, where I belong.

I know where to look first. No matter how small, a scenario existed that kept Jake not only uninvolved in the shooting, but unscathed. Maybe he cut school. It would not be the first time. He and his friend Max had just served detention for going to McDonald's for lunch one day last week.

I latch on to that idea like a crocodile. That's a bad analogy, actually. After a crocodile latches on to something, it dives into the murk, spinning its victim, breaking bones and drowning its prey. This latching on might be the opposite. I hold tight and let the idea lift me out of the murk, into the light. It is all I have left.

Some of the hope vanishes when I check the time. Somehow, it is 3:45. Where could he be?

First, I call Max's house. No one answers, so I leave a message asking them to call me back. Next, as I drive, I sift through the countless memories, files I'd built over the years of being with Jake and Laney near enough to 24/7. I decide that if Jake cut by himself (no one else is missing), he must have been upset about something. Girl trouble, maybe, although he never mentioned girls to me. I vowed to check with Laney when I got back, even though the thought felt absurd once I spawned it.

If Jake was struggling, where would he go? I had an idea. The three of us used to walk in the woods off a park by the house. Deep in the foliage, we'd come across an old church. We felt like we'd found something lost to history. When we came across old gravestones, most from the period between the American Revolution and the Civil War, the experience touched Jake. I could see a little explorer born. Laney got creeped out, so we didn't stay long that first time. Jake and I, however, had returned many times after. In fact, while leaning against the remaining stones of the chimney, I once asked him if it had been weird having a dad who stayed home.

Jake laughed. "No, it's just weird having you as a dad."

"Funny guy," I said, putting him in a gentle headlock. I let go. "But seriously, did anyone ever say anything to you about it?"

"Sometimes. I remember one or two teachers reacting kind of funny."

"Really, like how?" I said.

"Nothing big. Just like it was different. But the kids always thought you were pretty cool. Max said I was lucky. He thought you were pretty laid-back. I mean, you let us eat cake for breakfast sometimes."

I laughed. "Laid-back? That's funny."

"Why?" Jake asked.

I didn't answer him. For days after that, I'd felt really good. That seems so long ago now.

I park the car off the road and get out. The path runs between a local handyman's house and a big colonial with perpetually shaded windows. My body feels as if someone else sits behind the wheel. I move, with purpose, yet a haze falls over reality and I meander through it. If I stop and think about the fact that I am visiting an ancient, uncanny graveyard hidden deep in the woods, then I might consider how others might view the fact that my son felt a connection to this place.

I walk among the high, straight trunks of oaks, my pace chopped and rapid. My movement among the underbrush creates a kaleidoscope view as I scan, searching, praying that Jake will appear out of this awful dream, blissfully unaware of the tragedy engulfing our lives.

The closer I get to the spot, my destination, the slower I walk. Dread and I become magnets, opposing poles, pushing against each other. I need to get there and find Jake; yet, in getting there, another shard of hope might peel away, falling into the pit that I dare not even consider.

The path before me narrows. Briars and grasping branches pull at my clothing as I push past. A few feet ahead, it opens. I take my first step into the clearing that once held a house of worship. The ghosts of the past hover over the place, blanketing the mossy ruins and the sinking stones scattered around the hilltop like old bones.

"Jake," I call out.

The call of a red-tailed hawk answers, its screech far in the distance. I look up for the briefest of moments, trying to find it. I don't know why I do that.

"Jake," I whisper.

I search the ruins. I jog among the long dead, as if I might find him hiding behind a bush, smiling, waiting to jump out and surprise his old man so that I might clutch my chest and laugh. I know Jake is not there, but I look frantically nonetheless.

One corner of the old church still stands. It rises up, block upon block, to where I assume the roof once rose. I slow, placing a hand on the cold mortar and stone and bend around, looking into what once was the interior of the church. My heart misses a beat.

A doll hangs in the air, dangling from a frayed green cord of twine. The noose around its neck is perfectly tied. I stare at the weathered face of the doll, one eye gouged out, the other eyelid drooping closed, the red-painted lips stretched and smeared by rain, the once-blond hair jagged and jutting out in matted, dirty clumps. I fall to my knees, the tears exploding from me with violent pulses. I cannot breathe. I cannot think. I sob, coughing and sputtering, and I am not sure I will ever stop. For the first time, I truly doubt my son.

Darkness lifts me out of darkness. The sun sets behind the skeletal tree trunks. Icy pain radiates from my knees, whether from the age-related pain of kneeling for too long or the frigid wetness seeping up from the ground into my bones, I am not sure. All I realize is that I have knelt in the remains of the old church for too long. Time I could have spent looking for Jake is now lost. I must get hold of myself. What kind of father am I? Yet the doll haunts me. At first, I cannot touch it. What it hints at cripples me. The fact that it hints at anything makes me feel the betrayer. Worse, it makes me feel like a stranger.

I have to support myself as I stand, the circulation grudgingly returning to my jellylike legs. The doll, with its insane eyes and tattered and mildewed clothes that look more like melting skin, overwhelms my vision. It is all I see, but I can't let anyone else see this abomination. Staggering, I lunge for it, trying to tear it from the rusted support rod to which it is tied. The weathered twine catches and I notice the intricate knot securing it to the rod. I tug again but it does not budge.

I have a small Swiss Army knife attached to my key chain. Rachel, who travels all the time, tells me this is crazy, that I'll never get through airport security. I never travel, so I have left it there for years. Now, I fish it from my pocket and pry open the thin, small blade. Reaching up close to the rod, I slice through the twine. The doll tumbles to the decaying leaves below. Snatching it up and tucking the rancid thing under my arm, I head to the car.

"It's Doug's." I laugh to myself. "Jake would never touch a doll."

Once the last word leaves my lips, I convince myself. I look around, afraid someone might hear me. I press the doll deeper under my arm, blocking it from view. It dawns on me that I am breaking a law, a very serious law. Rachel would say I am obstructing justice. It might be the second time that day.

When I reach the car, a warning flag waves in my head, telling me I should rethink taking the doll from the scene. At the same time, I think about the other evidence I have removed, the note. I pull it out and reread it. Could this doll be what Jake was talking about? If so . . .

"A *crime* scene," I say, shaking my head.

I know what I am doing is wrong, but what would the police think if they found that thing hanging there? It would be bad enough if they found out Jake liked to hang out at some old cemetery. It would paint a false picture of him, one they would use to accuse him of this shooting. I can't let that happen. It would ruin his life.

Taking a deep breath, I open the door to my wife's car, throwing the doll into the backseat. I almost toss the note there as well, but stuff it back in my pocket instead. Getting in, I try to think, to decide where else Jake might be. The batting cages? He went there sometimes. I decide to head to the open space where Jake and his friends play football every Sunday afternoon. Maybe he's there. Or maybe Max is. I could ask him. He would know where to find Jake.

Doubt creeps through my thoughts. If Jake was okay, why wouldn't he have shown up? He had to have heard all the commotion. Not if he was on the run. I force the thought down, bury it where it cannot breathe life into other, more damaging considerations.

Absently, I push the key into the ignition. Her engine growls to life. It is a familiar sound. When the kids were younger, it was the sound I could not wait to hear. It harkened Rachel's return, the instant in every day (at least the days she was not traveling) when I no longer had to be responsible (at least not fully) for our children.

Jake Connolly.

My son's name hangs in the air around me, confusing, frightening, until I realize the radio has turned on. My heart freezes as I listen, expecting Jake has been found.

> *Police now believe that Douglas Martin-Klein did not act alone. According to one source inside the department, another senior, Jake Connolly, was with Martin-Klein less than an hour before the shooting. Officers are in the process of searching the boy's home. As we have reported earlier, unconfirmed reports are that the body of at least one of the shooters, Douglas Martin-Klein, has been recovered at the scene of today's nightmarish massacre.*

My hand shakes as I reach for the knob. I manage to turn off the radio as cold sweat beads on my face. There is no denial; no outrage; no pain; just utter, numbing shock. I cannot explain how it feels to hear something like that about your son because I have no idea how I feel. Instead, there is a void of feeling, a void of understanding, a void of action. There is nothing. Absolute but not final.

CHAPTER 11

JAKE: AGE NINE

My mother arrived at noon to watch Laney. I had already dressed in a button-down shirt and a pair of black Dockers. Rachel liked to say I was the only person she knew who bought the black ones. I tried to think of someone else but couldn't. At the same time, the tan ones made me feel like I might attend a college formal.

"Simon?"

"I'm upstairs."

I heard footsteps as she walked into the kitchen.

"Laney-poo!"

Having seen this greeting a hundred times before, I pictured my daughter launching herself into the air, awkwardly engulfing my mother's torso. The two of them shared a wide, toothy grin, passed on to yet another generation of Connolly women.

I stood in the closet, debating. Since leaving my old job, I had worn a tie exactly four times. Three of them had been meetings with my growing list of medical-writing clients and one had been Rachel's brother's late-in-life re-wedding to her new sister-in-law, a wire artist from Pasadena. As expected, she and Rachel did not have much in common. Mark now shared fifty-fifty custody of the children he had raised so perfectly. I missed him, although after that one night life had too many times gotten in the way of us bonding.

I decided against the tie. For some reason, I tried not to wear jeans to school, even though I wore them 99 percent of the time. I thought it would reflect poorly on the kids. A button-down and Dockers would do, though, so I headed downstairs.

My mother sat on one of our counter stools, leaning in and gushing over one of Laney's drawings.

"That is the best tree I have ever seen."

"It's blue, Grammy," Laney said, her head tilted.

I smiled. "Where's Jake?"

My mom rolled her eyes. My skin burned as my blood pressure rose higher than it should.

"What?"

"What?" she asked back.

"What happened?"

My mother sighed and looked out the window. "What did I do to become the hated grandmother?"

I looked at Laney, whose little eyes grew wide.

"Come here," I said, trying to keep my voice calm.

She followed me into the den. I shut the two swinging doors so Laney couldn't hear me. Then I checked the room. Sometimes Jake read his book with a flashlight under the table next to the couch. I didn't want him to hear the conversation. The coast clear, I turned to her.

"You can't say stuff like that in front of her," I said. "Shit, you shouldn't say that kind of stuff ever."

"Watch your language."

I took a deep breath. "Jesus, you always do that. You try to deflect."

"What are you talking about?"

"Jake!"

"I just wanted to know what I did to make him mad. When I came in, he didn't even look up from his book."

"I've told you a hundred times before, he's just like that. He does that to everyone. He's just a little awkward sometimes."

"It wasn't a hundred times," she said.

"GOD! Please stop that."

She blinked. "What?"

"Just back off him, okay? He's nine. You're the adult. Stop taking it so personally."

"I just thought things were better. I tried so hard to be nice to him, and now we're right back where we started from."

I covered my face with my hands, pressing into my temples as I slid them down. "Please, Mom. He's my son. Do you think I don't talk to him about it?"

"I just don't get it," she said.

I barked out a laugh. "Are you serious? Where do you think he gets it from? Remember when your friend, Mrs. Masterson next door, offered me candy and I said no because she was a stranger?"

"That never happened."

I turned away from her, attempting to hide my frustration. "I have to go. I don't want to be late for his conference."

Swinging open the doors, I walked into the kitchen and called out, "Jake."

"Yeah, Dad," he responded from the basement.

I walked down slowly, thinking. I found Jake in one of the beanbag chairs. He had two football-player figurines in his hands and he was making bone-crushing noises. He did not look up at me when I walked down.

"You okay?"

"Sure," he said.

"Did you say hi to your grandmother when she got here?"

He glanced at me through red-rimmed eyes. "I forgot."

"Buddy."

"Sorry, Dad."

A fat tear pooled and then dripped clear down his face. Another followed.

"Come on, none of that," I said.

"Sorry."

I often wondered if Jake's heart might be a little too big. I knew he cried because he felt he did something wrong, and that maybe he hurt his grandmother. It made making the point all that much harder, but I still had to do it.

"It's okay. Just try to be nice to her, okay? She thinks . . ."

"What?" he asked.

"Nothing. Just try, okay?"

He sat up straight. "What were you going to say?"

"Nothing. I have to go to your conference."

"I hope they don't say anything bad," he muttered, looking away.

I laughed. "They never do."

I texted Rachel from the parking lot of the school. Waiting a minute for a response, I decided to head in. One of us had to be on time. Although I'm sure the teacher wouldn't actually yell at us, I wasn't taking any chances. We had been a few minutes late to Laney's and I felt awful.

I waved to the two women working in the front office and turned down Jake's hallway. Parents of a kid I coached in recreational soccer stood outside the room next door waiting for their conference to begin. I waved.

"Hey there, Coach," the dad said. His wife smiled.

"How's Marcus? Ready for next season?"

"You bet."

I walked past them and peeked through the window of the door. The meeting before ours was still in progress, so I turned back to the parents in the hall.

"Tough loss in the play-offs," he said.

"That team seemed stacked."

"You're coaching in the spring, right?" Marcus's mom asked.

"Definitely. As long as Jake still wants to play."

Jake and Marcus weren't buddies. They got along fine at soccer but I don't think they talked to each other at school. I got along well with his parents, though, so we chatted until Jake's teacher called me into class. I glanced down the hallway hoping to see Rachel, but still no sign.

Ms. Jenkins smiled as she ushered me into her room. Colorful drawings papered the walls, jaunty lines melding together from picture to picture, creating a motif of nine-year-oldness. A table toward the back of the room held a troop of bottle people, little effigies of history's finest—Amelia Earhart, Albert Einstein, Thomas Edison—made out of empty designer water bottles. Looking at them, I wished our last name began with an *E* instead of a *C*. Who'd we have on our team? Bill Clinton and Casanova?

"Have a seat, Mr. Connolly." Ms. Jenkins looked over my shoulder, her expression comically troubled. "Is Mrs. Connolly going to join us?"

"She's running just a little late," I said.

Ms. Jenkins motioned toward a low, round table. One full-size chair rested on her side. An array of three miniaturized versions lined our side. I took a step in the direction of the real chair but Ms. Jenkins landed in it before I could. She looked at the little chair.

"Should we wait?" she asked.

I tried to fit my rear on the tiny seat, teetering back and forth until I found a semblance of comfort. When I turned to Ms. Jenkins, I realized I had to look up at her. I instantly felt like a child, folding my hands in my lap and waiting to get in trouble.

"I guess not," I said.

"Are you suuuure?"

She looked at me as if I might not be allowed to make important decisions, and I wondered if she had figured it out yet. Did she know I stayed home with the kids?

"Okay." She shuffled a folder around. "Let me start by saying Jake is a great kid. I really enjoy his perspective on things."

What's that supposed to mean?

She continued. "Here are his scores. He's right where he should be."

I scanned the paper. One column listed the subjects/skills: math, reading comprehension, social studies (at nine years old? ha), etc. The second column had a number, I assumed from 1 to 100. Jake earned 90s in all but one. On the right corner of the sheet, I noticed a column labeled class average. To my amazement, those scores were in the 90s and high 80s as well. How could the class average be so high? It was the first time I truly realized that we had moved to an area of high achievers and I suddenly felt like a total slacker.

Already feeling insecure, my eyes returned to Jake's lowest score, well below the class average. I traced it over to the subject.

"What is citizenship?" I asked.

I seemed to remember something from my grade school, maybe a good citizenship award for some girl who sold her stuffed animals and gave the profits to charity. Her mother made her, but no one mentioned that. Jake, it seemed, struggled in this department. He scored a 54.

"Well, citizenship is the responsibility of all students to understand the best interest of everyone in the class and act accordingly. We strive to teach our children the core values on which to build toward becoming enlightened, contributing members of society."

This came out like a rehearsed speech. I paused, making sure she was finished before speaking.

"How did Jake manage to get a fifty-four?"

My question, at first, had more to do with such a precise grade given for such an ethereal concept as "citizenship." That's not the question Ms. Jenkins answered, however.

"I wanted to talk to you about this. Jake, sometimes, he doesn't always fully engage in class."

My chest hurt. Up until that moment, no teacher had ever spoken negatively about Jake. In past years we had been told that he always helped other students, that he never said anything negative to anyone, and that he was a general joy to have in class. Once or twice a teacher had mentioned that he shied away from groups, but not in a critical way. More with a smile that said, *That's just our Jake*. Ms. Jenkins caught me totally off guard.

"Wow," I said. "What do you mean?"

"For example, last Thursday." She cleared her throat. "We performed a class play on the plight of Rosa Parks. I assigned roles to each of the students, randomly, mind you. Jake was supposed to be the bus driver. When it came time to read his lines, though, he wouldn't do it."

"What do you mean 'he wouldn't do it'?"

"Just that. He didn't read his lines. Even after the appropriate encouragement."

I lost track for a second, trying to figure out what she meant by "appropriate encouragement."

"Mr. Connolly?"

"Oh, yeah. Well, I know he doesn't like a lot of attention."

"I see," she said, nodding gravely. "Jake is a shy kid. I've noticed that."

The hair on the back of my neck stood up. "He's not shy. He has lots of friends."

Ms. Jenkins leaned back, as if assessing me. I fidgeted, and the door to the classroom opened. Rachel burst in, crisply attired in her business suit. The tension broke, making room for all new tension.

"Mrs. Connolly, glad you could make it. I'm sure you're so busy"—she looked my wife's business suit over—"with work and everything. I just don't know how you do it all."

Rachel and I stood together out in the parking lot. The telltale crinkle in her left brow told me she was pissed. At what, I hadn't decided yet.

"You okay?" I asked.

"Did you hear her? What the hell was that about?"

"I know." I let out a huge breath and the tension left my shoulders. "Can you believe she called Jake *shy*?"

Rachel's head tilted. "He is, Simon."

My eyes narrowed. "What?"

"He's shy. At least when he's in groups. But he's doing great. He has his friends and they have fun. That's all he needs."

My mind spun. She'd never said that before. I did not agree, either. In fact, her comment made me angry. Jake was not shy. Judgmental, maybe, but not shy. When he was uncomfortable, he got quiet. That was it.

"That's not at all what I was talking about. You know she's married, right?" Rachel asked.

"Huh?"

"All that crap about *Ms.* Jenkins. She's married, for Christ's sake. And she calls me *Mrs.* and she has to comment on how I'm too busy."

"She did?"

Rachel scowled. "You are so oblivious sometimes. You know, this isn't easy, for either of us. You think I don't know why you get insecure with the guys in the neighborhood, or why you coach everything? It's hard on me, too. Every day, I feel guilty. Every story I hear about the kids doing something fun, a little part of me aches. But we decided this is what works best for us, right?"

I nod. "I guess we did."

The next day, the kids had a day off. More parent/teacher conferences were scheduled; I was still reeling from ours. Jake and Laney didn't wake up until after Rachel left for work. They padded into our room together, whispering. Already awake, I lay silently on the bed, my entire body growing warm, a silly grin spreading across my face.

I loved to hear them talk to each other when they didn't know I was listening.

"Alex said I had a fat face," Laney said.

"He's stupid," Jake quickly responded.

"Yeah."

"You want me to talk to him?"

"No." She sounded incensed. "I told him he was short like a fire hydrant."

"Good one. What's up with that kindergarten kid that keeps licking the window?"

"He's not right."

Jake laughed. I tried not to. I felt their little eyes on me.

"Maybe we should just turn on the TV," Laney whispered.

Jake spoke nicely to his little sister. "Nah, I'm hungry. Plus, it's a day off. You want to play swords while Dad makes breakfast?"

"Sure, yeah."

I turned my head, still smiling. "Hi, guys."

"Hi, Dad!" they screamed together, jumping up onto the bed. Jake snuggled in on one side and Laney on the other. I did not want to move. I knew that someday this would all end, that it would be uncool to snuggle with Dad. So I absorbed and savored every second like it was my last.

When they finally grew fidgety, we got up. I started making breakfast and the two took their seats at the counter. The phone ringing startled me and I splashed some of the egg I scrambled out of the bowl. I looked at the clock. It was only 8:30.

"Hello," I answered looking at the caller ID.

"May I please speak to Jake," a young voice asked.

"Sure, hold on."

I thought it was Max, Jake's football buddy, but when I checked the ID, it read *Unavailable*. I handed the phone to Jake and listened in as I continued to make breakfast.

"Hey. Yeah. Let me ask my dad."

Jake did not cover the receiver when he spoke to me. "Can I go to Doug's?"

I motioned for him to cover it, but he just shrugged. I took the phone from his hand and did it myself.

"Doug?"

"Yeah, I went to his birthday. Remember?"

Jake liked to think me senile (though he didn't know the word for it yet).

"I don't know," I said.

"Why not, Dad?"

He did not whine. Jake never whined, but his flat tone caused me to second-guess my decision all the more.

"Tell him you'll call him back."

I gave Jake back the phone and he did as asked. After the call ended, he asked me again.

"I think we'll go to the park today. And Laney will want you there."

"I don't want to go to the park," Laney chimed in, sitting beside Jake. "I want to go to Becca's house."

"I just think we should hang out together today. That's all."

"But I told Doug that we could finish the fort."

Again, Jake's tone hinted at an absence of emotion behind his plea. He simply stated a fact, like his mother might in the courtroom. Knowing him as I did, I got it. I could see his disappointment.

"We'll see. Let me call your mom and then I'll decide."

He appeared fine with that. A terse nod and Jake buried his head back into the football book he'd read about a dozen times. I considered my motives as I scrambled Laney's eggs. She liked them barely cooked, with a sprinkle of cheese.

Other factors complicated my decision. Tairyn had, in fact, called earlier inviting Laney over. I really had no excuse, but something itched at the back of my mind. I could not admit to myself, particularly considering the lesson that had led to Doug and Jake being friends, that I simply did not like the kid, or for that matter, his father. I'd run into him a couple of times since the birthday party and we'd shared, at a conservative estimate, three words.

I set Laney's plate down in front of her and grabbed the phone. Walking back into the den, I dialed Rachel's office.

"Hey there," she answered.

"Question. Should I let Jake go over to the Martin-Kleins'?"

Rachel paused before answering. "Did they invite him?"

"Yeah."

"How about you have him over to our house? Then you can get to know him better."

"That's a good idea," I said, although I thought I knew him pretty well already.

"Why do you think he shouldn't go over?"

"That kid's crazy."

"How do you know?"

"Karen said he goes to the guidance counselor, like, every day."

She laughed. "So now you're listening to Karen? I seem to remember last month you called her a wolverine trapped in the body of a mime."

"I said that?"

"Yup."

I smiled. "That's a pretty good one."

"I didn't get it," she said, deadpan.

"She's a vicious animal that can only passively act out her insecurities and loathing."

"Anyway," Rachel said. "Do you know the kid?"

"I know his parents. His dad is a weirdo."

"By your own admission, you've said a total of seven words to the guy. Maybe he's just *shy*."

I caught the change in tone on that last word. It cut me. I knew she referred to my reaction after the parent/teacher conference. My lack of response to her opinion chafed Rachel still. A stealth argument had brewed since the day before. I wanted no part of it.

"I'll take him over then. No biggie."

"You don't have to." Her voice reverted to a more genial tone, one I hadn't heard since the morning before the conference. "You could bring the kids in for lunch."

"No, it's all right."

Once I answered, I regretted it. I should have just said yes. I knew she cherished any time she could get with the kids. Plus, I didn't even want Jake to go to Doug's. I really don't know why I didn't take her up on her offer. Maybe it was the *shy* comment.

I picked Jake up early that afternoon. Once again, he waited outside with Doug. I took a good look at the kid this time. He appeared nondescript. Clean, well dressed, but not in an awkward way. I still couldn't put my finger on my misgivings. He did look up when my car rolled to a stop, watching me. I felt there was something calculating behind his expression, his thin lips, his soft stare through hard eyes. Shaking my head, I thought about what Rachel often said to me, that I assigned adult intentions to children.

Jake beamed when he saw me. A wide smile on his face, he gave what looked like a hearty thank you and good-bye to Doug and ran to my car. He jumped in and I could see he was excited.

"You should see our fort. It's awesome."

"Your fort?"

"Yeah," he said. "We worked on it all day."

"Where is it?" I asked.

"In his backyard, kinda. There's woods back there and a pond, so it's a little past."

"Can you see his house from there?"

"I dunno," he said.

He went on to describe in ecstatic detail the building he and

Doug worked on. It did sound cool, but I felt uneasy the entire time. When Rachel got home that evening and the kids made it to bed, I brought it up.

"They couldn't even see his house," I said.

She smiled. "Simon, Jake's a boy. That's what boys do. You raised him right. I trust him. You have to let him grow up a little bit. What's going to happen?"

I couldn't answer that. My brain could. It flashed gruesome pictures of dismemberment, debauchery, defilement, every awful *de* word I could imagine. That's how I knew she was right. I had to ease up. Not just for the kids' sakes, but for my own, too.

CHAPTER 12

DAY ONE

When I leave the old church, I drive straight to the Martin-Kleins' house. When I turn into the neighborhood, I know right away that I will not get close to the house, at least not in the car. Police vehicles block off the street starting at least five houses down the way from the Martin-Kleins'. The cordoned-off area begins just past that and a line three deep of people stretches across the street and up onto people's yards. A nervous energy permeates the scene.

I park the car and get out. As I do, I notice the doll conspicuously resting on the backseat. People turn and look at me. Most recognize who I am. They look distraught and angry, and a murmur passes through the crowd. More eyes track me as I take a step toward the yellow police tape.

Reporters with cameras move toward me. I imagine the shot, me standing outside Rachel's car, a creepy one-eyed doll in the backseat. Even I have enough sense to back away. As the cameras near, I turn and rush back into the car. They film me driving away.

I pound the steering wheel, frustrated by being balked. I drive past the neighborhood three times, but nothing changes. So I turn my attention to everywhere I have ever known Jake to be. I pass the football field, his friends' neighborhoods, Max's house (which looks empty), even the grocery store for some reason. I find nothing. While I meander through the neighborhoods surrounding the school, my phone rings. It is Rachel.

"They found the hotel."

"Who?"

"The media."

"I figured—"

"No, Laney is down in the lobby. Alone."

My heart sinks. "Why? How?"

"The elevator's taking too goddamn long. I'm going to the stairs. We didn't know. She wanted a water."

"I'm coming."

I race out of the neighborhood and onto the highway. I enter the city in less than five minutes. From three blocks away, I see the news vans laying siege to our hotel. Like the crenelated parapet of a white watchtower, they line every street bordering the Marriot.

I swerve over to the right lane and turn, slamming Rachel's car into the first spot (legal or not) that I see. Once the car stops, I tear the keys from the ignition and bull my way out of the door. At a full run, I cross through an alley and end up across the street from the hotel. I expect a throng of reporters. Instead, an eerie silence greets me, scaring me to the core.

I pry the lobby doors open to get inside faster. I see the mass of bodies, like hopping vultures vying for carrion. Although I cannot make her out, I somehow know Laney is at the center, Rachel trying to shield her from the frenzy.

"Hey," I shout.

My shoulder barrels into the back of one of the cameramen. Someone curses and I push him (I think it is a male) out of the way.

I see my daughter for the first time, her eyes wide and glistening with tears. Rachel is with her, holding her close.

"Daddy," she calls out.

I elbow someone, then sweep my daughter and wife up as if hiding them under a wing.

"Mr. Connolly! Mr. Connolly!"

Green lights flash to life, like devilish spider eyes, threatening and surreal. I hold Laney tighter and she presses against me. I feel her shaking.

"I just wanted a water."

"Leave us alone."

"Are you surprised by what your son did?"

"Were there warning signs?"

"Are you aware of what your son posted on the Internet?"

"Have any of the victims' parents tried to contact you?"

The questions meld into a shrill torture. My head throbs and I push into the mass of reporters, Laney in tow.

"Get the hell out of the way!" I shout.

More questions lash out at us as I plod toward the elevator.

"Any comment on the drawings they found at your house?"

"How long have your son and Doug Martin-Klein been friends?"

I pound the up arrow just as the city cops arrive. They begin what I expect will be a long process of ushering the reporters out of the lobby. Laney sobs; I hear it over the chaos. A reporter grabs my shoulder.

Events unfold as if someone else guides my actions; a gremlin usurps control of my nervous system. I swing at the guy. Luckily, he dodges back. There is no contact, but those green lights tell me I have been taped. Closing my eyes, I back up toward the elevator door. It opens and I nearly fall inside, Rachel right behind me. Laney's crying grows louder as the doors close. I hold her. What else is there to do?

"It'll be okay, peanut," I whisper. "It'll be okay."

Rachel stands staring at the closed doors. My head tilts as I look at her. Laney bolts out of the carriage when the door opens, racing to our rooms. Rachel does not move. She looks lost.

"What?" I ask.

Once I say it, I know I should have remained quiet. No matter how I react, this pallor will hold tightly to my family, unable and unwilling to loosen its piercing grip. In this instant, I understand what I saw in Rachel's eyes. Hopelessness. This is something I have never seen before, not in her.

Rachel is a rock. She has never faltered, not once. Over the years, our marriage may have, but she never did. It is one of those things that drives me crazy. When we fight, there is no reaction. I cannot get to her. Yet all this has.

I lead her back to the room she shares with Laney. The hallway is silent. I imagine eyes pressed against peepholes watching us toil down purgatory. When we reach the room, Rachel's hand trembles as she attempts to insert the key card. I reach forward, but her shoulder shifts, blocking me. Laney cries softly beside her mother.

When the card finds the slot and she gets the door open, Rachel leads Laney into the room.

"Can I lie down?" My daughter's voice is paper thin.

"Sure, sweetie," I say.

Rachel darts a quick look at me and moves to settle Laney in one of the two queen beds.

"Will you sit here with me?" I hear Laney whisper.

Rachel responds too softly for me to hear. Once Laney is settled, my wife walks over to me. She passes and nods for me to follow her into the bathroom. My limbs remind me of a zombie as I shuffle toward her. Nothing makes sense anymore.

"We need a plan," I say. "I need to do something."

"In the morning, I think we should talk to Max. Maybe he knows something," she says.

"I left a message."

Or did I? I honestly cannot remember. The past hours have lost all clarity. Inexcusably, I think about the movies. Those parents, caught up in some awful tragedy paralleling our own, act the heroes, persevere against all odds, track down the clues and find the answers, gun in hand, nursing a nonfatal wound to the shoulder. For me, it is nothing of the sort. Instead the tsunami of reality pushes me, all of us, along, forcing us down this path of inactivity, bureaucracy, and flashbulbs. It is a wave of staggering weight that holds us captive to the nothingness.

"I'll go over now," I announce, unwilling or unable to stop fighting the storm.

"It's almost midnight," she says.

"It is? So what?"

Rachel stares at me for a time. "In the morning."

I take a breath. "I went to the Martin-Kleins' house."

"What?"

"I didn't get close. The police have it closed off." I leave the doll part out of the story.

"I don't know what to do," she says. "We need to know what's happening. I think Laney will feel better having you here. That shit downstairs got to her."

I nod. I understand this. I need to stay close, protect my family. Although my family, in its entirety, is not here. I rub my eyes, walking into the other room and sitting down on the end of the bed. My wife returns to our daughter. As the door between the rooms slowly closes, I turn on the television. I feel like I have been here before. The moments revolve like I'm trapped on some hellish hamster wheel. Time is on a loop. Before I focus on the television screen, this thought troubles me. A loop implies there is no past and no future, there is only repetition.

Then, I see and hear the outside world, those not stuck on our awful little wheel. My soul breaks in the minutes that follow. At first, it is an instant collage on the screen, people I know, facts I know, and places I know all folded into an enormous nightmare. Snippets stand out, punctuating the horror:

Karen appears on the television. She stands outside our house. Her face swoops, a somber and premeditated curve of the mouth and eyebrow in unison. I've seen this look before, as if she's prepared the ultimate backhanded compliment. I can't remember what she said in the past; I will never forget what she says now.

"He was a quiet kid," she says, peering into the camera. "A loner. He never really joined in when my son, Bo, had all his friends over. I tried to reach out to his father, but he was sort of standoffish, I guess. His wife, Rachel, was always more friendly. Although they kept to themselves a lot."

A girl I have never seen before speaks to a reporter just outside the cordoned-off area surrounding the school. Her blond hair hangs just above her eyes in perfectly coiffed bangs. The rest bounces behind in a jaunty ponytail. She speaks with an accent reminiscent of the Valley girls of my youth.

"Doug and Jake hung out all the time. The two of them always had their heads together. It was, like, really weird, you know? They kept to themselves all the time. No one really talked to them that much. I remember this one time, like, forever ago, Doug invited me to this birthday party. My parents wouldn't let me go. They must have seen something, even then. I guess, you know, I'm just not all that surprised."

A local anchor looks seriously into the camera. Even they are now reporting the story throughout the night.

"It is thought that two seniors at the school, Douglas Martin-Klein and Jake Connolly, planned and executed a horrible massacre this morning, killing thirteen. The body of Martin-Klein has been positively identified after he took his own life, apparently after running out of ammunition for the assault-style rifle he used in the shooting. The whereabouts of Connolly are currently unknown. Let's go to Lisa Ann, at the scene."

The camera cuts to a woman standing outside the school, surprisingly close to the same angle of the girl a minute before. She wears a windbreaker with the logo of the local station. Her appearance hints at the beauty she must have been ten years before, yet the makeup cannot entirely hide the passage of time. Beside her stands another woman, most likely in her seventies, who stares at the camera with unabashed anger.

"Hi, Kevin. I'm here outside the school where police are still searching for Jake Connolly, a high school senior thought to be one of the shooters. With me I have Donna Jackson, the owner of property adjacent to the school. She claims to have seen someone fleeing through her property at the time of the shooting."

"I saw that kid running through my field," Donna Jackson spits out. "Right as rain, I did. He ran into the woods toward the neighborhood back there."

"Was this before or after the shooting?"

Donna Jackson's eyes look strangely vacant. "Sure was."

Lisa Ann narrows her eyes. "Okay. Well, are you sure it was Jake Connolly?"

"The police showed me a picture. This kid had the same dark hair, if you know what I mean."

Lisa Ann's eyes widen, as if that was not part of the script. She pulls the microphone away from Donna Jackson. "Back to you, Kevin."

Tairyn appears next on another local station. Her gaunt face and lined neck clash with her $200 haircut and her diamond earrings. She wears expensive running clothes. I realize my thoughts are cruel, but all I can do now is protect and in protecting lash out.

"Jake was raised by his father, really. His mom wasn't around all that much. My daughter played with his daughter, so I'm one of the few people around here who have been in the house. I always tried to be nice to Simon, to include him in neighborhood activities, but I think he sort of looked down on all of us, the 'stay-at-home moms' here. I know he let Jake do things that I always wondered about. Even at a young age, I would see him playing with swords . . . and probably guns, you know, violent stuff like that. I guess . . ." She swallows her apparent emotions. "I guess I should have seen this coming. Those poor kids."

Tairyn can no longer talk. She is choked up, waving at the camera, but the shot lingers. She tries to brush it away, her eyes brimming with tears.

"I'm sorry, I can't."

The camera pans to their front door. There stands her daughter, Laney's old friend Becca. She happens to be wearing a high school hoodie. Although I expect Tairyn to react poorly, to cut the scene and tell them not to film her daughter, she motions Becca over. Becca wraps around Tairyn, who hugs her daughter close. It reminds me of how I held Laney in the lobby, but something is different. The two cock their heads in the exact same manner and I am reminded of a women's glamour magazine.

"It could have been her," Tairyn says, dabbing at an eye with a tissue. "My daughter was there when the shooting happened."

Although it looks as if Tairyn beckons her daughter to speak, Becca does not. She stares vacantly into the camera for a few seconds. She looks like she might be in shock.

"He was a quiet guy," another man says, one of the Martin-Kleins' neighbors. "Kept to himself mostly. Never came to any of the neighborhood parties. I'm sure he was invited, though."

The reporter nods. The conversation continues, rehashing much of the same judgment every "eyewitness" has shared since I turned the TV back on at six this morning. Finally, the reporter finishes up with this neighbor and looks thoughtfully into the camera.

"We may never know what caused Douglas Martin-Klein to turn on his own classmates. Violent video games, bullying, or mental illness, time will tell. Back to you, Jake."

Jake. Adrenaline pumps through my system, a jolt of draining energy that disappears as quickly as it came. Simply coincidence, but the sound of someone speaking to *Jake* is both hopeful and devastating.

The anchor introduces another field reporter. This one, somehow, has gotten himself into the library at the school.

". . . as first reported by Gawker.com, Douglas Martin-Klein's Instagram page paints a sad, grisly story of a boy crying out for help. This troubling image, a picture of a red fist bound by a gray cord, was used as his profile picture on the widely popular Web site."

There is something familiar about the image, but I don't remember before the reporter continues.

"Many may recognize the image from an album cover nearly a decade ago by the band Metallica. I went back and listened to the songs. What I heard will shock you. Here are just some of the lyrics:

> "'*Invisible kid*
> *Locked away in his brain*
> *From the shame and the pain*
> *World down the drain*'

"It makes we wonder how we failed this sad young man."

Never a huge heavy metal fan, I did recall that album, *St. Anger*. Strangely, I didn't remember it being one of their most popular, or best. I did not, however, know the song the reporter quoted. *World down the drain*. Sad, but not exactly Sylvia Plath. For that matter, it did not sound all that angry or violent.

The screen catches my eye, cutting off the thought. High school yearbook pictures pan like a police lineup. I see Leigh and James. Amanda's smiling face brings back memories of her being at our house, playing with Laney. A couple of unfamiliar kids are shown, and then one of the pictures hits me like a fist to the face—Alex Raines.

. . .

On one particular afternoon, around two months ago, Jake came home and I could tell immediately something was wrong. Anger flared on his face, reddening his cheeks and darkening his eyes. He went up to his room and closed the door. I stood in the kitchen, listening to see if he came back out, but the house was quiet. I tried to give him some time but my own curiosity kept those better intentions from being realized.

I knocked and waited. When Jake finally opened the door, he looked calm, normal.

"What's up, buddy?" I asked.

"Nothing, Dad."

"You looked upset."

He gave me a look I knew all too well. He couldn't lie to me if I asked a direct question but he didn't want to talk about it. I pushed, so he told me about Alex Raines. I knew the name from baseball. Alex had been big at an early age, a good hitter who never wore anything that did not sport an Under Armour logo. He was the first kid to rock a Mohawk, albeit a coiffed one, in the second grade. I'd never really heard Jake talk about him, positively or negatively, before that day.

"I was talking to someone and accidentally backed into him. He pushed me. I guess I hit a locker. It sounded bad but it was really no big deal. Just hallway stuff."

"You look awful mad for just hallway stuff," I said.

He lifted an eyebrow. "Amnesty moment, remember?"

I let it go and by dinner, Jake was his normal self.

That evening, the guidance counselor called.

"Hi, this is Phil Hartman, school guidance counselor. May I please speak to Mr. or Mrs. Connolly?"

"This is he."

"Mr. Connolly, there was an incident at the school today. I thought we should discuss it."

"Yes, Jake and I talked about that."

I felt proud of Jake for telling me, and maybe I wanted to show it just a little.

"I'm not sure what details you received from your son, but I wanted to let you know that neither student will be receiving any punishment. We feel they both acted out but were remorseful about it."

"Both?"

Mr. Hartman cleared his throat. "Well, yes. Best I can tell, Alex started it. When he called Jake a name, Jake put his hands on Alex."

"'Put his hands on'?"

"He pushed Alex, Mr. Connolly."

I felt off balance, unprepared. "What name did he call Jake?"

"Well, he . . . he called him a 'loser.' I spoke to the Raines boy and he apologized. I just would like to see that nothing further happens in retaliation. Can you reinforce that from home?"

"Of course," I mutter. "Thank you."

The call ended and for the first time I realized something profound. Jake's life was not the open book it had been when he was younger.

I reach out and turn the television off. Alex Raines. His picture still seems to float in the room, hinting at the unthinkable. It is a tie I want to cut, a clue leading to the worst possible reality. I push it back, deny it, and let my mind cloud over.

Instead, a new picture thrusts out of this nightmare. I see Jake, huddled in the dark, alone and frightened. He shakes, his pale skin glowing in the moonlight. Tears trail down his cheeks and he rocks back and forth, full of shattering regret.

Would it be better to find him? Or should I hope that he escapes, runs away and starts a new life in hiding? He would be alive, free. But why? Was Jake bullied? Alex sure seemed capable of that, with his elementary school Mohawk.

I need to talk to Rachel. I need to figure this out. I am plagued by thoughts darker than I can handle. Whereas before, I was sure Jake was alive and well, somehow having avoided this nightmare altogether, now my mind has altered, against my will. Could Jake have done this? My heart tells me, begs me to believe, that such a scenario could not in any way be true. The television, everything else around me, tells me something else entirely. The world claims my son murdered children today. An even more unfathomable thought pops into my brain. Could that be the best outcome—alive and free?

I stagger to the bathroom and heave. Nothing comes up. My body lurches to near bursting, but there is no relief. I crumple to the cold tiled floor.

CHAPTER 13

JAKE: AGE TEN

The morning dawned with the uplifting sounds of spring. Robins chirped from the bush outside the living room window as the sunlight spread across the kitchen, shining in Laney's eyes. She sat at the table, coloring a picture she'd brought home from school. Jake sat beside her, a figurine in each hand. One, a monster of some kind, seemed to be getting the best of the blue-clad, futuristic soldier he held in the other hand.

"Don't forget to eat." I glanced over my shoulder at them. "Jake, what do you want in your lunch?"

"Bologna and cheese," he answered.

I busied myself making his lunch, occasionally checking the clock. A Wednesday in February, the morning progressed no differently from most. Rachel left for work before eight AM and the bus arrived at eight forty-five AM. After the bus stop, I planned to go to a coffee shop nearby. There I'd spend a few hours doing work for one of my freelance medical-writing clients.

"Hey, Dad," Jake said, still playing with his figures. "Can I invite Doug over after school?"

I turned away from him before answering, hoping to avoid showing my discomfort. Although Jake had visited the Martin-Kleins' house a few times, we had not reciprocated.

"What about one of your other friends?"

"Like Max?" Jake asked in a flat tone.

"Yeah, that might be easier to arrange."

I lied to him (kind of). A pang of guilt caused me to shake my head. I rarely lied to him, or Laney. I tried to be as honest as I could all the time, yet I lied to him about something as benign as a playdate.

"That's okay," Jake said.

For a second, I thought he excused my lie. Then I realized he spoke about having Max instead of Doug. I picked up my phone and texted Max's mother, Jen. We'd become friends. She texted back quickly.

"Max's mom will drop him off after school," I said.

"Great."

That was that.

I glanced at my watch as I walked Jake and Laney out to the bus stop. On any given day, fifteen or so adults might congregate at the corner, socializing as the kids waited to leave for school. I used to say that I had a hard time talking to so many people before my morning cup of coffee but, truth be told, I'd drunk two cups already. I always had a hard time talking to so many people.

I crossed the street and shuffled to a stop beside a group of six or seven moms. The sound of their conversation warbled and waxed as I acted like something needed fixing on Jake's book bag. As I fiddled with it, I glanced down the driveway at the eight boys, all around Jake's age, playing basketball.

"Why don't you go down there with the boys," I whispered to Jake.

"No," he said.

"Why not?"

He ignored me. Laney scuttled away, finding Becca and a couple of the other girls, some as much as three years older than she was. She melded into their game like a pro. I put my hand on top of Jake's head. He did not tell me to remove it.

Tairyn turned slightly and mouthed "Hi" to me.

"Hi," I said.

The conversation went on, bouncing within the tight circle of their bodies. I shifted my weight, feeling like I should try to talk to them but having absolutely no idea how to break into the flow.

"Go ahead and play," I told Jake.

I didn't mean to press him. Honestly, I just needed to say something to someone. He happened to be the easiest target.

"Dad." He looked up at me with wide eyes.

I gritted my teeth together and Karen watched me. I looked away. The bus rumbled into view. When I spoke to Jake, my voice rose, as if wanting others to hear what I had to say.

"Remember, Max is coming over after school."

No one reacted. I hurried back across the street after the bus pulled away. Walking into the house, my body jittered, as if a surge of adrenaline had just worn off. I barked out a sarcastic laugh, realizing neither Jake nor I talked to anyone else while at the bus stop.

Thinking about how easily my daughter melded into "the group," I wished, not for the first time, that I could be more like her. I also wished (although I would never admit it) that Jake could be more like her, too.

Jen waved from her candy apple red minivan as she backed out of the driveway. Max, his yellow hair like a comet, sped past me. Jake met him and the two disappeared down the basement stairs. The sound of their excited voices slowly faded but I could hear their din even after I gently shut the door behind them.

My work done for the day and the kitchen floor recently swept, I eased down onto the couch in the living room and picked up my book, some geopolitical author predicting the near future. Leafing through to find my page (lost due to Laney's tendency to pretend that she is reading my books), I listened to the sound of the boys playing downstairs as it mingled with the sound of my daughter and her friend Becca playing in her room. Contentedness served up like a pancake breakfast and I actually sighed.

Time, as it tended to do when my kids were having fun without me, passed so quickly that I felt disappointment when the doorbell rang. Hesitantly, I put my book down and rose from the couch. Through the decorative glass of our front door, I saw the comically distorted face of Tairyn. I turned the knob.

"Hi, Simon." She stood on the front stoop.

"Hi. Come in."

Tairyn entered. She looked around, stepping about three feet into our foyer.

"Did the girls have fun?"

I nodded. "It's like they're not even here. I don't think I saw them the entire time."

Was that the wrong thing to say? I thought. I wondered if it implied I didn't watch the girls enough. At the same time, I worried that it would seem odd, or creepy, if I was around them too much. My cheeks flushed and I had to look away.

"They are buddies," Tairyn said.

I walked to the stairs. "Laney, Becca's mom is here."

Muffled voices seeped through my daughter's closed bedroom door. I waited.

"Laney, did you hear me?" I called.

"Yes, *Daddy*," she yelled back, but the door did not open. I thought I heard the girls laughing.

"Sign of a good playdate, I guess," I muttered.

"Excuse me?"

I turned to Tairyn and shuffled my feet. "I guess they had a good time. Don't want it to end."

"Oh, I know," she said, her voice suddenly animated. "When they're at my house, it's constant begging to stay longer. It's cute."

"Yeah," I said.

We stood in the foyer. Time ticked by, each second an exponential increase in the awkwardness between us. I could not think of another thing to say. With Jen, Max's mom, I could always turn to discussing a teacher at school, or sports (Jake and Max played flag football together). Tairyn and I, on the other hand, shared less in common with each other.

She ended up being the one to break the silence. "Are you and Rachel going to the progressive dinner?"

I squinted. My reaction, in turn, caused Tairyn to look more uncomfortable, as if she suddenly wondered if we had been invited. I had no idea.

I came up with, "No, we can't make that night."

Tairyn did not push the issue, most likely because she still wasn't sure we'd received an invitation. As I turned, intending to hurry the girls, the basement door swung open, slamming into the wall loud enough to startle Tairyn. She jumped and made a tiny, squeaky noise as Jake and Max crashed into the kitchen.

"Bang! Bang!"

"Ra-tatatatat!"

My son, holding a plastic AK-47, sprayed the house with pretend gunfire. Max dove behind a chair, wielding two pistols like Jean-Claude Van Damme.

"I got you," Jake yelled, laughing.

"Semtex!" Max pretended to lob something at Jake, who screamed and dove out of the way. Max made a break for it, passing within a hair of Tairyn as he stormed out the door.

"Excuse me," Jake said, standing in the foyer, gun aiming at the floor.

With a stunned expression on her face, Tairyn took a step back. Jake calmly walked past, leaping off the stoop and breaking into a sprint. The sound of their fun echoed through the open door. I stepped forward and closed it.

"Oh-kay," Tairyn said, her lips pursed.

I swallowed down my reaction, but I could not help looking at Tairyn. She had three girls and no boys. I chalked her reaction up to that. Thankfully, Laney and Becca appeared at the top of the steps.

"Bye, Laney," Becca said, hurrying down the steps.

Laney followed her. "Bye, Becca."

They hugged before Becca sidled up to her mother.

"Say thank you," Tairyn singsonged.

"Thank you," Becca mimicked.

"You're welcome," I said.

Laney waved and wandered off. I watched Tairyn and her daughter follow the front walk to her black Lexus. Tairyn eyeballed Jake as he ran past, shooting at Max. I closed the door and closed my eyes.

After the kids went to bed that night, I tried to keep it to myself but failed miserably. Within five minutes of sitting on the couch together, I turned to Rachel.

"You know there's a party in the neighborhood and they didn't even invite us?"

She blinked. I suddenly felt stupid without yet knowing why.

"We are hosting one of the stops," Rachel said.

"Oh."

Rachel laughed. "No wonder they don't invite you to playdates."

I looked up and Rachel stared at me. Her head tilted.

"Relax," she said. "I'm just kidding. I think these years at home have your head spinning a little bit. I've never known you to think everyone was out to get you."

"You think I think that?" I asked.

"I don't know. I do think you overthink some things when it comes to the neighbors, and the kids, for that matter. And . . ." She paused. "Maybe us."

"I don't overthink us," I said.

She laughed again. "Maybe that's the problem."

I let her words hang for a second. At that time, I would not have said we had a "problem." I would say that we lived in two very different worlds. Both no doubt had their positives and negatives. The funniest part, or maybe not so funny, was that I bet we both wanted to trade places. I yearned for the less complicated, more adult world of the office. I had a strong feeling that Rachel wanted more than anything to be with our kids more.

On a whim, I said, "Let's play hookey tomorrow. All of us. We can take the kids to that amusement park in Lancaster."

Rachel squinted. "Well, I have a . . ."

I stared at her. She smiled and said, "That's the best idea I've heard in a while."

The next day, I awoke half expecting a major disappointment. I knew things at Rachel's work were crazy, and I half-expected her to have to cancel on our plan. I'd even decided to let her off the hook. Her workload paid for a large portion of our lifestyle. I needed to be more understanding.

When I opened my eyes, I heard the shower running.

"Be cool," I whispered to myself.

"What, Dad?"

"Whoa!"

I spun around and found Jake reclined on Rachel's side of the bed, reading. He smiled, but his eyes remained mostly hidden under those unruly bangs.

"What's up?" I rubbed sleep from my eyes.

"We're going to the Wonderpark," he said.

Jake liked amusement parks, particularly the games. Laney, on the other hand, loved the rides, the scarier the better. Which explained the shriek of excitement that blasted from my daughter's room.

"Daddy," she called out. "We're going to Wonderpark!"

"I hear that," I called back to her.

The shower turned off as I talked to Jake about his book. I got up and knocked softly on the bathroom door. Rachel opened it, her hair wrapped in a green towel.

"I guess you're playing hookey," I said.

She smiled. "Guess I am."

CHAPTER 14

DAY TWO

At two in the morning, my phone rings. The sound reverberates off the bathroom walls, bouncing against my skull, at once returning sanity and tearing it asunder.

"Jake."

I have not even answered the phone yet. I hit receive and press the cold, lifeless plastic against an ear. My skin feels like it is burning hot.

"Jake?"

No one says anything. I can't even tell if the line is connected.

"Jake, is that you? Please."

The call ends. I feel I have the coordination of a toddler as I bring up the list of recent calls. It reads *Unavailable*.

I press the display, an impotent attempt to call the number back. Nothing happens. I am confused, then suddenly remember I have to tell Rachel about Karen . . . and worse, Tairyn. It is going to break her heart.

Holding on to the toilet for support, I stand. My head spins and my chest feels light. I bull through the sensation and open the door between the rooms. Darkness meets me. I push the button on my phone, illuminating the display. Through the faint light, I see Rachel and Laney. They lie prone on the bed, wrapped in each other's arms. Their steady breathing calms me. I stay there for a moment, battling with my need to move, letting my breath sync with theirs.

Closing the door as softly as I can, I step backward until I feel the bed against the back of my legs. I sit, my mind still doing nauseating somersaults. I try to rationalize the phone calls. Although I want to remain hopeful, there is no way it was Jake. He would have spoken to me. I start to talk softly to myself.

"Maybe he's lost somewhere the reception is bad."

"I must be missing something."

"Could Jake be hiding more from me? Like the doll?"

That's the breaking point. My defenses rise up. I feel inexplicably angry, my thoughts returning to the statements shouted by the reporters. Immediately, the faces of Leigh Marks, James George, and Amanda Brown flash behind my closed eyes. I shake my head, trying to make them go away, feeling guilty that it is not sadness that I feel. It is something darker, something I cannot face.

I need to do something but it is two AM, and the world sleeps. The reporters, their visages becoming vulturelike in my mind, said something about the Internet. I grab my iPhone. I think to go online and find out what they might have been talking about. Opening Safari, I don't even know where to start. I knew Jake had a Facebook and an Instagram page but I do not. That is Rachel's domain to police. I think about waking her up but instead search Jake's name on Google.

I get three letters in—J A K—and he pops up as the first option. I don't click his name on the drop-down menu. I can't because it sickens me to think of the millions of people who have done just that, mutating my son's name into an often-searched term on Google. I finish typing it out, pausing. I begin to realize what will appear when I enter my request. Closing my eyes, I do it anyway, flinching a little as if about to be struck.

Every major news outlet appears—CNN, local networks, national nightly news pages. I visit each, right down the line, looking for clues. These stories, however, regurgitate what I've already seen on the television, story after story alleging my son's involvement in the shooting. Scrolling down, I find the link to Jake's Facebook page as if I'm searching out the illicit. When I go to the page, there is a picture of Jake from a flag football game and a message that says

Jake Connolly's private information is only available to friends.

I'm his father. I try to find anything, the smallest shard of information that could help, but I get nowhere.

I ask myself, *Did Jake have a Twitter account?* I do not know. I remember hearing about Instagram, but honestly have no idea what it is. When I search for him there, I find nothing. Putting his name in again, I delve deeper. On the second page of responses, a message board catches my eye. It is for a video game Jake liked to play called Modern Soldier. I hit the link and it takes me to a conversation. Jake's name appears as one of the entries. His post reads:

My clip of a 360 quick-scope.

He embedded a video with the post, which was dated five months before. I watch it. The shot is a first-person point of view, someone carrying a sniper rifle. The scenery suddenly spins and the gun lifts. I look down the scope and the crosshairs alight on a man dressed in a black uniform. The gun fires and the man falls dead. The video ends there, a total of fifteen seconds long.

Understand, this video is familiar to me. I have not only watched my son play this game, but I have played along with him as well. I am awful, although Jake always tries to make me feel better about my inability. But this video causes my heart to sink to my feet.

I try to delete it. My attempts are frantic and end with me failing, throwing the phone to the ground. I lower my head into my hands and try to catch my breath. If people see that, they will think my son did it. I am powerless to do anything about that, though.

I need to refocus. I've spent the day hiding evidence, trying to protect him from what people might think. Instead, I have to find him. That's all that can matter . . . either way. Picking the phone up off the ground, I hit the button and the Web forum shows up again. I notice that there are pages of comments. I start to read them but stop quickly. Every one of them has been posted in the last twelve hours. They all call Jake a murdering monster.

I cannot remain in the hotel any longer. I slip out of the room, riding the elevator down to a nearly empty lobby. A single young woman stands behind the check-in desk, busying herself. When she turns to look and sees it is me, she blanches, immediately returning to what I assume is pretend work on her desk.

After I slowly pass, I feel her eyes return to me, boring into my back. I stop, attempting to see through the tinted glass doors despite the darkness outside. The faint white outline of a van materializes, as does another.

"There's a side exit through the parking garage," a thin voice says from behind me.

I turn to see the young lady. She makes eye contact through a pair of stylishly swooping glasses. A white, wide-collared shirt peeks from beneath the fitted navy uniform. I notice she could not be much older than twenty.

"Excuse me?" I say, trying not to frighten her.

"There's another way out. Those camera people and the report-ers are still out there. Why don't you go through the exit door down the hall to the right?"

I pause, having to look away. I need to ask a simple question. *Why are you helping me?* It is bizarre how the mind works. Just as I think that, a landslide erupts. Why wouldn't she help me? Maybe if she thought my son shot those children. Then the cement crashes into my already vulnerable soul. *Maybe he did.*

It is difficult to explain how I feel in this moment. I realize I have wavered. At times I am so sure of my son's innocence. Then, like a physical interruption, a thought flashes across my consciousness. Something I hear on the television, some new development, causes me to think the worst. Either way, the fact that I am unsure devastates me because of what it implies. If I'm not utterly positive, then maybe I just don't know my own son.

I say nothing to the girl. My head bowed, I walk down the eerily silent corridor. My feet barely come off the carpet. The thoughts press at my temples. The pressure grows. I will burst. Then there is nothing. My skin feels damp, cold. My eyesight is foggy, unclear. I slam into the door marked EXIT, cross a short industrial hallway, and hit another door. Fresh air washes over me and I shiver. But I feel better.

The parking garage empties out onto Orange Street. I see two vans parked there and decide to keep moving through the shadows. I see another green EXIT sign beckoning through the black night. I head toward it and find a pedestrian exit onto the street behind the hotel. I slip out without being seen.

With quick yet stunted steps, I make my way to where I parked Rachel's car. Thoughts of action replace those other, more troubling considerations. I no longer think, *What if?* Now I think, *What should I do?*

I will go to the school, search the fields behind the building, call out for my son, and hear his lost voice in response. That is my lifeline. That is our salvation. And that is all I can think as I climb into the car and drive off into the predawn night.

· · ·

The stars hang in the sky above, nearly as bright as the silver moon that rests on the horizon. The road stretches out before me, hollow and void of life. Dim security lights illuminate the vacant businesses I pass. Even the structures sleep, awaiting a new day, one in which the trickle of early risers will inject life into the somnolence that surrounds me.

For now, I am utterly alone. Silence sits beside me like some corporeal beast, feeding off my hopes, devouring them one by one until my mind is left with doubts and horrors. I continue to push back, trying in vain to find some plausible scenario that leaves our lives intact. Every second that passes chips away at that possibility, leaving me with the other options, the ones that make my stomach turn.

The ring of my phone startles me. I pick it up, hoping.

"Hello," I say, and even before I hear her speak, I know it is my mother.

"Simon, I've been up all night. Your brother and sister called. I've called your house fifty times. Why haven't you called? What is happening? This can't be true!"

"It's okay, Mom." But it is not. I have no idea what to tell her. I have no idea what I even know.

"Where is Jake? Laney?"

"Laney is here, with her mom," I assure her. "She's okay. So is Rachel . . ."

"Jake! Where is Jake?"

"Mom, I don't . . . I don't know."

"The television is saying he killed . . ." I hold the phone away from my ear. I feel the tears running down my cheeks. I did not know I was crying.

"Simon."

My dad has taken the phone.

"Jake did not do this."

My dad makes this statement. I cannot respond because, I realize, I do not have the same confidence level. Not anymore.

"Are you there?" he commands. "Did you hear me?"

"I don't know, Dad," I whisper.

"Jonathan will be calling you in an hour."

I startle. "Dad, no. We don't need a lawyer. I mean, I don't think—"

"One hour," he says.

I hear my mother wailing in the background before he terminates the connection. I am left holding the dead phone to my ear while I drive down a dead street. Jonathan, my father's business partner for the past decade, is one of the most powerful lawyers in New York City. Although I'm not even sure he still practices law, he had been a high-end defense attorney. Together, they also amassed a veritable restaurant conglomerate. Oddly, neither Jonathan nor my father cooked a single meal for themselves, probably ever. They simply brought a ton of cash to the table and ran the business with a deftness that astounded.

I think to call Rachel. She can't stand Jonathan because when anything legal comes up in a conversation, my father refers to him, ignoring the fact that my wife is a lawyer as well. I see where she's coming from and feel I should warn her.

Before I dial, I see the time. I don't want to wake Laney. Instead, as I drive, I text Rachel.

My father is sending Jonathan. Will try to stop him.

As I type it out, I hear the ghost of my son's voice.

"Dad, don't text and drive."

Nearing the school, I turn off into an adjacent neighborhood. Behind the glow of perfectly stationed streetlamps, I can see the facade of each home as I pass. Built not more than five years before, the homes vary only in shades of the same earthy white. Even the mailboxes, oversize and a pure white, are identical. With my mind distracted already, I miss the turn I meant to take and don't even realize it until I've passed two other streets. Backtracking, I leave my headlights off and coast down a cul-de-sac, rolling to a stop between two houses.

From the street, I can see the path. It runs from one of the backyards along a stubby rise, bending around a copse of trees and coming out onto the far end of the sports fields behind the high school. I climb out of the car and ease the door closed, afraid to make even the slightest of sounds. I feel like a criminal, but I hurry down the path and onto school grounds.

"Jake," I call out, halfway between a whisper and a shout. "Jake."

With so little moon, the fields are dark. I peer through the gloom, hoping to catch some sight of movement or maybe a soft sound, the type you hear when something, or someone, is trying not to be heard.

When I see the dugouts for the baseball field, my bearings return. I remember what I saw on the television. Witnesses claim to have seen Jake out there, beyond right field where the tree line meets school property. I begin to jog, the sound of my shoes on the infield mix reminds me of my time with Jake, coaching Little League, how I felt when he hit that home run.

"Jake!" I call out louder this time. "Jake, it's me. Dad!"

I am running when I reach the grass. I head toward the trees, my breath coming in jagged huffs. It seems I look in all directions at once, the scene becoming a dark kaleidoscope. This is where my son was. *Is!* I have to think *is*.

"Jake. Come out. It's okay. We'll figure this out. I promise."

A sound! I spin around, nearly falling over. I hear footsteps. My heart races. I've found him!

Then a light blasts over me, shining in my eyes. I try to shield my face but the muscles of my body have given up. I might fall to the ground.

"Jake," I whisper.

"Hold it there, don't move," a voice calls out. "Keep your hands out in front of you. What are you—"

Although I still cannot see him, I know this is a police officer. When he pauses, I know he's recognized me.

"On your stomach. Now!"

"Look, I'm just trying to—"

"Down, now."

I hear what might be a gun being pulled from his holster. I remain standing.

"No." I say it calmly, but I will not get down. All I can think about is how little these police officers have done to find my son. I will stand up to them.

The light inches closer. I am still blinded. "Down, NOW!"

"No," I whisper.

The officer takes me down. It happens so fast that I don't have time to resist. My hands are cuffed behind my back and I am lifted off the ground.

"Why couldn't you just listen to me?" the officer asks.

He sounds young. I can make out his face now that the light is out of my eyes. I think I've seen him before.

"I know who you are," he says. "What are you doing out here?"

"I'm looking for my son," I say.

"He's not here. We've been through every inch, even with the dogs. Nothing. There's a lot of smells, but . . . We've checked everything out. He's not here, sir."

When he calls me sir, this officer stops being my enemy. I even wonder why I thought he was or why I resisted. My mind is not clear.

"Look, how'd you get here?"

I explain where my car is parked.

"I have to escort you off the property, but I'll let you go. Go home, get some sleep. We'll find your son."

I don't say anything. What is there to say? That I can't go home.

That the only reason I think they are looking for my son is to arrest him. Instead of speaking, I let the officer lead me back to my car. When we get there, I pull the keys out. The officer turns and looks at the car. His expression changes. Suddenly, his light is back on. He shines it into the backseat. That's when I remember the doll.

"Shit," I say.

The officer turns the light on me, shining it into my face. "I think you better come into the station with me."

CHAPTER 15

JAKE: AGE ELEVEN

I stared at the phone, knowing I should call her back. Our conversation ended poorly again, although I didn't even know what set it off. In fact, I could barely remember what we'd talked about. The words melded with all the others coming before them over the past few months. I sat down on the couch in the living room and closed my eyes. Afternoon sunlight shone on the backs of my eyelids, the world a pink and orange glowing blanket. My head leaned into the pillow.

Since Jake's birth a decade before, life failed to follow the path I'd expected. I tried to think back to when I was young and full of dreams. Had any involved being a stay-at-home dad? I laughed out loud. During one neighborhood guys-night-out, Tairyn's husband, a tall, muscular guy with a surgical haircut and hairy arms who claimed to have played minor league baseball, looked me in the eye and said, "I always wanted a sugar mama."

"Yeah, Sam," I had said to him. "Guess you're not handsome enough to pull it off."

We traded barbs after that. In my opinion, I won. Later that night, however, as I drove home, I really thought about what he'd said. Normally, I'd bemoan a missed opportunity to zing him with some delayed witticism. That night, though, I truly considered his statement—had I always wanted a sugar mama?

After my call with Rachel, the absurdity of that statement struck me harder than at any other time. At twelve, I had finagled a paper route out of a friend's older brother. At fourteen, I took a job at a fish store, being paid under the table to bleach maggots out of their dumpster on trash days. By the time I was sixteen years old, I'd worked at an ice cream shack, a clothing store, two department stores, and a long-extinct video rental place. I worked odd jobs all the way through college, including internships and co-ops. One week after college graduation, I started my first "career" and did not go a day unemployed until Jake was born.

Every day since, I've felt guilt. In the morning, watching Rachel scurrying around in the dark trying to find her matching shoes, I convinced myself that she must feel contempt as I remained in bed, waiting for Laney to wake up and jump in to snuggle for a few minutes. During the day, when both kids attended school, I often imagined the people in the cars driving by the house glancing through my windows and shaking their heads with disgust, asking themselves, *What kind of man does something like that?*

On occasion, I talked to someone about my lowering self-image. Once I even visited a professional for a total of three visits. She reminded me (at the last one) that I raised two children (at the time under seven) while making a living as a medical writer and without the help of a nanny or in-laws (Rachel's parents tended to stay away from me when she was not around). I canceled my next appointment. I did not need someone to charge me $150 to regurgitate the obvious at me.

Often I told myself that Rachel and I were at the vanguard of a new world order. We were the Rosa Parks (admitted delusion of grandeur on my part) of gender equality. But in some ways, it was true. She brought home the bacon and I fried it up in a pan (yes, I stole this from an old commercial), yet somehow I was supposed to never, never, never forget I was a man.

To be truthful, my psyche had actually improved over time. When the kids were younger, my aggression level had skyrocketed. I used to fantasize about getting into fistfights with the mailman who looked at me askew when he saw me cutting the grass at noon on a Tuesday. I'd coach Jake's soccer team and tear into some father who questioned me, basically daring him to take a swing. I was not proud of this. On the contrary, it made me sick, but it happened.

By Jake's tenth birthday, that portion of my journey had passed. I'd calmed down. Outwardly, some might say my swagger had returned. Inside, I knew there were still some lasting changes. I worried about the kids, probably too much, and men aren't supposed to worry. I also didn't put in enough effort with Rachel. I'd admit it, even to her, though I felt she didn't put in the time with me, either.

My phone rang and I knew Rachel would be on the line. I picked up, telling myself I would apologize and end this fight, a fight whose beginning I could not even remember.

"Hi."

"What's up?" I muttered back.

For the second time, I told myself to chill, to let this all go, to start over and end it. Instead, the conversation lulled. I stood up and paced the foyer, my footsteps echoing through the empty house.

"Did you want something?" I asked.

She did not answer right away. It was a stupid thing to say. We had been fighting for three days, barely speaking to each other. It was not the first time, either.

"I am just really tired of being in the doghouse," she said.

I snorted. "You say that all the time. It is such BS." The floodgates opened. "It's an excuse. You do whatever you want. I get upset about it, then you spout off about being in the doghouse."

"You are always mad at me, Simon. I work late sometimes. You know that."

"That's not the point. I don't care how late you work. My issue is when you say you're going to be home at one time, but you come home three hours later without bothering to let me know."

"I had a meeting with Frank. What was I supposed to do? Be like, 'Hey, boss, hold on a minute, I have to call my needy husband.'"

My face grew hot. "Nice."

"I just mean I can't always get in touch with you."

"It takes two seconds to text me," I said, my tone icy.

"You've just forgotten what it's like to work in an office."

My business had been slow for a couple of months. I had not heard from my biggest client in half a year. I took her words as an intended affront and hung up the phone. I threw it into the couch cushions and stormed upstairs, ignoring the muffled ring behind me.

"Daddy," Laney moaned. "When's the game over?"

I looked down at her. She sat in the grass just off the sideline of the flag football field, a book open but upside down on the ground before her. Her big greenish eyes blinked and I couldn't help but think how cute she looked in pigtails and sweatpants, her normal attire. Considering her soccer shirt, I knew it was no wonder the moms (at least those with daughters) tended to tilt a head or tsk under their breaths. They all thought I ruined Laney by the way I let her dress. Although I fretted internally about this, I did nothing to change it. I liked her that way. She made me smile a lot.

"Soon, sweetie," I said, tousling her hair.

I glanced out on to the field. Jake, thick for his age but not fat, a good, sturdy black Irish in my opinion, hiked the ball to Max. Jen's son looked like a natural quarterback, dropping back, arm cocked, eyes scanning the field. The two kids running routes did not match his skill level, though. One danced with the defender, comically wiggling, flag twirling around his hips, but not getting anywhere. The other followed a pretty good pattern but refused to look back for the ball.

Although not exclusively, I watched Jake. He blocked one of the opposing linemen well. Two others, however, got past their blockers. Max, in my opinion showing uncanny pocket awareness, broke. He sprinted down the field, Jake plodding after him.

"Go, Max!" I called out.

"I want to go home," Laney said.

A safety pulled Max's flag at about midfield. "Nice run." I turned back to Laney. "We have to stay. Mommy's not home yet."

"Mommy's never home," she said.

I reconsidered my response and realized I should not have said that. I'd teed that one up for sure. I felt like a bitter divorcé.

"It won't be long. The game's almost over. Do you want to play on my phone?"

She brightened up. "Yeah."

I gave her my new iPhone and she tapped away like a pro. I watched her for a moment, amazed at her generation's deft electronics coordination.

"Looking good out there."

I spun around to see Jen, all smiles. She liked nothing better than to watch Max play football. A sporty-type mom, she wore a performance jacket and leggings, with expensive running shoes.

"Hi there," I said. "Like Jeff Saturday and Manning, huh?"

She laughed, getting my reference to the Indianapolis Colts center and quarterback. "Not Manning. He could never break the pocket for a first."

I smiled. "True that."

We stood next to each other watching the game. Other parents hovered around, as intent as we were, but I rarely if ever spoke to them. I never knew what to say. Plus, I had a hard time remembering which kid was theirs. Jen and I commented through the rest of the game. She shared a pithy one about the ref who, officiating at a ten-year-olds' flag football game, wore the full outfit, from stripes to white pants.

"He's hoping to get the call up to a middle school game. Big leap, you know."

She laughed. Despite myself, I looked at her again. The sound of her voice breaking out in real amusement warmed me from the inside. Not in a sappy way, either. I actually felt warm. She met my eyes and her smile broadened. I had to look away, suddenly uncomfortable. Not with her, with me. A thought rudely butted in line. I used to talk to Rachel like this before kids.

"Whatcha playing?" Jen asked Laney.

"Cut the Rope," Laney replied without taking her eyes off the small screen.

"Nice. Max likes that one."

The very official official blew his whistle, signifying the end of the game.

"Do you even know what the score was?" she asked.

I shrugged. "Don't they all end in a tie?"

"That was so last year," she drawled.

I laughed again as Max and Jake raced over. Max hugged his mom. I thought that was nice, the star quarterback hugging his mom in public—a good kid.

"Can Jake come over?" he asked his mom.

Jen looked at me and shrugged.

"Sure, if it's okay with you?"

Jake tugged at my arm. I bent down and he whispered in my ear, the earnest way kids do.

"I'm supposed to go to Doug's, remember?"

Crap. Maybe I had remembered. Maybe I simply did not want Jake to go to Doug's house. He'd seen a lot of the Martin-Klein kid since school had started back up. I glanced at Max and wondered if he had noticed. I probably transferred my emotions on to the kid, but it all happened so fast.

"Don't worry about it," I whispered. "Go have fun with Max."

I could see Jake considering it, fully. He took his time, his face pensive.

"I don't want to upset Doug."

"I don't think anything was set in stone," I said.

This was not an outright lie. The boys talked about it, but not the parents. I assumed that it was just kid stuff, wavy gravy as they said.

I pressed Jake. Eventually, he gave in. With a smile that I took to mean he would rather have been with Max anyway, the two boys sprinted to the car.

"What time do you want me to get him?" I asked.

Jen shrugged. "Five-ish."

"Sounds good. See you then."

"'K."

Jen walked away. I felt good about myself, feeling like I'd steered my son down the right path, at least in a big-picture manner; I watched her go. She looked very good in her leggings, and she walked with the grace of a feminine athlete. It had been nice talking to her.

My mind went where most men's go. The thought materialized, fuzzy and incomplete, yet arousing. What we did to each other, or with each other, popped from one disjointed scenario to another, all variants of some moment I shared with a female from my past. Disheveled clothing, unique combinations of undress, and daring moments of acceptable bravery, to name a few.

A little hand grasped my finger. I looked down at Laney as she peered up at me. She looked so much like her mother that I flinched. Laney's lip pouted and my soul flooded with pounding, burning guilt.

"Come on, sweetie. Let's go get some ice cream."

CHAPTER 16

DAY TWO

I am a bit player on a prime-time cop drama. I drag through the steps—fingerprints, photo, search, confiscation—and wait. They impound Rachel's car. The officer has brought me to the local city station. Eventually leading me to the holding cells, I pass a half-dressed woman sitting on a bench, picking at her nails and cursing at no one. I see a homeless man I recognize, a man who smells of urine and melted candy. He mumbles to himself. The police officer, the uniformed cop who processed me, a nondescript man I prefer to forget, cuffs me to a bench across from the smelly man. I don't care. The officer walks away. I sit for what feels like an hour.

My bladder burns inside my gut. The need to urinate permeates every part of me but my impetus. I do not ask to use the bathroom, as I see others do. Instead, the discomfort, near pain really, fuels me. Little by little, it awakens my senses again. I float toward the moment, inch by inch clawing closer to the agony that sent me to oblivion. I know already that I will never be the same. Something broke inside. But I am not a quitter.

I am trapped, about to be locked up. Even though the logical part of my brain, the part that seems to chug along despite the storming emotions, devises a plan, a series of steps. First, I will get released on bail. Second, I will get one of our cars back. Third, I will find Max and talk to him. Fourth, I will go to the Martin-Kleins' house. Maybe I will return to the school, or hire a private investigator.

For a brief instant, my mind clears. I ask myself what I am basing this plan on. I wonder what prior knowledge I have of a situation like this. Movies? Television? Fiction? In those stories, it would be all dramatic action, life-or-death moves, stunning discoveries. That is not how it is happening, though. Instead, the situation calls the shots. We are being moved from one point to the other. What I must do is fight it, leap from the grid, call my own shots. That is the only way I can hope to find my son. I will not give in, or give up.

At the same time, I am afraid. I fear any real news, because it is impossible to fathom anything good coming from it. I fear finding my son because my mind can light on only two plausible scenarios: he is dead or he killed. Once everything is known, one of the two becomes real. At a base instinctual level, I cannot let that happen.

My eyes reopen and I see reality. I have been arrested. Through the fogged pictures, I remember the charge—obstruction of justice. It makes little sense to me, but I do not care. When I am set before someone, I will not grovel. I will find out what they are doing to find my son. I will not give in to fear. I owe my son so much more than that.

I do not wait for long. A detective enters the holding cell. The woman, an emaciated fifty-year-old in a red dress and tilted wig, spreads her legs. I look away.

"We'd like to ask you some questions," he says flatly.

"I want to make a phone call first."

He leads me to what looks like half of a phone booth attached to the wall. He steps ten feet away. I call Rachel.

"Where are you?" she asks.

"I've been arrested."

"What?"

I try to explain it to her but my actions seem ludicrous. When I am done, she is silent for a moment.

"Is Jonathan there?" she asks.

"No."

"Is he coming?"

"No," I say, afraid that if I say yes, she will be even more furious with me.

"Don't say anything. I'm coming."

I hear what she tells me to do. It is not, however, what I do. I acquiesce, following the detective without a word. I am not worried about their questions. I want answers.

He leads me to a small, square room with a table and two chairs. I chortle when I see the "mirror" on the wall. Like it fools anyone.

"Have a seat," the detective says. His voice sounds rehearsed, especially compared to his earlier monotone.

"Okay." I sit.

"Do you know why you're here?"

I smile. "Because you charged me with obstruction of justice."

"Do you know why that is?" His voice inches closer to normal.

"Why don't you tell me," I suggest.

The detective reaches down to a box on the ground, one I had not noticed. His hand rises, gripping a large bag. The doll from the woods presses against the clear plastic. It ogles me with its haunted eye. Limbs bend in unnatural angles. I look at it, not away.

"You tracked that down, huh? And what have you done to find my son?"

The detective drops the doll onto the table. "Your son is a suspect in a mass shooting. At this time, the safety of the community is our number one concern. We also understand that you attempted to assault a reporter today."

I did, but I ignore his comment. "You have no idea where he is, do you? Have you talked to anyone? Have you put any thought into it?"

My body shakes. I feel like I might lunge at the detective. Not a violent person, I had not been in a real fight since the fifth grade, yet I hunger to hit this man.

"Believe me, sir, we'll find your son before he hurts anyone else."

I smile. "You shouldn't have said that."

The detective blanches. This is funny to see in a man of his stature and temperament. He understands why I said that. The conversation is taped, no doubt. Any kind of bias will be brought up if there is a trial, civil or criminal. When you are married to a lawyer, you pick things up here and there.

"How long did you know your son had plans to hurt people?" the cop asks.

Before I can answer, the door opens. Jonathan, my father's business partner, saunters into the room as if he is walking into his own office.

"Nice to see you, Simon," he says. He turns to look at the detective. "May I have a chair, please?"

A uniformed officer appears at the door, motioning the detective out. My father's lawyer sits in his recently vacated chair. Jonathan's blasé demeanor changes in a blink. He turns on me.

"How'd you get here?" I ask.

"Car service."

"No, really. How'd you know I was here?"

"Police scanner."

"You listen to police scanners?"

He laughed. "I have staff who do. What did you tell the police?"

"Nothing," I assure him.

"You told them something. What did you say? Tell me everything."

I try to remember verbatim. He takes particular interest in the doll. He smiles, though, when I tell him what the detective said about Jake and my response.

"Put him on his heels, huh." Jonathan laughs. "There's definitely some of your father in you, son."

I ignore the fact that I am over forty and being called *son*.

"Did you find anything out about Jake?"

I know Jonathan must have just gotten into town, but he is good. Very, very good.

"My office poked around. The police removed some circumstantial evidence from your home. Violent drawings. A story Jake supposedly wrote about a fight after a football game. There's something in there about a kid getting his skull cracked. They also found his cell phone and are searching that."

"No," I whisper.

"What?"

I don't tell Jonathan. Immediately, I feel a blazing anger fueled by senseless shame. I picture these strangers sitting in an office, hearing the phone ring, and glancing down at my number on the display, over and over again. I imagine them listening to the messages I left for my son, the raw words that poured out of my mouth in utter anguish. I feel murderous.

Just as quickly, however, that emotion blinks out. It is replaced by a numb hopelessness. This news, that my son never had his phone with him, shatters my hope that it had been Jake on the line when I called. I now know it was just a cop. I guess I didn't realize how important that had been to me because I feel very empty.

I picture Jake that morning, putting his phone on his desk, finding a pair of socks, and walking out without it.

"He was always forgetting it," I whisper, my eyes burning.

"Are you okay?" he asks.

I ignore the question. I am tired of feeling helpless. "Look, we need to get them out there looking for him. Why are they so sure he did this?"

"Because a kid told the police that he left school looking for

Doug. And a janitor claims he saw two kids with guns coming in through the gym exit just before the shooting. There's also something about one of the victims, Alex Raines, but the police were not too forthcoming with details."

I tell Jonathan what I know. I can see it does not paint a good picture. He nods and changes the subject.

"But I agree. We need them to find Jake. Nothing else matters at this point."

"How?" I ask.

"That's the hard question. We can't go on television and make a plea. Right now, the public does not think Jake did this." Jonathan looks me in the eye. "They know he did."

"They don't *know* him!"

Jonathan shakes his head. "They know what they've seen on the television."

The detective reenters the room, halting our conversation. He carries a chair under his arm. Jonathan stands and takes it, placing it beside mine. We are all sitting again, facing off. I am too stunned to speak.

"What are the charges?" Jonathan asks.

"Obstruction of justice," the detective says.

"So you've decided to charge Jake Connolly with a crime?"

The detective blinks. "Not at this time."

"So what justice, exactly, is being obstructed?"

"The criminal investigation into the school shooting today. The one where thirteen *kids* were murdered."

"And this doll," Jonathan pokes it with a well-manicured finger, "had something to do with the shooting?"

"We don't know yet. That's what we are trying to find out."

"Where did you find this doll?" Jonathan asks.

"In Mrs. Connolly's car," he says. "Your *client* was driving."

"Did he give you probable cause to search it? Was he pulled over? How exactly did this happen?"

The detective gets up and walks out again. A minute later, he returns.

"You can go," he says, handing me my belongings.

"But you pressed charges," Jonathan says, arching an eyebrow. "You can't just *let* him go."

"We never finished the paperwork," he mutters.

They ushered us from the station, me holding my envelope of personal belongings, him smiling like a cat, the Cheshire or the one that swallowed the canary, I am not sure.

"Did you just try to talk them into keeping me in custody?" I ask.

"Just yanking their chain. What were you thinking, anyway? Where'd you get that doll? The reason you're out is they have no idea where it came from. You were never going to be officially charged. They just wanted information."

"I found it—"

"Shhh," he hisses. "I don't want to know. Not right now. We need to get to work."

"Finding Jake?"

He looks me in the eye. I see a glimmer of sadness there. It surprises me. "That . . . and preparing for the worst, Simon."

That makes me angry. "Worst?! How can it get worse? Are you serious?"

Jonathan touches my shoulder. "We'll talk about it. Let's get out of here first."

I let my eyes close for a second or two, fighting back the teeth-jarring anxiety that courses through my muscles. I can't breathe or swallow. I feel like someone whose body is both paralyzed and palsying all at once.

When my lids rise, I see her. Rachel walks into the station in front of us, frazzled and out of breath. She sees me first and her eyebrows rise. Then she sees Jonathan.

"What the hell," she spits out.

Jonathan extends a hand. "Hello, Rachel."

Her entire attention is on me. She ignores his hand, placing hers on her hips. I know that stance.

"You said he wasn't here."

"He wasn't," I say. "He just showed up. I had no idea. But he helped me get out."

She shakes her head. "Oh, he helped you, did he? You know, I left our daughter to get over here. Thanks for letting me know everything was *under control*."

"Rach, I . . . I just got released."

She seems to accept this, but turns her back and walks away.

CHAPTER 17

JAKE: AGE ELEVEN

Over a span of ten months, I picked up Jake from Doug's house way too often. Each time, my irritation grew. I had yet to talk to the kid, or his mother, for that matter, all the time they had been friends. To be frank, his father just annoyed me. I tried to ask Jake about it, subtly trying to coax out bits about Doug and his family, but my son gave me little to nothing. Not in an evasive way. I believe that, as a kid, he just didn't pick up on what I was trying to get at.

He popped into the car, full of excitement. "Hey, Dad."

"Hi, buddy." I looked over my shoulder at him. "How you doing?"

"Great," he began, then the floodgates opened. "Doug had his Airsoft gun and we shot at one of those turkey vultures out by the pond."

"Whoa," I said, my voice rising. "You shot an Airsoft gun. Isn't that like a BB gun?"

"No, it just shoots these little balls."

"Yeah, like BBs."

"No, Dad."

I accidentally yelled at him. "Yes, son, they are."

Silence followed my outburst. I glanced in the mirror to see Jake staring out the window. My grip on the wheel tightened. I wanted to bring back the excitement he'd shared but the words disappeared before catching hold in my brain. I floundered for something, anything, to say. Unfortunately, the enigma of a preteen boy is legend and I came up with nothing. The silence expanded, filling the void between us.

When we arrived home, Jake got out of the car and headed inside. I followed him, reading his body language. His confident stride did not change. I listened as he greeted his mother and found his voice sounded normal, as if nothing had happened.

I sat down on the couch. The moment weighed on me, probably more than it should have. I wondered if Jake would even remember it. To me, it turned his path, ruined his chances at a well-adjusted life. He came to me so happy, and I bashed it to pieces just because I didn't like his friend. I felt like some junior high bully, or the pretty and mean people in the high school lunchroom. As I tended to do, I likened it to my own childhood. I filled out a mental list of my early friends. Frankie, whose parents divorced, ended up holding a kid at knifepoint at the park for his pocket money and was charged with, of all things, kidnapping. One of the others, Greg, cut me with a razor blade on the bus and ended up surviving a debilitating car accident. The Stewart twins set a fire in the woods behind the neighborhood and are now software guys out West making a boatload of cash and living it up in the sun with their attractive wives and inexplicably athletic children.

Rachel caught me stewing. She entered the den and shook her head.

"What's got you thinking?"

"I don't like that Doug kid," is what I came up with, but the truth was far more than that. "I just feel like we should keep Jake away from him. Jake needs other friends . . . more normal friends."

She sat down beside me. "Look, I don't like that kid, either, to be honest. But what you're forgetting is that Jake is an amazing kid with one of the best heads on his shoulders I've ever seen. I trust him."

"Yeah, but he doesn't even play with Karen's kid. He refuses to, no matter how much I try to make him. I mean, he's so shy sometimes. What if he ends up all by himself? I—"

"Stop," she commanded.

I looked at her. She met my eyes without a flinch.

"I know, I'm worrying again," I grunted. "I'll try to act more *manly*."

"Maybe you should."

"Maybe you should . . ." I stop myself, snorting. When I continue, my voice is soft, probably icy. "I know we have problems. In fact, our problems are more the norm now. It's like our good times are becoming the outliers."

"I don't disagree," she said.

Rachel rose and walked out of the room. She never even looked over her shoulder. Instead, I listened to her footsteps as she went up the stairs. Soon, laughter echoed through the halls, my son's, my daughter's, and my wife's. I remained on the couch.

I could have walked upstairs. They would have welcomed me into the fun. At the same time, I could have made less of the discussion with Rachel. I might have even had those thoughts while I sat there. Yet the evening played out, warts and all, like someone else wrote our story, someone I'm not even sure I liked all that much.

A scattering of parents sat in the elementary school gym, watching the makeshift stage in the back. Jake, with his friend Max, along with about a hundred fourth- and fifth-graders were trying out for the annual talent show. I did not have to be there. A lot of the parents weren't. But I really wanted to see the boys perform.

When their turn came and the two walked onto the stage, I slid to the edge of my seat. Both wore black suits, the kind boys their age might have worn for a wedding, and black wide-rimmed sunglasses. They carried the guitars Jake and Laney had gotten for Christmas a couple of years before to the front center of the stage. A track of the theme song from *Rawhide* began and they mouthed the words, air-strumming on the guitars along to the music. Halfway through, the music screeched to a halt. The two looked at each other, befuddled. Suddenly, Natasha Bedingfield's "Pocketful of Sunshine" started up. They slid the guitars away and began to do something that looked a little like the Cabbage Patch. To be honest, the act lost focus at that point and the two just went nuts. I could hear the other students in the wings of the stage laughing and calling out. The teachers, however, didn't appear to get the juxtaposition of the country-western bar scene from *The Blues Brothers* with today's pop culture phenom.

For my part, I tried not to laugh. Although this may sound unbelievable, I had nothing to do with their choice of act. In fact, I had no idea where they got the idea from. Their creativity, however, amazed me. Whether they made the show or not, I was impressed.

When their act finished, I meandered into the lobby and waited for them to come out. While standing there, staring at an antibullying poster next to a posting of the school's strict visitors policy, I got to thinking. I glanced out to the parking lot and saw the steady flow of parents coming and going, picking kids up from after-school activities. With the change in parenting style of my generation, organic play had been replaced by hyperorganization. The school had a running club, a chess club, a Lego club, Girl Scouts, Boy Scouts, rec sports, acting class, and after-school language enrichment.

Watching the swarm of parents picking up their young from the "hive," I wondered how this all happened. My mind slipped back to my own elementary years. My mother went back to her teaching job and I went to a neighbor's house in the mornings to wait for the bus. They plopped me in front of the television but never taught me how to change the channel. Instead of *Tom and Jerry* or *Looney Tunes*, I watched the *Today* show every morning. I vividly recalled the tally of days during the Iran hostage crisis. I watched the hunt for the Atlanta serial killer, Wayne Williams. Most important, the story of Adam Walsh swept the nation, if not the world.

I remember it being right around my tenth birthday when I first heard the news. Adam Walsh, only a couple of years younger than me at the time, had gone missing. Still summer, I only heard tidbits, but I recall a change in my parents' demeanor almost immediately. My mom stopped letting me linger behind or wander ahead in stores. My father eyeballed strange men nearby, something the usually docile man would not have considered polite before that. These were small changes, nothing drastic. All the kids still roamed the neighborhood. I walked to the pool with my older sister. After a couple of days, I stopped noticing.

Then school started back up. Again I found myself plopped before the screen, watching the "news" every morning. The awful details, repeated over and over again, seeped into my soul. The boy's head had been removed (after death, the anchor assured us). At one point, I remember a reporter talking about cannibalism. A shocking reality, but one seen very differently through ten-year-old eyes.

Over the course of months, maybe years, the media picked at the story like jackals. Adam had been left to watch some boys play video games at a Sears when his mom continued to shop a couple of aisles away. Total time, they say, away from his mom was six minutes. Although it came out that a security guard dispersed the boys, kicking them out of the store, I believe *that* six minutes changed the world. The thought of losing a child that quickly became a scar on the minds of all parents. A scar that, unlike a physical wound, did not fade over time. Instead, it gaped.

Abductions surely occurred before Adam Walsh. There is no doubt about it. But no case had ever been so nationally televised, so morbidly dissected, at least not that I knew of. It set the stage for first monthly, then weekly, then daily stories of abduction, torture, rape, beating, starving, even cannibalism. The dark corner of humanity, the formerly silent minority, changed over time, becoming a vocal majority when it came to hours covered by the media. Previously unfathomable nightmares assaulted parents and kids alike every day. The parents absorbed the horror, but kept on living. The kids, however, grew up to be parents, parents with a pale, jagged scar in their minds that changed their parenting style forever. All it takes is six minutes out of your sight. I believe that this awareness doomed the days of childhood freedom, replacing the dinner bell with the car pool.

This was what I thought when Jake appeared at the far end of the hallway, head together with Max, both smiling. I watched them, feeling content for the moment. Then my heart jumped. Doug Martin-Klein walked out of a stairway right in front of the two. I watched the scene unfold.

Jake looked up and saw Doug. My son stutter-stepped and said something, still smiling. Doug responded through thin lips, his eyes trailing toward Max. Max spoke next and the tension became obvious. Jake spun on Max. I saw anger flare in my son's eyes. Doug walked away, his body language cold. Max shook his head and said something to Jake. The two boys separated and Jake, head bowed, walked toward the lobby. Max followed close behind.

My short-lived sense of well-being crashed so suddenly that I choked up. Fighting it back, I waited for the boys. The walk out to the car and the ride to Max's house was silent. When we dropped him off, I hoped Jake would say something, but he did not. Instead, I had to ask.

"What was that all about?"

Jake pulled at the strings of his hood. "Nothing."

"Just tell me. I won't get mad."

"It was nothing."

"Jake, you know it's better to tell me. I just want to help."

He sighed. "Do I have to?"

"I would." I laughed.

Jake did not appreciate the awkward attempt at humor.

"Max just said something to Doug. Now Doug's mad at me."

"What did Max say?" I asked.

"He called Doug *weird*." Jake paused. Maybe it was just me, but he seemed to be trying to convince himself when he continued. "He's not weird. He's just quiet."

I had to find the right thing to say. This was one of those watershed moments. I took a second and looked out the window.

"Did Doug get upset?" I asked.

"I think so. It's kinda hard to tell with him."

"What did you say to Max?"

"I told him he wasn't being very nice. That what he said was *impolite*."

"Impolite" was Jake's favorite word, at least to describe what he considered misbehavior. A teacher once called him hypercorrect in a conference. I felt proud. Rachel did not. She talked to me afterward, saying maybe we should loosen the reins a little. I tried after that. Probably not hard enough.

"Did Max get upset?"

Jake gravely nodded. "He did. But he should not have called Doug weird . . ." He paused. I could tell he thought deeply before continuing. "Even if he thought that."

The crack in the door appeared before me. I thrust my foot through without thinking.

"Do you think that?"

Jake squirmed. "I don't know, Dad. He's quiet, I guess. But everyone says I am, too."

"You're not quiet," I protested.

He did not respond. When I looked at Jake again, he held a book in his lap. I doubted my handling of the situation, but I had no idea what to say to salvage it. I started the engine and pointed the car toward home. After a minute, I added my final say.

"It'll be okay. Don't worry too much about it."

We drove the rest of the way home without speaking. The entire time, I found it hard to believe that Jake could take those words seriously considering the source.

CHAPTER 18

DAY TWO

Laney sits in the backseat on the driver's side, alone. I feel the tentative control I have over my emotions falter. Since the time they were both in car seats, Jake and Laney always sat on their side of the backseat. When Jake reached "front seat" age, he took shotgun, but when we were all together, Laney sat behind the driver, Jake behind the passenger. His seat looks so empty.

Rachel stares out the window. She has not spoken to me since we left the hotel. Jonathan drove ahead to scout out the house. We are returning home. The police have given us the okay. All three of us have been crying most of the morning. At this point, I have nothing left. I feel empty, numb, and confused. When I look at Laney, I just want to scoop her up and run away from this world, keep her safe, make her whole again. I know that's not possible. It is simply what I want more than anything I have ever wanted before.

About a mile away from our neighborhood my cell rings. I glance at the clock on the dashboard display. It is 10:25 AM. The hours lost at the station weigh on me.

"Hello."

"It's Jonathan. Be prepared."

"For what?"

"Look, these kinds of . . . situations bring out the worst in people. They assume they know just because they heard 'allegedly' on the television."

"What are you saying, Jonathan?"

"There are people outside your house. Media, but also people from the community. There are some signs, stuff Laney shouldn't see. Maybe you should think about going somewhere else."

I speak to Rachel. "There are people at the house. Reporters, and maybe others. Jonathan thinks we should go somewhere else."

"We are going home," Rachel says.

I turn to look at Laney. Her expression is vacant and her body is twisted away from the center of the car, as if avoiding a ghost. I hang up the phone and drive. Rachel turns away again, looking out the window.

"Sweetie," I whisper.

Laney does not answer.

"When we get close to the house, duck down, okay? There will be cameras there, people trying to take your picture."

"No," she says.

My head jerks back, startled. "What?"

"No, Dad," she repeats in a calm, shockingly mature voice. "I won't hide. They don't know Jake. They're stupid, every one of them. If they knew him, they wouldn't be saying stuff like they are. He didn't do it. I know he didn't. And I won't hide from any of them."

I look at Rachel, my head feeling heavy. She looks back at me, maybe for the first time since leaving the police station. She knows what we will see. We have seen news reports about other shootings. An understanding passes between us. This is a moment where we must decide. Do we allow Laney to continue to think everything will turn out okay, or do we make her face reality, accept that Jake is gone, that he's left us in the most horrible way possible? None of us, not anyone who knew Jake well can understand this. Maybe Douglas Martin-Klein brainwashed my son. For the first time, I wonder if maybe it is . . . was drugs. I just don't know, but I note that my mind is finally accepting it and looking for the *whys*. Now we must understand if Laney's should, too.

Rachel, again reading my mind like only she can, shakes her head. I nod. We go back to ignoring each other. I assume her stomach twists and turns like mine as we near our shattered home. Is it still home? I don't know how to know. I simply drive.

It hits me how little time has passed, at least from a normal perspective. I received the initial text about the shooting less than twenty-eight hours before. Nothing is normal now, though.

As we turn in to the neighborhood, Rachel climbs from her seat into the back. She sits in the middle and I realize that she, too, must fear the ghost in the car, the ghost that follows us everywhere. She wraps around Laney, who lets her mother take care of her while she stares defiantly out the window. Even in my grief, I feel a stab of intense pride in my daughter. She is stronger than I could ever imagine.

Cars line both sides of the street when we are still five houses down from ours. Through the sentry-straight trunks of two pin oaks, I see a throng of people in our front yard. I swallow, fighting not to turn the car around and flee. The decision is made. We will face it now.

A man with a camera, the first to see us, sprints down the rise in front of the house. A well-dressed woman in her forties tries to keep up, her heels sinking into the dewy turf. Others realize what is happening. Their mouths salivate (I am sure) as they sense the arrival of their prey.

I struggle to make eye contact with anyone outside. They meld into a throbbing, soulless organism. I hate them for what they are putting my family through. Some hold signs reading: HOLD THE PARENTS RESPONSIBLE. Others mouth what look like obscenities. One man, older and dressed like a farmer, someone I am sure I have never seen before, kicks the side of the car.

"Fuck you," I hiss, forgetting Laney is in the car. I don't think she hears me. Her wide eyes do not blink as they stare at an array of humans who despise her lost brother.

Then I see Mary Moore, mother of Jake's homecoming date, Kandice. Kandice is dead. I realize this as I take in the loss and sadness, the confusion and need on Mary's face. Any anger I feel vanishes. What is left cannot be described. It is guilt piled on to emptiness and set afire.

"Lord God," I whisper.

I am not present as I inch the car up the driveway. I must have opened the garage because it beckons like the gates of Hades. A single uniformed officer keeps the perimeter as I park and shut the door behind us. Light fades and we are in the dark. None of us moves. The only thing I manage to do is push the ignition key so the engine cuts off before we asphyxiate.

Rachel helps Laney out of the backseat. They pause, letting me go ahead. My hand hesitates on the knob. I finally turn it and open the door into the den. This is not our house. Everything looks different. The couch tilts slightly askew. A lamp leans against the wall. I walk slowly into the kitchen. Drawers remain opened. The light is on. Nothing is as it should be, as I left it the morning before.

Rachel pushes past me. Somehow, maybe by the pace of her stride, I know where she is heading. She goes to Jake's room. I freeze, straining my ears. There is only silence until the door slams shut. Another door slam follows, our bedroom. I turn but Laney has disappeared. I walk, as quietly as a cat, up the stairs. The floor creaks as I near our room. I freeze again, listening. I hear crying, two sets. I can differentiate Laney's sobs. I picture her as a baby, crying in my arms. Then I can hear Jake as a baby again, too. His wails deeper yet more lusty than his sister's.

My phone rings. I answer, thinking it is Jonathan. It is not.

"Youfuckingmurderer."

The words slur together, the voice heavy from alcohol.

"Who is this?" I shout.

"You know who the fuck this is. Your son killed my boy. That worthless piece of shit of yours killed my Alex."

It is Alex Raines's father. I close my eyes and it hits me that he is also the man I saw in the golf shirt the day before. I want to hang up but something keeps me on the line.

"That coward of yours did it on purpose."

"What are you saying?" I hiss back at him.

"Your son. He can't fight his own battles. My son showed him." Mr. Raines (I cannot remember his first name) coughs and laughs at the same time. "I'm going to come over there and kill you," he slurs. "I mean it."

"What was going on between Alex and Doug?"

"Don't act stupid . . . murderer."

The line goes dead.

"Why'd Alex call you a loser?" I had asked Jake that day, two months before, when the guidance counselor called.

He sat outside on the back patio reading a book for school. He looked up over the spine, his shaggy dark hair shadowing his eyes. I was unable to read his expression.

"Amnesty moment . . ."

I shake my head. "You're too late. Phil Hartman already called."

Jake knew that amnesty moments were about telling me things before I found out on my own. I noted just a slight twitch to his eye, like he'd stepped on unsure footing.

"Uuuuurrrrrrr." Jake shot his arms out, book still in hand, pantomiming Frankenstein. I laughed despite myself.

"Funny. He told me there was a little more to the story than you admitted."

Jake brushed his hair back and looked at me. "You'll make a big deal out of it."

"No I won't."

Jake laughed. "Yeah, and I'll get a buzz cut."

"Is that a bet?"

My son thought about taking me up on it. Instead, he leaned back and looked at the sky.

"Why'd he call you that? I never knew you had a problem with Alex."

"I don't," he mumbled. "At least I didn't."

"So, why?"

"He didn't call me a loser," Jake said.

"That's what Phil said."

Jake barked out a laugh. "Ha. You're quoting guidance counselors now? But really. He didn't say it to me. He said it to someone else."

"Who?"

"A friend I was talking to. Alex was being a jerk. I don't even know why he came over and started to mess with us. He bumped into me, but I just ignored that. Then he . . . Well, I shouldn't have pushed him."

"Who was with you?" I asked again.

"Don't freak," he said.

I paused, waiting. He looked back up at the sky when he answered.

"Doug."

CHAPTER 19

JAKE: AGE TWELVE

Jake, now in middle school, sat in the living room reading. The doorbell rang and he did not look up. I put down the dish towel I was using in the kitchen and walked by him.

"Did you hear the bell?" I asked.

"Yeah," he said.

That was it. I shook my head and answered the door. The delivery guy handed me our order and I paid in cash.

"Thanks," I said, tipping the kid who was probably only five years older than Jake. He nodded and walked toward his car. I shut the door.

"Is that dinner?" Rachel called from upstairs.

"Yeah."

I went into the kitchen to get everything ready. I got everyone plates for the pizza and left Rachel's salad in the plastic takeout container. I put the order of wings at the center of the table and grabbed a bunch of napkins. Maybe five minutes later, Rachel and Laney came down from upstairs. Laney had a Nintendo DS in her hand.

"No games during dinner," I said.

She rolled her eyes just a little. "I know, Daddy."

With dinner on the table, Jake still hadn't come. I called him again and got no answer. When I poked my head into the living room, he walked past me.

"You could have answered," I said.

"Sorry."

We sat down and started eating. Rachel asked the kids about their day.

"Good," Laney said, a wing in her hand and sauce on her cheek. Jake kept eating. I looked at Rachel and she shrugged.

"Three things," she said.

"Three things" was a policy created by Rachel. The concept dripped with simplicity. The kids had to tell us three things about their day. In practice, it resembled more and more a trip to the dentist as the kids got older.

Laney dove into the request. She mentioned what she played at recess, who got in trouble in class, and something about the bus I did not fully understand.

"Well, they sit by themselves, so they end up taking third-grade seats. It's just not fair."

"Did you talk to the bus driver?" Rachel asked.

Laney shook her head. "No way. I'm no rat."

I laughed. "Your turn, Jake."

"I dunno."

"Come on," Rachel said.

Jake took a bite of pizza and spoke while chewing. "I had a test in math."

"How'd you do?"

"Good."

I waited for more, but that was it on the subject.

"Two more," Rachel said.

"I didn't have a test in social studies," he said, smirking.

I laughed. "Good one."

The conversation continued along in that vein. Laney carried the load a little more than Jake, but the years showed on our children. Little flashes of adult mixed with preteen moods, giving off the air of the true person each would become when out from under our tutelage. It was at once infuriating and amazing.

When dinner finished, we had to remind them to take their dishes to the sink. Jake retired to his book and Laney to her DS. Rachel helped me clean.

"They're growing up fast," I said.

Rachel nodded. "Yeah."

Finishing, I hung the dish towel and turned to her. She checked her phone.

"I'm going to head downstairs to work out."

"Okay."

Watching her go, I picked up a book and joined Jake in the living room.

Maybe a week later, one evening after helping the kids finish their homework, I heard the garage door open as I slid the last plate into the dishwasher. Like a spouse of a deployed soldier returning home, I felt the urge to rush and meet Rachel at the door, scoop her up into a giant hug and tell her that she is my best friend in the world. Instead, I calmly folded a kitchen towel and hung it from the handle of the stove.

Rachel entered the house. I listened as her footsteps neared. They sounded the slightest bit tentative, yet I knew they were not. She did nothing without conviction, a trait I'd fallen in love with long before.

"Hi." She said it first.

I turned and looked at her; forcing my voice to sound chipper. "Hi."

"Guess what?"

Her tone sounded playful. I cracked a real smile. "What?"

"We are going on a date tonight."

My eyebrow arched. "Jake has a basketball game. And what about Laney?"

"Tairyn offered to have her overnight, so I called Jen up and asked if she could take Jake. She said Max would love to have a sleepover. Looks like we are free."

"Nice!"

We both paused. I imagined Rachel felt similarly to how I did. The divide between us caused the concept of date night to be layered with a nagging fear, like we would mess even that up.

"I got us a room at the Ritz-Carlton."

"Philly?"

She nodded. "Thought we'd get some sushi, maybe walk South Street."

I laughed. "Like the good old days."

Our date night soared beyond my expectations. At one point, while we drank a deliciously adventurous carafe of warm sake before dinner, I realized something. Away from all the chaos and worry surrounding child rearing, no doubt exaggerated by our gender pioneering, we quickly recalled what brought us together and led us to the miracle of childbirth in the first place. We talked for hours, just the two of us, as if no one in the bustling Old City of Philadelphia mattered. We walked Market and down Second, passing hip youngsters, a crowd that the rest of the nation would never imagine stalking the chronically misunderstood streets of the City of Brotherly Love. The place crackled with energy and we drank it up and walked on by, greedily hoarding, not sharing with others, only each other.

Rachel and I sneaked a kiss as we walked a long, quiet Third down to South. Once there, the hipsters melded with the chaotic. Unlike Old City, South Street probably earned the city's reputation. Police officers dotted the corners as partiers, thugs, and high-schoolers jostled along the sidewalk, some ducking into exotic shops with feather-lined hats and multicolored condoms while others scanned the throng, predatory eyes searching out weakness. What they did with it, I do not know. Having grown up visiting South Street, I was adept at avoiding those looks, and trouble in general, for that matter.

Hand in hand, we visited a classy Irish restaurant and pub for a couple of pints, and even hit up the Troc for some dancing. We didn't last long in that mash fest. Walking the streets for another half hour, we simply basked in our freedom. Amazingly, we did not talk about the kids for most of the night. After hailing a cab, I turned to Rachel and smiled.

"We needed this."

She wrapped her arm around mine and snuggled into my shoulder. "Yes, we did."

Back at our room, we never bothered to turn on the lights. When our bare skin touched, I whispered in her ear, "Too bad this place doesn't have a tiny kitchen."

I called Jen as we headed home Saturday morning.

"Hi, Jen."

"Hi, Simon. How was your date night?"

I could not tell if she was being playful there or not. Not that she would be.

"It was great. We had a lot of fun."

I glanced at Rachel. She paid me no mind as she wove through traffic on I-95.

"Well, I just dropped Max and Jake off at the Caseys' house for their Saturday football game."

"Great," I said. "We'll just pick him up from there. Was he good for you last night?"

Jen laughed. "Jake? Ha, has he ever been bad?"

"He has his moments," I said.

"Right. They all do, I guess. But it is hard to imagine Jake's. He actually offered to wash the dishes last night. My jaw hit the ground."

"Wish he'd do that at our house. Are they finishing up at the normal time?" I asked.

"I assume so. Those boys are like clockwork."

I laughed. "Thanks again for having him."

"No problem."

"We owe you one. Talk soon."

"Bye-bye."

It took us about twenty-five minutes to reach the Caseys' neighborhood. The entrance lane crossed over a small red bridge spanning a meandering creek. Two men in thigh boots stood in the shallow water fishing for trout. Beyond the far bank, the left side of the road opened up into a wide field with a backstop in the far corner. The boys, six in all, played football, orange plastic cones marking the sidelines. Rachel eased the car to a stop, two wheels on the grass. She cut the engine and we watched for a time.

"Why didn't we buy here?" I asked.

Rachel laughed. "Too much nature for you."

As corny as it sounds, I felt warm inside watching the boys play ball. I could hear their voices, still high at times, right through the closed windows. They dove and bounced off each other, playing harder than any one of them ever would for an organized team, as if this game meant so much more.

As we watched, Jake snagged a pass over the head of another kid. Cutting back the other way, he eluded one tackle, only to be plastered by Max. The two hit the ground hard. When Jake pulled himself up first and put out a hand to help Max, I felt so good, almost teary, although I probably should not admit that.

At the same time, I tempered my happiness, knowing that, as a dad, I rode life like a giant roller coaster. I let the highs get too high and I let the lows get too low. Seeing Jake having so much fun was great. The next day, however, could bring about something totally different. My plotting mind imagined weeks at home, sadness and alone, bullying and depression.

Rachel, somehow sensing my thoughts, took my hand in hers.

"I heard what Jen said. You did a great job, you know . . . with the kids."

I looked at her. Being married to someone for so many years, it was not hard to recognize true sincerity. My wife's words traveled straight from her heart. I knew it immediately. I felt it, too. In that moment, I felt like the best dad on the planet. But a modest dad at the same time.

"Laney would have been happier if you had been home with her."

Once I said that, I worried. Depending on my inflection, it could trigger Rachel's working-mom guilt. It did not, though, not this time. Our date night must have provided some fresh myelin for the frayed nerves of daily life.

"She loves you, you know."

"I know," I said. "Please don't misunderstand this, but it's always been kind of easier with Jake. I've just known how to play with him, and even, sometimes, what to say to him. Does that make sense?"

Her smile was so warm that it caught me off guard. Years later, I would be able to close my eyes and see her face at that moment anytime I wanted to.

"It does. You don't think I feel the same way? Sometimes, when I watch you two playing Wii or catch outside, I wish I was you. With Laney, I get it. You know? Not everything, but our thoughts are similar. At the same time, I feel something so deeply for Jake. It's like that difference makes it more intense."

I'd never heard her say that before. When she did, it triggered something inside my heart. I so totally understood what she said that I actually felt like I had said it myself.

"I would die for her," I whispered.

Rachel squeezed my hand. "I know. That's why I love you."

The entire household floated on a cloud of contentment for weeks after our date night. I remember considering the very real possibility that nothing changed outside of my own perceptions. I saw things as light and airy. A C plus in spelling for Laney—oh, just do better next time. A call from the guidance counselor over an argument on the bus—that's just boys being boys. I slept great every night, and in doing so realized I had not for years, maybe since the evening Jake came into this world. I watched television without each scene reminding me of some worry I felt. A kid getting bullied on a cop drama—oh, that's really an exaggerated problem these days. A girl in a sitcom being put on the fringe by her friends—so clichéd.

Then, one afternoon, everything changed. My old neurosis boomeranged right out of thin air, striking my ill-prepared brain like a cattle prod. It happened while I sat at the kitchen table. Jake walked in from the bus stop just before three PM.

"Dad, can you take me to Doug's house?"

I swallowed, failing to push the acid from my stomach back down. "Huh?"

"Can you take me over to Doug's?"

"Why? I mean, you haven't hung out with him in a while, have you?"

Jake shook his head. "Look, I know you don't like him. But it was you who taught me to be nice to people. The kids at school really have him down. They pick on him a lot. I just want to stop by there and see if he's okay. I'm not going to do it every day or anything."

"What about Max, and your football buddies?"

Jake's eyes widened. "What about them?"

"Do they like Doug?"

"No."

One of my greatest failure moments as a father dribbled out of my mouth. "Do you think they'll be okay if you go over there?"

Jake did not smile. "If they aren't, then I don't want to be friends with them."

The look on his face said it all. Every kid probably has that moment, the realization that their parent is full of shit. Jake had sucked up my grand advice like a sponge all his life. Suddenly, when the going got a little tough, I backtracked, took the easy road, failed to live up to my own lofty standards. For a second, I felt like I could see through his eyes. Jake looked at me, looked through me, and saw a human, a man as flawed as any other. From that moment on, he would make his own life. My hands were off the wheel. Jake was on his own.

"I'll get the keys," I said.

He turned away and muttered, "Thanks."

CHAPTER 20

DAY TWO

The phone rings again, startling me. It is Jonathan, so I pick it up.

"Hello."

"Simon, I'm outside. Parked across the street. I need to talk to you and Rachel. Unlock the front door but stay toward the back of the house. I will let myself in."

Jonathan hangs up. I push myself to my feet. The sobs behind our door have stopped. I knock lightly.

"Rachel, we need to talk. Jonathan's coming in now. But someone else just called."

I head to the front door and find it is already unlocked. The police must have left it that way, which surprises me. My head swivels on my neck, frantically taking in every inch of our living room and foyer. Even the yellow-gold paint appears different. Nothing about the place seems real anymore. I stand in someone else's house, a home for someone else's life, a life existing in a dreamlike world that cranks forward no matter how I try to plant my feet and stop the excruciating turn of the wheel. My feelings, made into words, make no sense anymore. All I can think about is Doug. And Alex. Did the doll have something to do with all this? Could I have missed something at the cemetery?

"Look, about Jonathan—"

"Later." Rachel walks down the stairs. "Who called?"

I tell her. Then I ask, "What do you know about Alex Raines?"

"I don't. Not much. Jake told me that they got into a fight at school. That's about it . . . Wait. Facebook. I checked Jake's page when you left last night. There was something there from Doug about a fight. I figured it was about that Alex kid, but maybe we can find more."

Rachel grabs her work iPad from the table by the door. She turns it on as voices rise from outside. I turn and the door opens.

"Can you comment on the report that his parents didn't even know the video games he played?" someone yells.

"They should be thrown in jail!"

"Murderer."

"Bottom-feeding lawyer."

"It's your fault."

I blink, sure that my mind fabricated that last one, if not all the others. Jonathan pushes through the entryway. I glimpse the back of a uniformed officer as he pushes the throng of media, and others, people who for reasons of their own have camped outside my house. Some look to judge, some look for answers that can't relieve their pain.

"Are you okay?" I ask, but I glance at Rachel. She is scanning pages on her iPad. Fleetingly, the irony of how much it used to bother me when I lost my wife to her electronic devices occurs.

Jonathan closes the door behind him. "This is what I expected. We need to talk—you, Rachel, and me."

Rachel looks up. I can tell she is unhappy about Jonathan but there is more. I want more than anything to ask her what she's found, but I see Laney standing at the top of the steps. Rachel follows my gaze. When she looks at Laney, our daughter runs down the stairs and sits beside her on the couch.

I take a step toward them, hands outstretched.

"Maybe this isn't—"

"She's going to hear this," Rachel says. "She needs to hear this."

I do not agree, but I do not protest, either. I sit down, my body so exhausted that I wonder if I will ever stand again. Laney will hear the truth; everything her brother was will be stripped from her memory, her heart, and cast into the darkest pit of someone's judgment.

"I'd advise—"

My wife cuts Jonathan off. "I don't need your advice."

Jonathan flinches, a funny sight from a man so well polished. Today he wears a perfectly tailored black suit with a classy striped tie and Italian leather shoes. His white hair, circling his head like a halo, falls perfectly in place, more a drawing than real. He smiles and the creases around his eyes look perfectly planned out, some artist's interpretation of a genteel man.

He decides to plow forward despite Rachel's comment. "Okay. I came over to lay some things out. First, the police are actively searching for Jake. They had a pattern radiating from the school, where the janitor claims to have seen him before the shooting. I can tell you they have uncovered absolutely no sign of him, or anyone else. I've also found out some details about the Martin-Klein boy. A couple of surveillance cameras captured his movements. He appears first entering the gym. No one is there and he proceeds into the lobby of the school. He then runs to a nearby classroom, opens the door, and fires randomly, it appears. Eventually, he steps away from the room, backs up against a locker, and . . . He dies of a self-inflicted wound to the head. It was the last piece of ammunition on his person."

I look at Laney. She watches Jonathan, her expression dull, as if she's asleep with her eyes open. I get no read at all from her. She seems to have tuned out. Rachel touches her arm but the two do not look at each other. I do not know what passes between them, but sense it nonetheless.

Rachel's voice is cool as she asks, "Is Jake on the video?"

Jonathan shakes his head. "No. The police claim that the video contains sound of unaccountable gunfire."

"Maybe it was an engine backfire," I say from out of nowhere. It seems a silly thing to say, but my mind nags on something. I think back to standing below the school and hearing something, seeing the police officer react.

"The police are conducting DNA analysis throughout the school. Your son's blood was found on the door the shooter used to get into the school and near the classroom where most of the shooting took place. A janitor, an Edwin Manner, reported seeing two kids enter the school through a door behind the auditorium approximately three minutes before the shooting started. Later, he told the police he wasn't sure he saw anyone. He didn't even know they were students. I doubt his testimony will be in play here."

"Did he identify either child?" Rachel asks. She uses her "lawyer" voice.

"Not positively, though the police did show him pictures of both Jake and Martin-Klein. There is a woman, too. She lives on the farm adjacent to the school's property. Her name is Donna Jackson. She IDed Jake, but not the Martin-Klein boy. We looked into her background. She's been through a couple of mental wards. Real 'black helicopter' type."

"Black helicopter?" I ask.

"Paranoid. Thinks the government is tapping her phone, that kind of thing. Also, three kids reported that Jake left school that morning heading to Martin-Klein's house about one hour before the shooting, prior to classes starting."

"Who?" Rachel asks.

"Three boys. Ben Campbell, Brian Cushing, and Max Turner."

My stomach rolls and I feel a chill, as if my skin suddenly turned clammy. "Max?"

I don't want to believe it. Jake's best friend for over a decade. Why would Max turn on him like that?

"Those are his friends," Laney whispers.

Jonathan somehow knows this. His nod is grave as he folds his hands on the tabletop.

"The media is worse," he says. "They dug up trash from Facebook and Twitter and are painting an awful picture. I have not seen it, but they are reporting that Jake posted something about assassinating someone in his class."

"That's a game!" Laney blurts out. "The seniors play it every year. They get assigned a name and have to 'assassinate' that person. It's just pretend. They use water pistols. It goes on until someone wins."

Jonathan pulls a pad out of his jacket pocket and jots something down. "Thank you, Laney. That was very helpful. They also claim Jake played violent war video games online."

"Everyone does," Laney says. "At least all the boys."

"There was a fight with this kid Alex Raines," I said.

I tell Jonathan the entire story. He shakes his head. He seems about to ask something more delving but stops himself.

"They'll run with that," he answers.

"Who's they?"

"The media. They've already put it out there that Jake was quiet; that he wasn't friends with some of the kids in the neighborhood. They are painting him into a very antisocial corner. I really think your family would be served by hiring a PR firm we've worked with. They specialize in image management." He pauses, sensing the sudden chill in the room. "I know this is a very trying time, but you have to think down the road . . . to future civil suits."

"Get out," I say.

Jonathan appears shocked. His mouth opens but no words

escape. Rachel looks at me. I sense something different, like a wall crumbling down between us. She does not smile, though.

"I'm sorry, Simon. I . . . Your father sent me to help. He's worried about how this will progress. He's worried about you all."

"Leave," I say.

I stand and Jonathan is forced to follow suit. He backs up a step toward the door but I pass him, swinging it open. The crowd outside reacts with a cacophony of voices that meld into a single, accusatory drone. I ignore it and hold the door for Jonathan.

"I'm sorry, Simon."

His expression says something altogether different. It says, *You are a fool.* I ignore that, too, and close the door behind him. When I turn, Rachel is standing next to me. She hugs me and cries against my chest. I do not see her move but Laney joins us. We hold each other, as we used to group-hug when the kids were young. It is all too much. I do not hide my tears from my daughter. Even if I wanted to, I couldn't. The truth, though, is I have no desire to. This is the reality of our life. She's a part of it now. Her childhood, in essence, fled once this began, as it did for all the children in her school that day.

Once Jonathan leaves, Laney slips away and Rachel and I sit down in our living room, eyes wide open.

"I don't think he meant to be so awful," I say, half thinking through my own thought.

Rachel's eyes darken. "What?"

"Jonathan. He just wants to help."

"Did *you* hear what he said?"

By the way she says *you*, I sense her feeling of betrayal. I do not fully understand it, not yet, but I know it's directed at me. I try to backtrack.

"I know. He was out of line. He should never have taken it that far."

She leans forward. *"Taken what?"*

It is almost as if those two words slip through the salivating mouth of some predatory animal. They pierce, tearing at what is truly behind her words.

"I mean . . . he should not have suggested we hire a PR firm."

"Why not, Simon?"

I sense being on the most frightening, unsure footing I have ever stood upon in my life. The tattered remains of my world hang in the balance. I do not know the proper response. I should remain silent, knowing whatever I say could push it all over the edge, into the abyss.

"It was thoughtless on his part."

"No, it was not. It was very thought out. I can't believe it. You think our son did this, don't you? Goddamn!"

To describe Rachel's expression would be an injustice. Her eyes bore through me, as if peeling away the imperfections of my outer layers only to find utter rot at the core. For the first time, I taste hatred in the air between us, a foul, acrid thing that dries my mouth like scalding coffee. I know now what I have done, but she is right. My head hangs.

"I don't. But where is he? What else could it be?"

She rises. For the first time in our relationship, Rachel towers over me in every sense. I look up at her, pleading, but to no avail. When she speaks again, her words hiss from her mouth like droplets of acid, burning, sinking down to my soul.

"That brain of yours, that whirling dervish of *what ifs*, is probably picking through every moment of the past, trying to find out how you caused this. What? Was it that we didn't take him to playdates? Or maybe we didn't push sports on him. God knows a star football or lacrosse player is *far* less likely to do something awful to someone. Right? Is that what you're doing to our son right now?

"You never could accept things for what they are. You have to pick it apart like scraps from a bone, leaving everyone and everything around you bare and exposed. You never once thought about it, did you? You've already forgotten how special he was."

Tears run down both of her cheeks, random tracks of sorrow plunging from her chin toward oblivion. Her words don't cut like I'd expect them to. Instead, I listen to each one. Could it be that I have thought too much, but not enough? The concept grates at my sensibility. Yet at the same time rings hauntingly but confusingly true.

I had been thinking too much. I thought that I failed Jake. I should have taken him to playdates. I should have helped him be a better athlete. I should have pushed him to be more social, more talkative. I should not have let him have a Facebook page or Twitter account. I never should have bought him a video game or a Nerf gun. More important, I should have seen this coming. How could I have not seen this coming?

What I need to grasp hold of, to pull forth and never let go of, is so simple. With each passing minute, a beautiful memory of my son vanishes, replaced by the angst and horror around me. The key is not to learn the now; it is to remember the *then*.

Before I can do that, Rachel hands me her iPad.

"Read this."

My wife shows me a conversation playing out on a Facebook post. I see Jake's name, his picture, and Alex Raines's as well. I begin to read:

Jake: Look dude I am out
Alex: Ha
Alex: Pansy.
Alex: Who asked you weirdo
Alex: You come by my house with that thing again it WILL be over
Alex: surpise surprise crazy U gonna be blocked

"I don't get it."

"Someone else originally commented."

"Oh," I say, rereading the thread. "So what Alex is saying is in response to someone else. It's probably Doug. You think he's talking about that doll?"

Rachel's hands rest on her hips. "What doll?"

I realize I never told her about it. When I do, finally, she is incensed.

"Why did you take it?"

"I thought . . . if they found it."

"What, that they'd think Jake did it?"

"I . . ."

"You need to find our son."

Our conversation is left at that simple truth. She leaves me; I hear her footsteps somewhere else in the house. Then she reappears, Laney in tow. My daughter looks at me and I am surprised that there is no accusation implied by her expression. But there is utter sadness.

"No, Mom," she says, tugging at Rachel's arm. "Don't leave. I don't want to leave. We need to stay together."

Rachel pauses. I understand now. She is taking Laney and leaving me. I predicted this moment, maybe even before the nightmare began. There is nothing that can stop it, so I remain silent, watching them. I feel no hope or anticipation. I simply feel the numbing cold fingers of loss tracing paths across my body. Rachel's words vibrate against my skull. I have failed again. I have not found Jake.

Rachel stares at me. My lack of fight gives her all the ammunition she needs.

"Laney, we have to go. Your father needs some time to think."

"I don't want to. Why can't you two just get along?"

Rachel's eyes look cold as well. "I need to leave, Laney. I need to get away from the house for a while. I think you should come with me, but I can't force you."

My wife walks away, through the kitchen toward the door to the garage. Laney breaks down, sobbing. She rushes to me and I hug her harder than I ever have before.

"It's okay, sweetie. Just go with Mom. It'll be safer for now. Once everyone outside leaves, I will join you. Okay?"

"What about Jake?" she pleads.

I hold her face and look into her tearing eyes. "I'll find him, peanut. I promise."

She looks up at me, wanting to hold me to my word.

"You promise?"

I pause, fully understanding this moment. She has spent years with me. She knows if I promise, it will happen.

"I promise."

The tears dry up and she steps back.

"Bye, Daddy. I love you."

I hold back my tears until she disappears into the kitchen. I hear her open the door and enter the garage. I am still her father. I am still Rachel's husband. I will protect them. Crying, I go to the front door and swing it open. The mob outside sees it is me. They pulse forward. Jeers and microphones assault me but I stand tall, watching the garage door open. No one seems to notice but me. I am the perfect distraction, the ultimate decoy.

"Mr. Connolly, Mr. Connolly, how did you not see this coming?"

"Do you think fathers raising children is causing this increase in gun violence?"

"Did you hear about the shooting in Kansas this morning? Ten more children were shot and the alleged suspect claims he wanted to outdo your son."

"Murderer!"

"Faggot!"

"This is your fault!"

I hear it all as I watch my family drive away, unmolested. A smile creeps across my face, no doubt it will fuel more negative reaction in the bloodthirsty media. I do not care anymore about appearances. My last gift, although it will never make up for my sins, will be to shield my family. I decide in that instant to be a lightning rod, to absorb the worst anyone can throw at me, knowing that each word I survive is a word Laney and Rachel will not hear.

As I remain aloof but present on my front step, a strange thing occurs. The crowd quiets down. The reporters, the first to notice what is going on, retreat to their vans. On deadlines I am sure, they have little time and quickly figure out this venture will get them nowhere.

Eventually, the others in the crowd, random strangers along with a few familiar faces, vanish one by one. I do not move as almost everyone walks from my lawn and disappears down the street, to God knows where. I think about what might have brought all of those people to my house. They spout hatred and anger, but I think I know the true motivation—fear.

They do not fear me, although I do not doubt they blame me. No, these people fear the unknown. They fear unpredictability. The specter of randomness pricks them and they react like an exposed nerve ending. They must be able to answer one simple question, *How do I keep this from happening?*

I wonder how my reaction on the front step will be interpreted. The crowd will see my lack of response, my smile, as a cold, psychopathic tendency. Genetics, they will say, are to blame. I tainted my son from the dawn of his creation. Luckily, they will think, my family does not have such tendencies. We could not stand up to such a barrage of righteous indignation without reaction. Therefore, our sons and daughters will not grow up to be cold-blooded killers . . . like mine. My Jake. The kindest, gentlest, most pure person I have ever known. But the doubt still lingers. Did I know him at all?

My eyes focus and I see that one person remains, Mary Moore. Her face has changed. It now drips with judgment and rage.

"Why my daughter?" she yells at me. "Why couldn't it have been yours?" This too, I absorb, for now. Once the door closes, my demeanor changes. Good or bad, I've done what I can for Rachel and Laney. Now I must keep a promise.

CHAPTER 21

JAKE: AGE THIRTEEN

"You promise?"

I glanced into the rearview mirror, looking at Laney.

"I can't promise. What if there is a lightning storm and it gets canceled? What I can promise is that I'll do everything I can to do the plunge. And you know Dad. I never break a promise."

"Well," she said. "You're doing the polar plunge with me, then. Because there is no way they are going to cancel the whole thing. It doesn't lightning in March. Plus, thousands of people will be there."

I merged my wife's car onto I-95 heading south. It was the Wednesday of spring break, early afternoon. Normally I would avoid the bottleneck of the interstate at the mall exit but I figured our random time of departure should help avoid that traffic. I was right and we sailed onto Route 1 with no problem. One hour and a half more and we would be basking in the briny air of Bethany Beach.

"Maybe hundreds, sweetie. And it can lightning in March. Just not too often. Are you going to run the five K with me?"

"No way!"

"I thought you wanted to run track in middle school?"

This conversation was retread at least once a week in our house. It got Laney fired up every time, but she really did want me to jump into the ocean with her. Honestly, I did not want to. The ocean temperature in midspring was significantly colder than, say, January, because the months of winter cooled it to a heart-stopping forty degrees.

Rachel plugged a movie into the portable DVD player we used in the car. The kids quieted down, their voices replaced by Ben Stiller's in *Night at the Museum*. A good choice because the dialogue was funny enough even without being able to see the picture. For some time, Rachel and I just listened, laughing occasionally.

"When is Jake's meet next week?" Rachel asked.

I laughed. "If you don't know, we're in trouble. I think it is Wednesday. The eight hundred is usually around four-ish."

"I think I might make that."

"Don't tell him unless you're sure."

I probably should not have said that. Jake had reacted a few weeks prior when his mom missed a track meet she had planned on attending. I did not want him to be disappointed.

"It's okay, Mom," he said from the backseat.

"Thanks, buddy."

I glanced over and caught the smile on her face. Although Jake contradicted me, I appreciated it. The moment passed and we continued to talk, the mundane of school-age children—schedule, schedule, and more schedule. Our cadence eased into normalcy and I grinned as we sped past flat, open farmland.

The movie wound down as we entered the beach towns. The first stoplight at Lewes, what Rachel called Five Points when she was a kid, signaled our arrival. I felt the tension slide down my back as if the asphalt had vacuumed it away. When we coasted through the bend into Dewey Beach, I craned my neck, peering down a side street to get my first glimpse of sand.

"It's the dogs again," Rachel moaned.

My wife did not like greyhounds. Irrational as it seems, the mere sight of their spindly legs and pointed snouts sets her teeth to itching. I laughed, not at her discomfort, but for the ironic fact that our favorite place on the planet also hosted an annual greyhound owners' convention. They were everywhere, walking by the Starboard and the Rusty Rudder, two staples of the Dewey Beach nightlife. Greyhound heads poked out of car windows and between guardrails on motel balconies. I counted thirteen as we waited for the light to change.

Rachel let out a sigh of relief (at which we all laughed) as we left town and drove along the isthmus between the Delaware Bay and the Atlantic Ocean. My kids, even as teens and preteens, loved to see the old watchtowers. Giant cylinders rising from the sandy dunes, acting as sighting points for a little-known, but highly fortified military installation during World War II, Fort Miles. During the war, the place bristled with dozens of guns, some able to launch massive shells almost thirty miles out to sea. Now, the towers stood as silent sentinels with their half-circle vertical slit windows facing out to a calm Atlantic Ocean.

At times throughout my children's lives, I have likened myself to those lonely towers. I imagined standing on the outskirts, a daunting figure on the horizon of their existence. I threatened any who dared to harm them, silently hinting at some great consequence. Yet, when life's pain washed over them like the waves of the ocean, constant and unstoppable, light shined on the truth. My threat, like those towers, was hollow. I manned no arsenal of destruction. Instead, as all parents inevitably do, I stood by powerless to stop the pain that must be a part of my children's lives.

I swallowed down that thought like a thick, chalky pill. Rachel glanced in my direction but looked away just as quickly. I think she sensed my doom. My kids chattered in the back, talking about walking to Candy Kitchen when we arrived at the house. I drove, letting the proximity to the ocean clear away the bitter after-thoughts.

That night, we took the kids to the Grotto in West Bethany. A local chain, I believed their pizza to be the most polarizing food in the mid-Atlantic. People who grew up going to the beach tended to love the strange pie with a swirl of blended cheese on top. Others, introduced to it later in life, despised it. Except for me. For the kids and me, Grotto was a must-have every trip.

"You don't sit at the popular table," I heard Laney say.

The two kids had been talking for some time while Rachel and I discussed our order. I barely paid attention but my ears picked up her comment.

"I didn't say we did, Laney, did I?"

"That's what Jesse's sister told her. She says Max and Ben are annoying."

"So what," Jake said.

"But they *are* annoying."

"You and Jesse just want the basement all the time. That's why you say that. I don't even know her sister."

"She sits at the cool table," Laney proudly announced.

"There isn't really a *cool* table. There's sort of a weird table . . ."

"Yeah, yours," she said.

"Laney, be nice," I scolded.

She crinkled her brow, so like her mother. "I was."

To my surprise, Jake laughed. I thought he would be upset or feel insecure but he looked nothing like either emotion crossed his mind. At that instant, I saw just how comfortable he was in his own skin.

I watched the two, my children, interact. The moment unfolded as if I had never seen it before. They carried themselves with confidence and happiness. I checked and found that Rachel watched them, too. Her expression mirrored what I thought mine must look like. I felt her shoulder touch mine. A second later, hers moved away, as if the contact had been accidental.

"Why are you always with those guys?" Laney asked Jake.

"Because we're friends."

"You just like to play that fools-ball game," she said in one of her accents.

They laughed. "No. We play Barbies a lot, too."

She feigned outrage. "You better not touch my dolls."

He smirked and acted as if his fingers were tiny, well-coiffed figurines. "Oh, Ken. Oh, Barbie. Smooch, smooch."

"Aren't you proud?" Rachel whispered, smiling.

"Actually, I am."

"Yeah, me too."

After dinner, we drove home. Instead of heading inside, we walked the block and a half to the beach, passing the houses with their sailboat motifs and grand, inviting screened-in porches. Fireflies speckled the tree line of an empty lot, blinking their silent story to the night. In the distance, the pounding growl of the ocean teased our ears. The air smelled of the sea and I heard another family on the next street over singing an old song.

> *"By the sea*
> *By the sea*
> *By the beautiful sea*
> *You and me*
> *You and me*
> *Oh, how happy we'll be."*

I stopped, straining to hear. My grandfather sang that song to us during our one visit to the state-owned beach bordering Maryland.

He didn't know the next line, though, so he hummed a few stanzas and ended with a resounding: "by the beautiful sea."

My family had gone ahead a few yards and Rachel looked over her shoulder, wondering why I stopped.

"What's up?" Rachel asked.

"Sorry, I was just listening to them singing."

I caught up to her and thought about explaining the significance, but my mind turned in a different direction. As some songs can do, the lyrics touched something inside me. When the kids were little, particularly during some of those tough times when I felt they were isolated from everyone else (or maybe that I was), and Rachel and I struggled with our role reversal, we talked about moving to the beach. Rachel would get a job in some retail shop and I'd try to pick up as much writing work as I could. Inland, the cost of living dipped to the absurd compared to the multimillion-dollar beachfront homes. Maybe we could make it work. The beach coursed through both Laney's and Jake's veins. It was our happy place. Why not embrace it fully?

The words in the song surprised me—"Pa is rich, ma is rich, so now what do we care?" They hit home. Every decision in life seemed so important. I thought about how important it had been for me to enroll the kids in the best school possible. We couldn't do that at the beach.

I noticed the problem with our theory during Jake's early parent-teacher conferences. Throughout school, I ranked in the top 10 percent of the class. The bottom quarter consisted of kids who would not go on to any education after high school. Some never graduated. Only about half my grade attended a four-year college. As bad as it sounds, I built a level of confidence in myself by being at or near the top academically.

For my kids, primarily due to my own decision to find the *best* school for them, they are smack in the middle of a school in which 80 to 90 percent will continue on to a four-year college, including some schools that my old classmates would not have been able to spell correctly. My kids, therefore, see themselves as average compared to their peers. Rachel and I had discussed this in the past, but decisions were made and were hard to undo.

The other family walking toward the beach peeled off toward an ice cream stand. Their departure brought my attention back to the present. I caught up with the kids, tapping Laney on the left shoulder but swinging around her right side. Jake lunged at me, grappling like a puppy. I laughed and the three of us, along with Rachel, carried our horseplay all the way to the sand.

The night proved to be one of the most beautiful I can remember. Long, fingerlike clouds passed in front of an enormous orange full moon. The light reflected off the ocean, painting the surf in a living array of yellows, oranges, reds, and purples. The waves crashed at the perfect rhythm and my heart seemed to change its beat to be in sync with nature. The brisk air reddened my cheeks, and refreshed, I took it in and savored the moment. This, I thought, was what the beach truly meant to us, to my soul. Peace.

At one point, Rachel and I stopped and the kids went ahead. We talked in hushed tones.

"Things have been tough," I said.

She nodded. "No tougher than for other people. I think it's just this time in our life."

I watched the kids as they played together. For a second, I felt like I was back on the beach that night so long before, when Rachel and I got engaged. I felt the urge to reach for Rachel's hand, to share that moment. My fingers even twitched, but they stayed by my side. The barrier between us became, for a moment, a corporeal thing, the manifestation between two people who very well may be growing apart. Yet through it all, two things pulled us back together, and those two things had gotten pretty far ahead.

Eventually, Rachel and I hurried to catch the children. We walked farther than normal that night, passing the houses crowding the dunes to the immediate south of our beach, on to the state beach beyond. I noticed the silhouette of a pickup backed up to the surf line. Three men sat in chairs, poles jutting out like giant antennae. They spoke softly to one another, their deep whispers accenting the tide. I waved and they all returned it.

"Should we head back?" I asked.

"Look. Mermaids," Laney called out.

I turned toward the water. As the moonlight reflected off the rolling surface, slashes of light created the mirage of a sparkling form riding atop the waves as they pushed toward shore.

"I see," Jake said.

"You're right," Rachel announced. She was the mermaid expert, the person who had introduced their existence to me almost twenty years before.

A tight knot, we stood together and watched as minutes passed into the night. My arm snaked around Rachel's shoulder and Laney leaned back against me. Rachel encircled Jake and he nestled in as well. I wrapped Laney up into another family hug as salty air brushed the back of my neck. I felt whole and at peace, sharing this moment with my family. The barrier weekend, fading into the night and becoming a shadow. I wished that would last until the end of time.

The weekend passed too quickly. The drive home consisted of contented silence and a couple of naps in the backseat. Home by dinnertime, we ordered out, P.F. Chang's. Laney and Rachel wanted to pick it up (since I drove home from the beach) and Jake and I went into the backyard and threw a baseball as the sun slid below the horizon.

"Getting too dark," I said.

He nodded. Baseball, unlike some other outdoor activities, became significantly more dangerous at twilight. The ball faded into the gloom only to reappear three feet from your face. The first few were exhilarating. After that, we were just asking for trouble.

"I'm hungry," Jake said.

"Let's get everything ready for when the girls get back."

We trooped inside and prepared for dinner. Jake fished aged chopsticks out of the utensil drawer, his favorite and Laney's. I grabbed some napkins and retrieved a beer for Rachel from the fridge in the garage, and a bottle of Pellegrino for myself. By the time I reentered the kitchen, I heard my wife's car pull up. At the same instant, the home line rang.

"That's probably Max," Jake called from the kitchen.

I expected him to pick it up but the phone continued to ring. It sounded three times before I made it to the kitchen. Creasing my eyebrows, I moved to answer it.

"Don't . . . please," Jake said.

"Why? Who is it?"

I could tell Jake did not want to tell me, but he rarely left a direct question unanswered.

"It's Doug."

I lifted one eyebrow.

"I just don't want to talk to him right now."

CHAPTER 22

DAY TWO

First, I call Jen. She answers and I hear sadness before she even speaks.

"Is Max okay?"

"Yes." She breaks down. "I am so sorry."

Strangely, I do not feel emotion in this moment. Nothing at all. "Can I speak with him?"

Jen pauses. It is a lot I ask, considering what has happened. Yet, considering what has happened, there is no way she can say no. When Max gets on the line, I can tell he's ready.

"Max? Are you okay?"

"I thought you'd call me," he says.

His voice breaks and tears roll from my eyes again. I set them free, allowing the droplets to course down my cheeks and drip from my face without wiping them away. I do not sob or heave, though. The tears are peaceful but more real than any I have shed so far.

I stay quiet. Part of me needs to know what Max knows. Another part has absolutely no idea what to say. Like the parents outside our house, he might lash out, blame me, or worse, blame Jake. Maybe he will tell me all of the signs that I missed. I don't think I can handle that, but I have to know.

My voice goes steely. "Talk to me, Max?"

"He didn't do it, Mr. Connolly. I know he didn't."

I take a deep breath. My heart—already broken for my son, my family, the victims, and myself—breaks again for Max.

"I know it's hard to understand. I don't know what to tell you, Max. I'm sorry."

"No, I mean it. I know he didn't do anything."

My brain feels numb as I comprehend what he said. I still believe this is simply adolescent denial. His young brain cannot comprehend the horrific facts so it has to change them. I understand that; I thought I saw it in Laney as well. But there is something about his tone, the way he makes that announcement, that sends currents tingling across my body. There is a very real possibility that Max knows my son better than I do.

"How do you know that?" I whisper.

Before he can answer, I dread what he might say because, for this split second, I can believe that my son had not taken part in this horrible tragedy. I can release a torrent of emotions that I did not even understand yet. Max let in a tiny, inconceivable hope that had vanished those first few hours after this ordeal started. Maybe Jake will come home to me, to us.

"Because I know. I know that kid Doug. He's crazy. Jake was just nice to him, the only one, really. He always tried to protect him. I never understood why . . . Maybe I do, now. I don't know."

I hear Max crying. I imagine how difficult it must be for a seventeen-year-old male to cry on the phone with another male. I realize, though, that Max cannot be thinking that way.

"It's okay, Max. None of this is your fault."

He settles down. I hear him swallow and clear his throat.

"Thank you," he says.

"Do you have any idea where Jake might be? Where I can find him?"

"I saw Jake that morning, Mr. Connolly. I talked to him. He said he was going to walk over to Doug's house. I had to tell the police the truth. But they just didn't care about the rest."

"What *rest*?"

Max cleared his throat again. "He looked scared. Jake did. I've never seen him like that before. He's a tough kid. He never really got upset about stuff."

In a different circumstance, hearing my child's friend speak candidly about his character would be utterly compelling, a spiritual treat. Under this circumstance, I hang on his words for a very different reason. I hunger to hear what makes Max so sure.

"He told me to stay away from Doug. He said something wasn't right, that he was freaking out. Jake felt he had to go over there to make sure Doug wasn't going to hurt himself."

Max's words became a chisel, chipping away at what I feared to be true.

"Did he say anything about hurting other people?"

"No." Max's reply sounds adamant. "Jake would never hurt anyone. You know that."

I did. Yet, possibly, I had forgotten.

"Did he say anything else?"

Max does not respond right away. When he speaks, his voice sounds guilty and unsure. "He told me to tell you that he was sorry."

My eyes burn and I have to swallow, but I cannot. I fall back into a chair, my legs giving out from under me.

He was sorry. For what? I do not understand. What did I do? What could I have missed? I failed my son. I failed on my most basic charge, protecting my own child. Nothing made sense any longer.

"What did he mean?" I whisper. To myself or to Max, I am not sure.

"I don't know," Max replies, breaking down again.

For a time we cry on the phone together, all pretense shattered. Finally, I can take it no longer.

"I have to go."

"I'm sorry, Mr. Connolly . . ." Max sobs.

"You are a great friend."

I hang up the phone and bury my head in my hands. The weight of my body presses into the chair. I cannot feel my fingers or my feet any longer. This cannot be happening. It has to be a joke, some sinister test.

One thing is certain. I have to get to the Martin-Klein house. I know for sure that's where Jake went yesterday morning. I grab my spare keys and go out through the den into the garage. It is empty and I remember that the police have my car and Rachel has hers.

"Shit," I growl, slamming my fist into the wall. I rush back into the house and throw on my running shoes. Their house is five miles away, less than one mile from the school. I burst from the front door and sprint through the renewed crowd. I feel a dark thrill as a few of them try to stay with me but fall behind like little yapping dogs chasing a car. The air rushes past my face and I feel alive. I am action now. I will not be stopped.

It is the fastest five miles of my life. My mind goes numb and my feet pound on the asphalt. I feel medieval as I push through the pain and the stares. I have one, and only one thought—getting to the Martin-Klein house.

When I reach their street, I stop, bending at the waist, hands on hips and panting as I take in the scene. Like our home, a ring of onlookers circles the property. This group, however, is different. The Martin-Klein house is not just dark, it appears long vacant. Although a few reporters stand on the fringe, within range of the streetlight half a block away, the rest skulk in the shadows. I instantly feel unsafe.

Pausing only for a moment, I walk down the driveway. These people will not stop me from finding Jake. I hear the threats as I pass among them, but no one touches me. I am through their midst and find open space surrounding the house. It is as if they fear being too close. I wonder. Are they afraid of getting hurt or catching whatever it is that allows a human to act as Doug has?

I approach the front door. The windows look like black soulless eyes staring at me. I press the doorbell and hear it echo behind the closed door. Otherwise, the house remains silent. I hear only the ominous murmur behind me.

I cannot take no for an answer. I pound on the door. As I stand, shoulders wide, on the threshold, I see my shadow expand across the side of the house and realize a camera is recording. I think back to the moment at my house and feel I am pushing it.

At the same time, I feel like the atoms in my body are vibrating, like I might burst apart and scatter across the universe. My hand pounds the glass. It rattles but does not break. Behind me, the crowd moves closer, like a torch-carrying mob. I take a step away from the door, toward them. I am ready to fight every one of them. Then I'll beat down the door and find out what Doug's father knows. Another step and a young woman appears in front of me. She has the look of a reporter, but her eyes are not jaded. She is not looking at me like I am an animal in a zoo.

"We have a police scanner in the van. The police are coming. Someone called them. Get out of here before they do. It won't look good."

My head tilts. This moment makes no sense. The absurdity of a reporter telling me to get away before the best story of the night unfolds right before her camera is not plausible. This bubble of humanity strikes me to the core.

"Thank you," I whisper. And I run home.

I return to an empty house. Worse, I have no car. I decide to call the detective. I will demand to know what they know. I will demand answers. Instead, I am put on hold.

Phone to my ear, I turn on the television. I do not know why I do this, other than it is a rote reaction to our generation's need to know more. Our children surf the Net to learn the news. For me, the golden box remains king.

Immediately, I realize something has gone wrong. A thick red band crosses the screen entitled BREAKING NEWS. I find myself reading the scroll at the bottom and not listening to the crisply dressed middle-aged man with the graying temples talk on screen. It reads: Shooting at Kansas school/Victims thought to include four children and one teacher/Police source names Jeff Jenkins primary suspect.

I listen to the anchor.

"Initial reports claim that Jeff Jenkins was obsessed with the Delaware school shooting earlier this week. On a Facebook page since taken down, we found this post: '13 is nothing. Wait until you see what's next.'"

I change the channel, my finger slamming the remote button down as if I can erase what I am hearing. A cable news channel shows much the same, except the host is now a young woman in a low-ish cut silk shell and a uniquely angled business jacket. A man in a crisp black suit with perfectly combed hair and soft jowls sneers out through the screen. He speaks as if his words carry a wisdom that he's decided the rest of us have forgotten.

"Parents should have known. We could have seen this coming. From all accounts, Jeff Jenkins was strange. He kept to himself; no real friends. Just like we see in the Delaware case. Schools, and God help us *PARENTS*, need to identify these children before they harm others. Open your eyes, people. Look at your children. If you're sitting there saying to yourself, *Wow, little Johnny is different*. But you're convincing yourself that he's just *special*, well, I say you are an accomplice to murder. There, it's out there. I challenge anyone to prove me wrong."

The host is visibly uncomfortable. "Okay, hold on there. I want to be sure that everyone understands that this is not a view held by this station."

Rage burns under my skin, warming my body as Muzak plays in

my ear. I slam the channel button again, daring them to show me more of this filth.

"Of course introversion is a personality type. There have been many successful people who might fall under that categorization. They are people who look inward, not outward. They seek quiet as opposed to noise. Their ideal night is spent at home, not at a party," a middle-aged professorial woman says.

The host nods along, smirking. When she speaks, righteous indignation seeps from her like a contagious illness.

"They kill, too, is that not right, Dr. Gregory?"

I turn off the television. Strangely, the anger abates. My mind latches on to a single comment I heard—*Just like we see in the Delaware case.* The woman referred to a child with no real friends. I will never forget the sound of Max sobbing on the phone. Never. It was the sound of a true friend suffering utter loss. The woman was wrong.

The hold music begins to grate. I look at the display. I have been on hold for over twenty minutes. I startle when someone knocks on the door. Hanging up the phone, I answer it. Jen stands before me, her eyes red rimmed and her face pallid.

"Can I come in?"

I nod.

As I back away from the door, I see flashbulbs pop. They are taking pictures of me letting this *other woman* into my house. Great.

I sit down without offering Jen a seat. She remains standing. When I look up, I see she is crying. Everyone is crying. My life has become a babbling creek of despair.

"There was another shooting."

"I know," she whispers. "I had to come over to make sure you're okay."

"They say the kid did it because of ours." It seems strange for a second that I take ownership of this tragedy; but it is ours now. No one touched by these events will be free of them, ever. If we don't own it, it will own us.

"They need to be able to explain it away. That's what all this is about. If they can't categorize what happened, put it in a nice, neat box, they can't sleep at night. . . . I've done it before. Now I see how awful it can be, though. It's like they want to pick at us until we are bare, exposed, just to make themselves feel better. They dissect our pain just so they can convince themselves they are immune to it. It is like someone suffering a horrible disease and finding someone who is worse off than they are and asking them, *Why?* Why are you worse off than me? How is your situation different from mine? Tell me, so I can go home feeling better as you stay here and die."

Jen begins to cry as she speaks. I want to get up, wrap her in my arms, and hold her, but I have no comfort left to give. I am used up.

She continues. "You know, it's been proven. If there is a suicide and the news reports it, particularly with their typical flare, the suicide rates actually go up in that area. This is proven. Kids can't buy cigarettes because they die fifty years down the road. But they can watch the news even though it might kill them in three days."

"Jen," I say, reacting to the tension in her voice.

"No, I mean it. If that's true for suicide, which it is, then why wouldn't it be true with school shootings, too? There are kids out there on the edge. Shouldn't we try *not* to push them over? Maybe that kid did copycat the Martin-Klein kid, but maybe it wouldn't have happened if those vultures out there just kept quiet, stopped making these troubled souls into superstars."

"It's okay." I feel impotent, unable to calm her. "Everything is going to be okay." My words are empty.

"No it's not," she snaps, her hands shooting up and covering her face. "Oh God, I am so sorry." She laughs, a sound totally lacking in mirth. "I came here to make *you* feel better."

I cannot take it anymore. I stand up and hug Jen. As my arms wrap around her, I imagine the reporters outside sneaking up to my windows, craning and jockeying, and finally snapping picture after picture of my staged infidelity. I think of Laney and how that would make her feel. My insides are a storm, a swirling tempest of neurons and guilt. Pulling away, I can't look at her.

"I think I need to be alone," I say.

Jen shudders, but nods. She backs to the door.

"He didn't do it," she blurts out. "He's a great kid. The best. Don't let them make you think he did. Don't let that happen. Promise me!"

I stare at her.

"Promise me, Simon! I mean it," she cries out. Her entire body shakes. "Don't let them do that to him."

She's too late. I have already returned to my senses. Jake could never have done anything like this. I knew *that* all along.

"Don't leave," I say.

"What?"

"I need your help."

Jen looks confused. "Okay."

"I need to take your car."

CHAPTER 23

DAY TWO

I am already sitting in Jen's car when Rachel calls.

"I see you have a visitor," she says after picking up.

"What?"

"Jen."

I am confused, thinking for a second that Rachel has the house under surveillance, which makes no sense at all. Then I remember the TV crews outside.

"I called Max."

There is a pause before Rachel speaks. Her tone is cool, protected. "What did he say?"

"That Jake couldn't have hurt anyone."

"I know that. What else?"

"He said that Jake was afraid of Doug. He was really upset."

"And Jen?" she asks.

"I don't know. Nothing. Look, we have to find Jake."

She laughs. "What do you think I'm doing?"

I pause this time. Strangely, I have no idea what Rachel thinks.

Our communication since this all started has been disjointed at best. At worst, we have split, a chasm opening (or opening wider) between us.

"I don't know," I say.

"I've called the police and threatened a suit if they don't find Jake soon. They're treating him like a suspect, not like a victim, so they don't care about the possibility that he is hurt somewhere."

My mouth forms words before I think it through. "You thought he was dead before."

"They can't just leave him out there somewhere . . . alone. No matter what."

I feel dizzy. I want to yell at her, tell her she knows nothing. Yet I realize I know nothing. Some part of me believes Jake is alive, maybe hurt, but alive. The rest of me is numb, thoughtless.

I go back to the one truth we share. We have to find our son.

"I think this all ties back to whatever was going on with Alex Raines. Can you check with the police, see if there were any complaints? I tried to call his father again but he won't answer."

"I'll try," Rachel said. "I'm heading to the station now. They might not release that kind of information, but I'll try."

"I'm going to look for him."

"You don't have a car," she says.

"I have Jen's."

"Good."

Rachel hangs up and I look out the window at the throng of people surrounding me. I can't take it anymore. I no longer care what anyone thinks. My back straight and my chest out, I get out of the car. About a dozen reporters see me and converge like turkey vultures on a roadside carcass. This carcass, however, still has teeth.

Microphones thrust at my face as questions cut through the air, more damaging than any bullet.

"What would you say to the families of the victims?"

"How did you not see your son's violent side?"

"What do you say to the people who think you should be held accountable?"

I let the questions peter out without a response. When the opening presents itself, I strike.

"Let me ask you all a question," I say, hoping my voice sounds as confident as I feel. "Why haven't the police found my son?"

Incredibly, silence answers my plea, so much so that I can hear the rumble of the news vans' engines in the background. One cable reporter (according to his microphone) pushes forward. He is a man with a clear opinion behind his squinted eyes and red-cheeked face.

"He's on the run. We hope they find him soon before more children are hurt," the reporter says.

"Where would a seventeen-year-old run to? Has there ever been a mass shooting where the shooter got away? The answer is no. The reason the police haven't found my son is that they are looking for the suspect, not the boy."

At least half of the reporters appear to understand what they have, a new angle, something unexpected to report. I see the hunger in their eyes and know they will let me speak.

"When children go missing, there are community searches, there are hotlines . . . and empathy. Why hasn't anyone asked about Jake? Asked if he was okay? No, he has been condemned, and with what evidence?"

My phone rings from deep in my front pocket. It might be Rachel, but I have an idea it is Jonathan. If my comments are playing live, he is likely having an aneurism. I do not answer.

"There is no security footage, to my knowledge, showing my son even at the school during the shooting. Where's the smoking gun? A Facebook post? Some teenage e-mail. Check the digital footprint of your own children. You might find it eerily similar.

"Instead of picketing my yard, go out and look for Jake. Help me find him, please."

I drive out, leaving the masses behind me. I am going to the Martin-Kleins' house. This time, I don't care what anyone thinks. I am going to find Jake.

CHAPTER 24

On the drive over, I call their number. Someone answers but the line remains quiet for a moment.

"Hello," a female voice says.

That disarms me. At first, I felt ready to lash out, tear into Dr. Martin-Klein, although I had no idea what that would have sounded like. To hear Doug's mother's voice unnerves me. I'd never spoken to her before.

"Is this . . ."

Somehow I know she was about to say *Jake's dad*. My throat tightens and I close my eyes.

"Hello," I finally mutter.

"Oh. This is Mary . . . Martin-Klein. I'm sorry, Mr. Connolly. You have no idea how sorry.

"Your son was a good boy. So good and nice. He was always nice to . . . nice. I hope you know. I don't understand how this happened."

I am broken inside and those rips allow vitriol to ooze out like puss from a festering wound. I am not proud of myself, nor am I in control.

"How could you not know? Didn't you watch your kid? What, did you just let him run around free, doing whatever he wanted? I don't get it! How could you not know? How could you be that ignorant?"

That last word hangs there. It is enough to awaken humanity. I shake from my toes to my throat. Could I honestly admit, even to myself, that I know everything about my own son?

"I'm sorry," I mutter.

Mary Martin-Klein weeps. She does not hang up or cover the phone. The sound cuts almost as deeply as my words. At least that is what I tell myself.

"I'm sorry," I repeat. "I . . ."

What is there to say, though? I am as bad as the rest. To my amazement, the weeping stops. Her voice returns, strong, shockingly resilient.

"I think Jake," she begins. The sound of my son's name startles me, but I try to concentrate on what she says next, "came to the house the . . . yesterday morning. He came here."

I feel suddenly sick to my stomach. "What are you saying?"

"He was here. The police told me. They found blood, traces of his blood in . . . in . . . our kitchen."

"At your house?! Have you seen him?"

Her voice sounds so distant. "He hasn't come around for such a long time. I . . . No. I . . . I don't think Jake hurt those children."

"I'm almost to your house. Will you let me in this time? No cops?"

"Yes," she whispers.

I can tell there is more to her answer but I hang up. Her words storm through my mind, freezing everything. The overstimulation causes me to shut down. I turn inward, not about Jake, but about what I just did, that I spoke so harshly to this mother who has suffered as much, if not more, than me. Am I evil?

. . .

Pulling up to the house, my first thought surprises me. I expect to feel violent hatred or overwhelming sadness. They both tie for second.

During my moments of weakness, those hours that I allowed the world to tell me my son was a murderer, I failed to remember just how small a role Doug played in Jake's life over the years. All in all, they spent maybe a year and a half as playdate-type friends. After that, Doug morphed into an acquaintance, one I am now learning my son looked out for at school.

I jump out of the car and rush up the walk, trying to breathe normally but panting like an overheated dog. My chest feels tight and my finger hovers over the doorbell. I need to get inside, to find Jake, but the thought of facing Doug Martin-Klein's parents is that overwhelming.

Before I ring, the door opens. Flashbulbs fire behind me as Mary Martin-Klein appears behind the screen door. Maybe they had been going off before, I don't know.

"Come in," she says.

I try to subdue the rage I feel but fail. "You were here earlier when I knocked on the door. I know it."

She nods. "My husband left. I was scared. I . . ."

I look past her. Expecting to see the doctor, I realize my anger is now solely directed at him. She tells me he is not there.

"He left. I don't know where. He just disappeared," she says. "I can't go. The lawyer told me to leave. But I can't go."

"Where's Jake? Have you seen him? You said he came here the morning of the shooting?"

She does not answer. I feel like I am waiting for a blank sheet of paper to speak to me. I understand. Looking into her eyes, I see she punishes herself. This torment acts as a penance. Mary Martin-Klein deems herself a murderer.

This is a moment in time where my very person, the character that acts as my foundation, is tested. I know this, even now. I step closer to Doug's mom and take her in my arms. I hug her and the world behind me erupts in madness. I hear shouts. Lights flash like an electrical storm. I drown it all out with a whisper into a mother's ear.

"It's not your fault."

I have never been more certain of a sentence in my life. I feel her body slacken, as if her bones turn to dust. I hold her up, support her weight as if supporting a bag of feathers. She shakes and I imagine her demons alighting into the air, off to haunt someone else.

It is not true, though. My words cannot heal her. The demons come back, as they always do. When she pulls away, deep circles ring her eyes, like the edges of two sinkholes threatening to expand and devour her whole.

"They found the . . . he was in here," she says.

I follow her into the kitchen. A yellow evidence marker remains on the linoleum floor. I kneel next to it and know my son once stood at this very spot, alive, but I know not for how long. I want more than anything to turn back time, to kneel here in the seconds before his blood spilt. I could protect him then, stand in front of him and force back a known threat, not one lingering in the shadows, stalking my son for so many years.

"The police knew," I whisper.

I reach out and touch my son's dried blood. My fingertip simply brushes the surface and I pull away. There is nothing for me. I feel no closer or farther from Jake. The spot remains nothing but a spot. I will not find my son here.

When I look up, Mary is gone. I do not know where she's gone. I am alone in the kitchen of a school shooter. Yet I still cannot find my Jake.

CHAPTER 25

ONE WEEK BEFORE THE SHOOTING

Maybe life is just a series of banal moments punctuated by tragedy. On Tuesday evening, I was hungry. Jake and I returned from his cross-country meet and I hustled into the house to check on the pork loins I had thrown in the slow cooker that morning with a bottle of barbecue sauce. Taking two forks, I pulled the meat into long strings. If I had taken the time to cube the pork, dinner might have been more presentable, but I worked all afternoon on a speech for a non-profit executive. The pay sucked compared to the medical writing I did, but the topics usually interested me.

Rachel and Laney sat in the living room, both reading. Laney flipped through a *People* magazine while my wife read a brief on her iPad. A familiar yet diaphanous annoyance colored my vision of what could have been a nice family moment. Instead, I blamed my wife for being a workaholic and at the same time wondered why Laney wasn't reading her assignment from school instead of a glossy periodical. I thought about saying something like: *"Did you pull the pork*?" but I let it lie. I had gotten pretty good at that over the years.

Instead, I turned my attention back to dinner. I tossed a bag of potato rolls onto the counter and pulled open the refrigerator, hunting for a bag of baby carrots.

"Damn," I muttered.

"What?" Rachel called back.

"Nothing. I forgot to make the coleslaw."

"No biggie," she said. "It's good without it."

I did not agree. Annoyed, now at myself, I banged plates and silverware around until my wife came into the kitchen.

"What's wrong with you?"

"Nothing," I said.

"No, really."

"I'm fine, just disappointed I didn't make the coleslaw."

Her phone dinged, announcing a new text. I watched as she read it. When done, Rachel turned and walked out of the room. I shook my head.

I plated up dinner. For Laney I made a small pile of pork, some carrots, and a handful of Tostitos, not much different than what I'd served her a decade before. For Jake and me, I slopped together two pulled-pork sandwiches apiece. I called everyone in and sat down. It was not until Rachel arrived that I realized I hadn't made her a plate. For her part, she did not seem to notice. She fixed her meal and joined us.

"How was cross-country?"

"Great," Jake said. "Max shaved thirteen seconds off his best."

I nodded. "He's got some endurance, huh?"

Jake told us about how they practice. I listened but could not recall the conversation afterward, probably because I was watching Laney. She looked at her brother as he spoke, her eyes wide and unblinking. I marveled at how much she looked like her mother. Their blond hair both pulled back in a ponytail with wisps falling along their temples. Her blue eyes shined in the light from the fixture above the table. I glanced up at that and realized I needed to replace one of the bulbs.

"How was your day, sweetie?" I asked.

"Great."

"Didn't you have tryouts today?"

She laughed at me. "Dad, they're called auditions."

"Yeah, right. Weren't they today?"

She nodded.

"Well, how'd it go?"

"Good, I think. You never know."

I asked her what they made her do and she told me. I forgot her answer, too, because as she spoke, I glanced at Rachel. She listened to Laney with a soft smile lifting the corners of her mouth. I felt a jolt of guilt for what I'd thought when I got home. Without Rachel, my life could never have ended up the way it did. I really did owe her everything. I vowed to show that to her, to treat her better.

Dinner ended and the kids went upstairs to "do homework." I noticed Jake grabbed his phone on the way up. I had begun to detect hints of a possible girlfriend, but I wasn't sure yet. He'd slip soon enough and tell me, so I didn't worry about that too much. It wasn't like the thought of Laney having a boyfriend. That was going to be too much for me to handle.

I did the dishes as Rachel finished up some more work. At nine o'clock, we both moved toward the den without mentioning it to each other. I sat down on the couch and turned on the television. We watched *Top Chef*. Neither of us spoke during it. Not in an uncomfortable way. The silence felt more apathetic than that. I checked my phone a few times for e-mails, although I didn't expect anything. Halfway through the show, Rachel turned on her iPad.

I must have dozed off because the next time I saw my wife, she stood over me, looking down.

"Hey, I'm going up."

I grunted something but followed her upstairs. Rachel and I

climbed into bed. She turned her iPad back on, I think to read her book club book. I rolled away from the glow, too tired to sleep. I vaguely remember the light from the screen going off and Rachel turning away from me. Then we slept, awaking the next day prepared to relive the one before it.

So many moments taken for granted. What I wouldn't give to return to that time.

CHAPTER 26

DAY TWO

Once again, my phone rings. This time, I know who it is before even a glance.

"I'm at the Martin-Kleins'. Did you get anything from the police?" I say.

Rachel has no time for greetings either. "A detective is coming out to talk to us. Jonathan is . . . here. He's helped. The police found blood, Jake's . . . blood in their house."

Although I've already learned this, hearing it again devastates me. "Why didn't they tell us?"

"Because they thought he'd killed those children. They thought he was a murderer."

I feel angry. Everyone stopped seeing Doug and Jake as people. Rachel's words could not be truer. The only thing anyone wanted to know about them was *why*.

Anger turns to guilt. I thought Jake a murderer, too. Jonathan told us to get out in front of the story. I doubted. I never stopped seeing Jake as a person, but he's my son, not some stranger I see through the television or Internet, introduced via some awful picture chosen from a Facebook site for its shock value rather than any likeness.

Did Rachel doubt? I never saw her waver. Maybe it is a *mom* thing. Maybe dads are pragmatic, impatient, and ill-equipped, just like they all claim to be. I do not know.

"The detective is coming," she says over the line.

"What?"

I hear muffled voices, Rachel sobbing. Jonathan speaks next.

"The police just handed Rachel some of Jake's things. Evidence they took from his room, his phone, some other things. She's . . . it's a lot to take. I'll take care of her. But I have to tell you first. They took prints off that doll. They match the Martin-Klein kid. None of Jake's prints are on it. The detective also just told us that the Martin-Klein boy allegedly threatened the Raines kid with a gun two weeks ago. When the police went to the house, though, they didn't find anything. There wasn't enough to press charges, just the word of two boys."

I have no words as Jonathan excuses himself to care for my wife. In any other circumstance, the irony of that fact would amuse me. Not now. Instead, I begin to understand.

Doug threatens Alex with a gun. The gun isn't found when Alex's dad calls the police. Jake wrote a note telling someone, probably Doug, to get rid of something. Jake's blood is in Doug's kitchen. Jake's blood is on the door to the school. That doesn't mean Jake was ever at the school. He never made it back.

The gun. Gun. Guns. Suddenly, I know why the police did not find anything. I know where Doug hid the gun. And I know, as only a parent can know, exactly where I will find my Jake.

CHAPTER 27

FOUND

My mind tears through the millions of memories, trying to find any detail that may guide my step. At the same time, I run, faster than I ever have before, racing through the side yard, leaving everything and everyone behind.

"Jake!" I shout.

At full stride, I break through the tree line behind the Martin-Klein house. Dry, late-fall brush shatters as I crash into the forest.

"Jake!"

I don't know why I am calling out. I just want Jake back. I need to find my son. And I am so angry. Why had I not looked there before? I had almost forgotten that's what the boys did all those years back. What started as such an enormous worry had petered out over time, replaced by the day-to-day stresses of two teenagers. But how could I have forgotten?

I have no idea how to find the fort, the setting for Jake's pretend battles as a child. I consider turning back, going to ask Mary Martin-Klein, but I don't even slow my pace. I also realize that I no longer have my phone. I must have dropped it in front of the house. Everything is happening so quickly now that I can't know for sure.

The brittle leaves snap under my shoes as I weave among the tall, straight oaks. The occasional evergreen breaks the stark grays of the forest's annual death. My voice echoes through the emptiness, stirring a blood red cardinal from a bush. It darts amid the trunks, quickly disappearing from my view.

"Jake! Where are you?"

I hear footsteps. The sound jumbles my mind. For a second I imagine my son will appear, smiling, laughing, racing toward me through the woods, a green hoodie tied around his waist. I grab him. Hold him. Press him so tightly that he cannot breathe. Torrents of relief and amazement storm out in streaming tears.

But this is a dream. The reality is that the footsteps come from behind me, not in front. I hear sirens approaching, more than one, and their call melds into a baleful moan. I push forward as if we are racing. I will find him first. No one else.

My eyes never look back. I scan the woods, looking for a path or a dark shadowy mass that might be a fort.

"Help me find you, Jake," I whisper.

I want a sign; I deserve a sign. I love my son with everything I have ever had. I know, I have always known, that I would die for him in an instant if need be. But nothing is that romantic, that dramatic. I was never given the chance to sacrifice for Jake. And now, when I plead for something to show me the way, a stag in the mist to guide me, the call of a red-tailed hawk, Jake's favorite bird, to bring me to my son, there is only silence and dread.

I stop, my head tilting back. I look up at the sky, cracked by the skeletal limbs grasping above me. A cloud floats lazily toward the late-autumn sun, softening the long shadows that streak across the landscape like the mythological remnants of some great lightning storm.

"I'm sorry," I bellow. "I'm so sorry."

When I look ahead again, through tear-clouded eyes, I see the pond. A snippet of the past comes clear. I remember Jake telling me about the pond behind the Martin-Klein house.

My walk turns to a run when I see the fort appear from behind a patch of massive fern. I trip over a thick fallen branch, dropping to a knee. My hand skids across a patch of exposed rock and pain sears up the length of my arm. I stagger back to my feet and keep moving.

The fort rests low to the ground. A lean-to, two large sheets of weather-stained plywood tilt upward, supported by three gnarled black limbs. Dirt, moss, and dried leaves form a thatchlike roof atop the sheets of wood.

Above, the sun thrusts through the blanketing cloud and the world around me brightens like a new beginning. Something sparkles by my foot. I bend down to pick it up. My fingertips touch cool metal and I lift the object off the ground. It is an intact round of ammunition.

My heart races. I look down and see more bullets. They scatter across the forest floor like pebbles in a streambed. For some reason, I begin to count them. It lasts only a fraction of a minute but I see more than fifty. My mind cannot focus. I still do not understand.

Then I see my son's shoe. It is a simple swatch of neon yellow but I know it immediately. The shoe is almost covered by fallen leaves as it rests undisturbed beside the large fern. I stare at it, frozen in place, unable to move, unable to see that it is not just a shoe, that it is my son alone in these woods, somehow forgotten until this very instant, lost and gone forever. All those thoughts are so unfathomable. They are the stuff of paralyzing nightmares, the reality of a life I never considered, even during my darkest parental neurosis.

I cannot move. I need to go to him, but I cannot accept that he is not there anymore. He's left us already. He's gone off alone. I can't bring him back. I can't talk to him anymore. We can't joke. We can't wrestle. We can't go out for dinner or eat pulled pork at home with Laney and Mom. I can't drive him. I can't pick him up. I can't wait for him. He'll never walk toward me, smile at me, be there.

Jake can only be inside me now. He can only speak through memories and impossible imagination. What ifs. If onlys. I wishes.

Dogs bark. Someone is close behind me. I think he's been there all along. It is the dogs, however, that awaken me again. I take a step and then two. I fall to my knees. I embrace what was Jake, what will never be Jake again. I hold him but it is not him. I cry and rage. And I never see the empty box of ammunition in his cold hand.

CHAPTER 28

AFTER

I am alone with Jake, the two of us now lost together behind the Martin-Kleins' house. Time must pass, birds must call out from the trees above the fort, but I am not there. Then I realize I am no longer alone. An enormous police dog, a German shepherd, tilts its head. I look into its deep brown eyes, my hand resting on my son's still chest. Someone once told me that I should never look into the eyes of a dog, that it is a challenge. That is not how I feel. Instead, this grand animal looks into my soul. I feel it tugging at some semblance of life and realize it must be mine. It is trying to bring me back. I am sure of it.

The dog does not move. I hear people approaching but our connection remains firm. In my head, we speak to each other, two animals in the forest contemplating the most basic fact of life.

He is dead.

Yes.

I can't live.

You can.

Why?

Because.

Is that good enough?

Yes.

I don't understand.

You do.

I want more than anything to die. I do not want to get up or walk out of the woods. I do not want to live a life of meaningless moments. I want to lie down and never leave my son's side. If there is a will to live, I think I lose mine.

Or do I? What is it that keeps me breathing? I would like to say it is Rachel and Laney. That is the correct answer, the human answer you expect to hear from me. If that is not the answer, then I am unlikable.

The honest reason I breathe is because I am scared. I fear death. I fear living. I fear loss. I fear change. I fear everything and nothing at the same time. Instinct, some leftover synapses from before the Ice Age, tortures me. It keeps me from turning off. It rewires my brain. I no longer think years ahead or days ahead or moments ahead. I don't even think one breath ahead. I simply take in air and let air out. I become an automaton of survival.

I let them take me away but I look back over a shoulder at Jake. I want to cry but I might be out of tears. Instead, I feel an icy chill radiate out from my torso.

"I can't leave him," I say, but it comes out as a whisper.

"It's okay, Mr. Connolly," an officer says. "We'll take care of him. I need to get you some help."

"I'm fine."

He leans into me as we walk down the barren, shaded path.

Something strange happens. I do not remember walking past the Martin-Klein house. I am not even sure where I am, except I know I sit inside the back of an ambulance. A paramedic holds a mask over my face. I breathe in the cooled air, unafraid. In fact, I feel utterly numb.

Rolling my eyes around, I see silver instruments, an IV drip, and a blood pressure cuff around my bicep. Three blankets lie atop me but I do not really feel their weight.

"Just relax, Mr. Connolly. Your blood pressure dropped. We're giving you fluids and a sedative. You'll be fine."

No, I won't, but he doesn't know that. Nor do I tell him. Instead, I close my eyes.

When I sit up, Rachel is there. She reaches out a hand and, together with the paramedic, helps me out of the ambulance. We hug. She has tears and they flow freely. She shakes in my arms. I hold her but I am still devoid of feeling.

I should be reacting differently. I look around, sure people are staring at me, wondering how I could be so normal, so nonchalant about my son.

"You feel cold," she says.

At some point she stops crying.

"I'm fine."

The scene around me clarifies.

I startle. "Where's Laney? She shouldn't . . ."

"It's okay. She's with my mom."

I did not know Rachel's mom came up from the beach. In fact, I never even thought of her parents during this entire thing. I never called my parents. I didn't call my siblings. I feel guilty about that, which seems absurd in the moment.

An engine starts. Another ambulance rolls slowly up the driveway. I want to climb in, as if Jake has simply suffered a concussion at a flag football game. But there is nothing else left for me to do, just take air in and let it out again.

CHAPTER 29

More than twenty-four hours have passed since I found my son, a series of empty moments at once agonizingly slow and blurrily fast. We were taken home, together. We cried, together. All three of us slept in the family room; the rest of the house remains as it was after the police search. At some point, the doorbell begins to ring. Then it never seems to stop. Covered dishes march into the kitchen as well-meaning neighbors, many of the same who blamed Jake a day before, return to our door bearing food, eyes empathetic, mouths wordless. A silence descends. Rachel takes Laney to her mother's condo. I am left to clean up the mess, which I do with numbing regularity.

That night, I learn that the footsteps I heard behind me when I searched for Jake belonged to a cameraman from the local NBC affiliate. He filmed the entire thing with a handheld. At four PM that afternoon, the police issued a report of their findings. Together, the story and the report play out on the television set.

Tonight, the final pieces of a national tragedy fall into place and a hero emerges from the carnage. The footage you are about to see was shot earlier today by a cameraman in Wilmington, Delaware. Once thought to be an accomplice in the school shooting on Monday, Jake Connolly's body was found in the woods behind the home of his schoolmate, the alleged shooter, Douglas Martin-Klein. Police issued a preliminary report this evening telling a remarkable but sad story. It appears that young Jake learned of Martin-Klein's intention to shoot students at the school. He confronted the boy in the Martin-Klein house where police believe Martin-Klein fired a shot from the same assault rifle used in the school shooting. The bullet struck Jake Connolly in the lower back. What happened after that is amazing.

Suffering from what police at this time believe would have been a mortal gunshot wound, Jake Connolly heroically ran from the house back to a fort the two boys built when they were young. There, he apparently scattered over one hundred rounds of ammunition before being shot down by Martin-Klein. Police believe that this action may have saved dozens of lives at the school.

The police have also issued a report that clarifies some earlier evidence that leaked to the press during those first days after the shooting. Although Jake Connolly's blood was found on the door leading into the school, it is now believed that the blood had been on Douglas Martin-Klein's hand following Jake's tragic attempt to stop the shooting. Eyewitness reports placing two shooters entering the building that morning have also been recanted.

I warn you that the footage we will show now may not be suitable for young viewers. It shows Jake's father, Simon Connolly, racing through the woods, calling out to his son, only to find his son's body at the base of his childhood clubhouse.

There was a note, too, found in Jake's pocket. Thankfully, the police returned it to me without it leaking to the press. I read it once and I can't read it again. Not yet. It read:

Dad,

I've needed an amnesty moment for a while now but I was afraid to ask for it. I think you already know what it is about. You've known for a long time, I think. Longer than I have. It's about Doug. But I guess it is also about me, too.

I am afraid. Not of talking to you but of how things have been lately and what I have been thinking about. I can't seem to figure out what to do. No options seem right to me. It's like I took a wrong turn somewhere and I can't find my way home.

I think Doug is a psychopath. I am not being mean. I actually researched it. He's not like what you see on TV. He doesn't draw bloody pictures or keep a stalker wall or anything like that. We all like violent stuff. It's something else, something darker on the inside.

Doug doesn't care. When Max makes fun of him, it doesn't make Doug sad or hurt him. It makes him angry, really angry. I've tried to get Max to stop, and he has really, but other kids do it, too. They won't just leave Doug alone. It is starting to make me angry, too. Why do people have to be so mean? Why do they have to rag on kids every day? Sometimes I wish the tables would turn. I wish someone could teach them a lesson.

Sometimes, you don't really know a person. Sometimes I feel like I don't even know myself. I wonder what I will

*do when things get worse. I wonder what kind of person
I really am. Doug has a gun. It's hidden in the clubhouse
we built when we were kids. I haven't seen it but I know.
He told me. I worry that he is going to hurt someone. He's
gotten scarier. He hung a doll at my spot in the woods. I
know it was him, and it was a message to me. I don't think
he'd hurt me but I should tell you. I think you can help,
but I know you'll tell the school or Doug's parents. If that
happens, I think he'd snap and do something really bad.*

*I'm going to try to talk to him one more time. If it
doesn't work, I'll give you this. Just promise me you won't
freak, okay?*

I love you dad.

Jake

Everything I needed to find him on one piece of paper. Unfortunately it came too late. Much as I did.

CHAPTER 30

DAY SIX

The line of people outside the church wraps around the block. Rachel, Laney, and I sit in the front pew. Occasionally, someone close to us kneels and offers their condolences. Laney sobs until Rachel finally takes her into a small room in the vestry that the priest offered to us in case anyone needed to get away. I sit there, my head bowed, listening to the soft music rolling out of the organ up on the balcony.

The viewing lasts for hours. Laney does not come back out. Time has lost its meaning, for as soon as one ceremony ends, the next seems to start. We are at the funeral now. People are talking about Jake. I am sure people feel like I should be up there, speaking, but I can't. The words are inside me but I do not want to share them. I am afraid to open that door because a raging storm lurks just behind.

I am okay, stable even, until after the funeral. People come back to our house. I don't want them to, but they do. I know Rachel feels the same because she sends Laney to be with her folks at their condominium. I try to talk to some of my closer relatives and friends, but what is there to say? They speak about Jake, about his bravery. I take that in. It does help, I guess. But then I see her.

I am sitting down in the kitchen, my legs feeling weak, when the front door opens. A woman takes a tentative step into the house. I recognize her immediately and bound to my feet.

"What are you doing here?" I say loud enough for over a dozen people to hear.

Mary Moore freezes. Her mouth opens but nothing comes out.

Rage fills me. This woman who stood in my yard, condemning my son, even wishing my daughter dead, dares to come into my house now that he's a *hero*.

"Get out," I say.

A room filled with more people than it can comfortably hold grows more still than it ever has been before. I feel the eyes on me, boring into me, but I can only look at Mary Moore. My jaw clenches and my hand trembles. I want to run, to lash out, and to collapse all at once.

Fingernails bite into my forearm. A harsh tug twirls me around to face Rachel. Her face is red, her eyes are afire.

"What is wrong with you?!"

"She . . ."

"NO!" Rachel breaks down crying. "No. You can't do this!"

I look around and see the eyes now. They are full of shock.

"What?" I ask Rachel, maybe everyone.

"Go upstairs," my wife whispers. "Get hold of yourself."

I sit on the edge of our bed. It takes only a moment for me to realize what I have just done. My emotions thunder and crash. It would be a lie to say I felt totally wrong. So many people vilified Jake. Now, they all come to our house and say how great he was. Where were they yesterday, the day before?

Another part of me realizes I just called out the mother of one of the victims. What kind of monster would do something like that? It is beyond contempt. And I wish I could turn back the clock and take it all back.

Eventually, sooner than it should have, the noise downstairs lessens as people trickle out the door. Rachel opens the door to our bedroom and stands at the threshold.

"I'm taking Laney and going to my parents' house for a while."

This is not a request or an idea, it is a fact. She is telling me she is taking my daughter away.

"You are not," I say.

"I am. And you need to get some help."

"What?"

"You need to talk to someone, someone who can convince you that none of this is your fault."

I feel my body trembling. "I never said that."

She laughs, a bitter sound that I've never heard before. "Really, Simon. I remember what you were like about the stupid little stuff. You used to tell me you ruined the kids because you wouldn't go to a playdate, for Christ's sake. I know you, Simon. I know that you think you caused all this. Even worse, I know that you feel like you questioned our son, that you maybe, for a second, thought he did this. And I . . . I know you . . . think that if you found him . . ."

"Shut up," I snap.

She does not move. She does not back down. "I know you, Simon." The tears return. "I just don't have the strength to help you right now."

Rachel turns and walks away from me. I am alone in our house, a bitter irony considering how often I wished I could be over the years.

CHAPTER 31

DAY TWENTY-SOMETHING

One day, I've lost count at this point, I rise from the couch. My muscles are cramped, rigid, and my mind lacks an anchor. It floats on the undercurrent like a ghost ship through the ocean mist. I find myself getting dressed, lacing up my running shoes, and stepping through my front door.

No crowd surrounds my house. I might be alone. Yet I break into a sprint, my eyes locked on each step my shoes make, seemingly of their own accord. They retrace steps from weeks before as if they align with a glowing path toward some end of which I am still unaware.

Halfway to the Martin-Klein house, my pace slows, for I realize that is my destination. I still cannot look around. I cannot understand why I am going, but now I know where. For a second, I consider turning back, but I do not. Instead, I press forward, speeding up. My breath, ragged and made painful by the cold air, seems the only thing fighting for my survival.

I do not slow as I leave the pavement and cross through the

Martin-Kleins' lawn. From a distance, I see a break in the dead undergrowth. With a leap, I am once again in the forest.

I do not go all the way. Instead, I stand near the pond, staring at the shadowy outline of the fort. A chilled breeze cuts through the skeletal trees, pressing its cold touch against my cheeks. My breath fogs, rising up before my line of sight, giving movement to the otherwise desolate scene.

First, one step. Then a second. Tentatively, I approach the scene of Jake's death. When I reach the spot, time ceases to exist. The sun sets behind a line of sentinel pines and long shadows creep across the forest floor.

How do I leave? How do I get up and walk away? Jake will be alone, even though I know he is no longer here. I cannot let that happen. Instead I stay by his side. I sit at the ending. And all I can think about is the beginning.

The alarm sounded at 5:50 AM on February 12, 1997. I still remember the song that played, TLC's *Waterfalls*.

> *A lonely mother gazing out of the window*
> *Staring at her son that she just can't touch*

I reached across Rachel, feeling the swell of her belly under my elbow as I gently press the snooze button. A slight pressure moved across my skin, or maybe I imagined it. The night before, I watched as his little foot pushed out and across her tummy (at least it looked like a foot). I watched for some time after the movement stopped, hoping to see it again. Rachel said he quieted down but I waited a little while longer, just to be sure. Then I turned our light out and went to sleep, the last time I would do that as just a man. The next day, I would be a father.

"Sweetie, it's time," I whispered.

Rachel stirred, making that noise she'd made since I met her, a soft purrlike grumble, as if to say, *I love you but let me sleep.* I smiled, hugging her (and my son).

"We can't be late," I said.

I'm not sure why I thought we couldn't be late. Five hours later found us sitting in a maternity room, anxious and bored at the same time. The induction began on time, right about eight AM and soon after the doctor broke my wife's water. I will not go into details on that one. Suffice it to say I will remember but will probably not bring it up at any parties.

As we played another sluggish hand of cards, my mind returned to a familiar thought: one I had on my wedding day; while I was sitting at my college graduation; during my first Holy Communion; and many other moments in my life. I expected some kind of grandiose display of amazingness in these pinnacle slices of time. Instead, during each one, I marveled at the utter triviality of the scenario.

"The baby's heart rate is dropping," the doctor said. "We have to consider a C-section."

Rachel's eyes opened wide. She had endured over twelve hours of induced labor. Before that fateful day, she confided in me that a C-section scared her to death. She had wanted more than anything to give birth naturally (not no-drug natural, just the old-fashioned way). Amazingly, she had never been under the knife in her entire life.

The machine buzzed and beeped at the same time, startling me. My son's beats per minute dropped to sixty-five.

"Oh God," I said.

No one heard me, or at least no one reacted. The doctor spoke softly to Rachel but I could not listen. Instead, I just stared at the monitor, willing that number to go up. I hate to admit this, because it will sound odd, but I did this other thing, too. I probably will not explain it correctly, but I reached inside. In my mind, it was like pulling out a piece of my soul that I thrust free and offered to the tiny life inside my wife's body. I tried to give my unborn son a slice of my own life. I felt the tug from my core as I held my breath, offering him everything. The number dipped even lower.

The doctor turned to a nurse.

"Prep delivery room four."

The nurse hustled out and the doctor leaned in toward Rachel once again. "We have to move you over to an operating room now. Your baby's heart rate has dropped too low. Everything will be fine, but we will start prepping you for a section. Okay?"

Rachel nodded. The doctor left the room and I hugged my wife. I could feel her sobs against my chest.

"It's okay," I whispered. "Everything is going to be fine."

"I'm sorry," she said.

Those words tore my heart out. "It's not your fault. You didn't do anything. The doctors will make sure Jake's okay. And I'm here for you. I promise."

Rachel did not say anything else. Two orderlies (possibly the same two we'd seen that morning) appeared in the doorway. Cautiously, they wheeled Rachel and her bed out of the room and down the hall. A nurse approached me as I watched my wife being taken away.

"Mr. Connolly, you can come with me. We need you to get scrubbed before you can go back with her."

There are moments in life when you are faced with an impossible decision; a choice must be made when you no longer live for yourself. Mine occurred at the single biggest moment of my life up until that day, the instant my son came into this world. Some details of that moment are my wife's alone and I would not share them. What I recall was sitting on a stool at the head of my wife's hospital bed. The nurses erected a screen just below Rachel's chest, blocking the operation from our view, more Rachel's than mine. I had been operated on in my life, but never awake like she was. I could not fathom what it must have been like for her.

I did my best to support her. I held her hand as her body shuddered, sometimes from her nerves, other times from the manhandling of the operation being performed on her abdomen.

"They're pulling me," she moaned, her voice thick from the epidural.

"It's okay." I spoke softly to her. "Everything will be okay."

The nurses and doctors spoke confidently while they worked. I missed most of what they said but it sounded as if everything was proceeding as planned. I tried to find the monitor on my son's heart but couldn't. Maybe that was for the best.

"It hurts," Rachel said.

"She says it hurts," I told the nurse.

"I'll see what I can do."

Tears rolled down my wife's face as she stared up at the ceiling. The droplets melted into the coarse fabric pillowcase, leaving a slowly expanding dampness. I wiped one away and she flinched as if my touch hurt.

"It's okay," I said again. I could not find any other words.

"He's coming," the doctor said. "Do you want to see?"

I stirred, a morbid curiosity piqued by her suggestion, but Rachel grabbed my hand. I looked down and she glared up.

"Don't look at me," she ordered through a clenched jaw.

I sat back down, nodding gravely. Neither the nurses nor the doctors took any notice. They continued their work.

When Jake finally joined us, I did not notice the exact instant. Or maybe I will never remember it. The span from Rachel telling me to stay with her and when a nurse placed Jake on a small metal table vanished or never existed. Who knows? All I can remember is turning my head and seeing him. His eyes locked on to mine. I know every expert or know-it-all would say that it was impossible, that babies cannot see more than light and dark at that point, or whatever. I know the truth. Our eyes met. He looked at me. Tears welled in my eyes and I blinked them away, needing to see my son, for him to see that I looked at him as well.

That look—it changed the world. Jake called out to me without making a sound. His tiny head tilted to the side, his red lips set in a straight line. He absorbed my everything, taking it in and holding so tight that I knew I'd never get it back. I disappeared that day, vanished and reborn as something entirely new. Not a stand-alone presence but part of a matrix of shared existence. At the time, I did not put a word to it, but later I would. The word, one I thought I understood before, but my prior comprehension fell woefully short, was *love*.

"Do you want to hold him?" the nurse asked.

I stood, my body feeling airy, almost ethereal, as if Jake might pass right through me. My arms reached out and the nurse, having already cleaned him up a bit, swaddled my son so quickly that I barely noticed and handed that little dream to me. I felt his tiny weight pressing down on my forearms and knew he was real, that he would always be real, no matter what. My son looked up at me, his expression so untouched, so new, that I could not stop crying. I bent and kissed his forehead, my dry lips warmed by his skin.

I do not know how long I held him. I lost track of everything but Jake until a nurse touched my shoulder.

"Let's give Mom a turn," she said.

My eyes widened a bit. I turned, slowly, and looked at Rachel. What I saw was a moment I could never undo. She stared at Jake, her eyes still so full of fear. Though the realization was never expressed as words, it swallowed us that day. This little infant, so small and frail, you would think him the vulnerable one. The truth is that the real vulnerability opened inside us. No longer did we live as ourselves. We lived for him.

There is no dog this time. No one is there to lead me out of the woods. In the end, it is weakness. The cold cuts through my damp running clothes and my body shakes violently. I close my eyes to the darkness and walk away, walk home, and sleep.

CHAPTER 32

DAY TWENTY-SOMETHING

The next morning, I get the mail. I do not want to, but I do. Once back inside, I walk calmly into our dining room. This is where I always put the mail. Today, it seems like a foreign place, a room I have never seen before. Paintings and family pictures still hang in the same spots. Sitting at my dining room table, I am surrounded by a border of floral wallpaper I'd meant to take down when my kids were young. There are pictures of Laney and Jake surrounding me. One shows them swinging side by side at the elementary school. Laney's full, downy hair flies behind her like the flames from a cartoon jet engine. Jake is . . . smiling.

I glance at each picture on the wall. Our dining room is a collage of their childhood, but my eyes focus on one thing—Jake's face. Smile, smile, smile. Okay, there are frowns, too. And looks of surprise. These are the pictures Rachel and I chose, picking the younger ones out of a box in the office upstairs and taking them to the photo shop she always loved, choosing the more recent ones from her laptop and printing them ourselves in black and white (or sepia if we felt particularly artful).

Life is kind of like that, picking the memories you want to frame. We all have an idea of how it should be, all smiles and swing sets. There are the more unsavory moments that we leave in the box stashed up in the darker parts of our psyche. We know they exist but we don't go flaunting them in front of the dinner guests.

In that moment, I frame my son's life. I see him rounding third, helmet brim low, mouth set with fierce determination. I feel that pride like it is happening right this second. I stand in the sand watching the waves roll over him, his body at once helpless and in such graceful control. I see him frozen in time, water cascading around him as he checks to make sure his little sister is okay. In my mind, in my heart, I frame a snapshot of him in the talent show, and jumping high in the air to catch a pass.

"Oh, Jake," I whisper, smiling despite the tears.

My memories are little flashes of light in the darkness. They sparkle and glow, but fade under the weight of what life has become. That darkness fuels the slow decline that is my life since the shooting. I don't know how to pull myself back up.

That's when I see the purple envelope. I reach out, tentative, like checking the sharpness of a knife with a fingertip. When the thick paper touches the pad of my index finger, I know it is real. It is something unexpected and I am frightened by it.

When my finger and thumb grasp the corner, the paper is cool to the touch. Slowly, cautiously, I slip it out from under the circular. It is a letter, the address scrawled in the unmistakable script of a school-age girl. My heart stops dead in my chest. For the letter is addressed to my son.

Why? My first thought—it is a perverse, sick joke. But that is not possible. I spasm into motion. In a jerky, desperate slash, I tear the envelope. My hands are shaking as I pull a sheet of notebook paper

out, one with a jagged line of flimsy barbs where it has been torn
from a spiral binding, so like Jake's final note. I read:

Dear Jake,

*My name is Jaimie and I am writing to you from
California. I wish you could read this letter. It is not fair
that you can't. When I saw the stories about you on the
news, even before everyone knew the great thing you did, I
understood. I hope this doesn't sound weird, but I felt like
I knew you. That maybe you and me are alike. See, I'm
quiet at school. I don't always talk to people. Sometimes
I don't talk to anyone. My mom tells me that it's just who
I am. I guess she's right. But just because your mom says
something, doesn't mean you believe it, right?*

*I guess it's strange that I'm writing this letter. If my
mom knew, she'd never, ever let me send it. And I doubt
it will ever be read. But you made a difference, not just to
those kids in your school that you saved, but to me, too,
even though I am so far away. Sometimes people say stuff
about us quiet kids, or any kid that isn't like everyone
else. That's what they did to you. Maybe now, now that
they were proven so wrong, they can see that just because
someone is different, it doesn't make them bad. That
maybe we should take the time to see what someone is
really about, like you, before we decide who they are.*

*When the time comes in my life when I can take the
easy way that's wrong or the hard way that's right, I am
going to think about you and remember what you did for
your friends. I just hope everyone else does, too.*

You will never be forgotten.

Love,

Jaimie

CHAPTER 33

The next morning, I cannot get that girl's letter out of my mind. Not entirely sure what I am thinking, I pace around the house, my lethargy replaced by a twitching potential energy. I feel the need to act.

The thought materializes out of the ether. Ill formed, it pulses like an amoeba. Where it originated, I cannot recall. I simply act, unfettered and without forethought. Using Safari, I find what I am looking for in a town in West Virginia. When I call and ask, the woman on the other end gives me the answer I hope for, the one I somehow knew she would have.

"We have one left, actually. A boy. If you can get down here to pick him up in the next week, he's yours."

"I'll be there tomorrow," I say.

"Isn't it quite a drive?"

I shrug, although I know she can't see that. "Six, seven hours."

She is dubious. "If you can make it . . ."

"Count on it."

I shower and dress for the first time this week. Standing in front of the mirror above the sink, I pull out the shaving cream and a razor. When I wipe my hand across the fogged glass, I see my reflection. Droplets of water distort my vision, diffusing the lines of my face. The shadow of my growing beard juts out, dominating the visage. I like it for what it represents—change. So I put the razor and shaving cream back in the medicine cabinet and walk downstairs, running a hand through the week-old stubble.

When I finally make it outside the house, the sun has risen to dance among the treetops. Long shadows crisscross the yard and a cardinal darts out of our landscaped bushes and alights on one of the skeletal branches. I watch it sit, motionless, on the limb, its vibrant red contrasting with the stark near-winter grays. I can look at it. It hurts, but I can do it.

The writer in me wishes the day to be spring. Winter signifies death, the end of a cycle. I do not feel that, at least not in the moment. Instead, I feel a new beginning. It is not one to be excited about, or even nervous. This beginning is tentative, full of nostalgia and longing. Nevertheless, my soul stirs and I think that tomorrow may dawn and the balance of my will might tip. As slow and gnawing as my decline progressed, it now withdraws at the same clip. It is a step in a direction. Right or wrong, however, seems to matter far less now.

Taking a deep breath, I get in my car and drive. I have three stops. Two I dread. When I reach the first, I park the car on the street and walk up the driveway. When I ring the bell, Mary Moore, mother to my son's homecoming date, opens the door. When she sees me, her eyes widen. I try to smile but know it appears forced. I jump in with both feet before she can slam the door in my face.

"I'm so sorry for what I did. I—"

She cuts me off. "I understand, Simon."

This is, I think, the first time either of us has used the other's first name. I feel a strange closeness to this woman, this fellow survivor, and think she must feel the same.

"I don't know why I said it."

She shakes her head. "I'm sorry. I should not have gone to your house that day. I just . . . ever since . . . I feel like I'm walking around in a fog. It's like there's nothing left to live for."

I take a step forward and she laughs, waving off my attempt at a supportive, yet awkward, hug.

"Don't worry. I'm out of tears. At least for the moment."

I nod. "Me, too."

There is nothing left to say. I realize I didn't need to say anything, but as I walk back down the drive, I admit to feeling slightly better.

The next stop is much harder. The second Mary. Just driving to the house turns my stomach, but I push through. I fight the urge to flee after I ring the Martin-Kleins' doorbell. I came to tell them that they are not to blame, even though I know they will blame themselves forever. I have no delusions of grandeur, I do not think my simple words will change their lives. But I need to say it.

I stand on the stoop, wetting my lips, waiting. The seconds tick by but no one comes to the door. Finally, after ringing the bell two more times, I turn to leave. Out of the corner of my eye, I am sure I see the curtain in one of the windows flutter. When I spin around, there is no one there. I stare at the spot for a moment longer. After that, I leave, knowing I won't come back again.

I drive to West Virginia over that night. Halfway there, I lower the window and let the chill air keep me awake. By the time I get to my destination, a tiny town at the base of a rolling green mountain, I check the time—5:30 AM. Too early to arrive, I turn the car and follow an access road up to the crest of the foothill. A dirt lot waits and I park in front of no less than three signs pertaining to hunting licenses.

I meander into the dark woods. Up ahead, I see a slice of deep purple sky through the towering trunks. After a few hundred yards, the view in front of me opens up. I can see the rolling mountain range to the east. Light peeks over the lower heights, painting the sky in the many shades of nature. I sit down on the leafy forest floor and watch the sun rise, alone.

I must have dozed, because when I check my watch, it reads 9:43. I pop up and head back the way I came. I find the car, no problem, and roll down the mountain. Once back on a main road, the GPS guides me to a farm. Classic post-and-rail fencing outlines sloping fields on both sides of a long and winding drive. I follow it to a modest two-story colonial with a wraparound porch and perfectly painted shutters. When I open the door to get out, I hear barking.

The woman I spoke to on the phone answers the door.

"Mr. Connolly, I'm glad you got here. I have three people interested but I held on to the boy for you."

"Thank you so much."

She leads me into the house. Off the kitchen, she built an extension, not for a breakfast nook, but for a puppy room. A half wall closes the area off. As I near, a perfect little yellow face pops up and disappears.

"He's a jumper, that one."

I don't even care. I stop and watch this puppy's head spring up and disappear, spring up and disappear, and there is no question.

"I want to take him home," I say.

She laughs. "That's why you're here."

She does not really know why I am here. Nor do I. I just act, not for the past, not for the future, just for the now. I reach out for the banal and pray I won't lose my grip.

CHAPTER 34

MY LAST CHAPTER

A week passes before I pull up outside the beach house. I see Rachel's mom sweeping the front porch. A second later, awakened by the lack of motion, someone else sees her, too. A tiny yellow tail frantically wags.

"It's okay, Bub. You did great."

The puppy, standing up now on the passenger seat, front paws on the windowsill, black nose leaving a streak on the window, whines. I have only had him for a few days, but already I can see the amazing dog he will become. There is something in his eyes that hints at the human soul trapped inside.

Rachel's mom looks stunned. Although the weather remains unseasonably warm for early December, she wears a lined windbreaker and a knit cap. Her hair, white now but still hinting at her blond days, dances in the salty breeze. The sun shines on her face, one full of guarded uncertainty.

"Hi, G-Ma," I say.

The puppy, my new puppy, tugs at the leash. An AKC certified yellow Lab.

G-Ma states the obvious. "You have a puppy."

I nod. "Are Rachel and Laney home?"

She puts down the broom and steps toward me. I expect a sense of trepidation, as if I might be unpredictable, if not dangerous. I figure the puppy adds to this profile. Instead, she gives me a hug as the dog jumps against her leg.

"They're down at the beach. Taking a walk."

"Thanks," I say. "Come on, buddy."

I turn and walk down the driveway toward the road.

"Simon," she calls after me. "Be careful with them."

Her words cause me sadness. But I know what she means. I need to be careful with them, now and forever. As they do with me. It is our lot now.

The puppy has a nose for the ocean. He pulls, leading the way. Through the silence, I hear the soft pound of the surf. My stomach flutters.

As I crest the dune and get my first glimpse of the ocean, I see them—Laney and Rachel. They stand above the foaming tide, daughter leaning on mother. I feel their longing from that distance, as if they wait for some miracle to appear on the horizon.

I do not walk to them right away. Instead, I let this sight settle into me. Finally, I move. It is not my doing but the dog's. He needs to greet these two strangers. He lets out a whine and a yelplike bark. Even over the crashing waves, Laney hears. She turns, eyes only for this poster-perfect puppy. She takes a few steps toward me before she realizes who I am. When she looks up and sees me, her pace does not stop, it quickens. She runs to me and I scoop her up, dropping the dog's leash. He dances at our feet as I embrace my daughter, holding her so close that not even air can separate us.

"I love you, sweetie."

"Oh, Daddy, don't leave."

I choke up. "I won't. I'm so sorry."

"Shhhh."

Laney's attention turns to the pup. I give her the leash and she promptly unhooks it from his little collar. The dog races free, Laney by his side. They dig in the sand and startle to the sound of gulls arguing over a ghost crab. I watch them and smile.

Rachel does not come to me. When I look at her, her eyebrows rise, as if asking what brought me here. I walk to her. We speak, not facing each other, but watching our daughter play with her new dog.

"A puppy?"

I shrug. "I don't know. I was on my phone, about to call . . . make a call, and I started searching for breeders. Then it just kinda happened."

She laughs. "That's not very Simon."

"I know."

She looks worried when she asks, "What's his name?"

I shake my head, as if to assure her that the thought, her worry, never crossed my mind. "Bubba."

She laughs.

We do not talk for a moment. When I continue, I find it hard to stop.

"I'm sorry, Rachel." I continue through her protest. "Let me say it. I'm sorry for not being able to turn my mind off. I think I missed so much with the kids because I couldn't just let it be fun. Everything had to mean something; everything became some kind of pivotal moment shaping them for the . . . forever. I forgot to make every minute special, with them . . . and with you."

Her hand takes mine. "You're okay, Simon. You've always been okay. Sure, you think too much but there's nothing wrong with that. You do it because it's you and because you love with everything you have inside you. We all know that. You don't have to apologize."

"But I feel like I worried so much about him that I never just enjoyed our time."

Although I wish I could say we did not cry anymore, we did, together.

"You're forgetting the good," she whispers. "Disney and all those summers here. That game you and the kids used to play in the surf, where you let the waves crash on you." She laughs and cries at the same time. "And you all yelled."

"Oh No," I say, filling in the name.

"Yeah. *Oh No!* Remember that stuff, okay?"

"I'll try. I want to remember everything."

We both read into that statement. The one thing we don't want to remember is the one thing we will never be allowed to forget. I struggle to get past that thought, but Rachel helps.

"You know, I like the beard."

I laugh. "Makes me feel manly. I bet Laney'll hate it, though."

Rachel looks me in the eyes. "She loves you so much."

"I didn't pay enough attention to her. It was easier with Jake. I understand boy stuff. I feel like I never spent enough time with her."

"You're fine," she says. "More than fine. What you gave her is better than all that. You showed her the kind of man she'll marry. A man who will love her with all his heart. A man who will do anything to keep her safe. A man who will help raise their children. A man who will treat her like she's the most special girl on this planet."

"How'd I do that?"

She squeezed my hand. "By being you."

I know she's leaving something important out. She knows, as well as I do, that we've lost something, she and I. This moment, I think, isn't about that. It's not about us. It's about survival and strength. It is about living, not without fear but despite it.

"You know that no matter how quickly we found him, it wouldn't have mattered. The coroner told us that."

"I know," I say, though I doubt I'll ever truly accept that. I will continue to blame myself, but I will live with that, too. "I'm sorry about how I acted. I talked to Mary Moore, Kandice's mom. I apologized to her. There was no excuse, but I am sorry about that."

I hear my daughter laugh for the first time in a long while. When I turn, Laney looks at us. Her eyes are hopeful. Ignoring the puppy, she rises and sprints to us. Her arms widen and I know what she wants. So does Rachel. We hug, the three of us becoming one as the ocean roars behind us. The sun shines on Laney's cheek and a sparkling tear rolls down her perfect young skin. It might as well be the first tear of joy to grace this world.

We hold each other. The tears dry up and the moment stretches toward normalcy. The puppy nudges Laney's calf. She turns with a squeal of excitement and runs, the dog playfully nipping at her ankles.

We watch our daughter go and it is some time before I realize Rachel and I remain holding each other. It feels right.

When Rachel speaks, it reminds me of a time long past, a time before Jake and Laney. A bitter memory now, but I can, at the least, conceive of the fact that it was once sweet, too.

"You just have Jake in your thoughts. You have always been so hard on yourself. Let it go. You didn't mess Jake up. You made him such a beautiful person that he gave up his life to protect others. He saved those kids."

"He did," I say, looking out at the ocean, listening to my daughter laugh. "And more."

She tilts her head. "What do you mean?"

I think of Jake. My son kept his dark hair on the long side. He loved to play football with his friends. As a big brother, he neared perfection, never treating his sister like a lesser life form. Jake loved his family with every part of his being. Smart and funny, maybe my son was a little shy. Most of all he cared about people the way we all should. Like Jaimie's letter reminded me, Jake can be a lesson to us all.

I'm not crying when I answer Rachel. Nor am I smiling. I look at Laney.

"He saved us."

ACKNOWLEDGMENTS

Michelle . . . my best friend, life with me may be heavy but you have a way of pushing me when I need to be pushed and understanding when I can't be pushed another inch. I love you.

Mom and Dad . . . you endured your own worries, so different than my generation's yet stemming from the same source. It couldn't have been easy watching me change majors five times. Looks like psychology was a good fit.

The University of Notre Dame . . . a place of history, culture, social dynamics and awe. My experience under your massive wing led me to an amazing, albeit bizarre, life.

Mrs. Long . . . my high school English teacher. I'm sure you'll never see this but if you do, you'll be as shocked as I am grateful.

Tracy Garozzo . . . just because I know how happy you'll be seeing this. You helped me survive one of the most daunting experiences of my life to date—my kids' preschool—by talking to me like an average person, not a stay-at-home dad.

Kari Reardon . . . the first person that read this story, thanks for making me feel like a better writer than I am.

Captain's Catch . . . you showed me that cleaning dumpsters at a fish store might not be my first choice for a profession.

Stephanie Kip Rostan . . . a better closer than Papelbon, that's for sure. Thanks for seeing potential and pushing me to realize it. And thanks for getting me.

Lyssa Keusch . . . for making me a better writer. I've learned so much in such a short time and it feels great knowing that it's changed how I work.

Rebecca Lucash . . . thanks for all the help in making me a better writer. Your thoughtful perspective gave me the confidence to think this story may speak to more than simply parents.

HarperCollins . . . I owe you one.

About the book

2 Behind the Book

11 Reading Group Guide

Insights,
Interviews
& More . . .

Behind the Book

I DIDN'T SET OUT TO WRITE A BOOK about school shootings. In fact, I still don't think I did, even though most reviews and summaries I've seen so far disagree. It may be closer to say I wrote a book about being a stay-at-home dad. I may have. Certainly I've been given the advice to "write what you know" a few times. At the base of it all, however, I wrote a book about introversion and parenting an introverted child. Even simpler, I wrote about parenting.

School Shootings

Not long ago, I read an intense and thorough book about the tragedy at Columbine High School—Dave Cullen's *Columbine*. It is the kind of book that you can't say you loved, and you can't say about it, "You should read this great book I just finished." Those are all high praise, but every once in a while you come across a book that is different. It is the kind of book that changes the way you think. It sticks with you for months, or maybe forever. That is the book Cullen wrote.

Two aspects of *Columbine* struck me the hardest. First was how deftly the author addressed the antagonists' story. Often, when a tragedy strikes, particularly one involving children, human nature leads us to vilify. I'm not saying this is a bad idea, or wrong, but it is not real. Factors influence violent acts. Some appear obvious—mental illness, feeling powerless, bullying, troubled upbringing. Some are convenient— the depiction of violence in our society, bad seeds, the "quiet type." In reality, another factor is always involved but rarely accepted. It is that which we cannot understand. We cannot predict everything that will happen. And we cannot explain away or understand all the bad in the world. It is just not possible.

Cullen provides factual insight into the lives of the two boys responsible for the shooting, Eric Harris and Dylan Klebold. In my opinion, there is no hyperbole or exaggeration. After finishing the book, I was left with the feeling that Eric Harris was the force behind what happened. Although I am in no way assessing more or less blame, it felt like Dylan Klebold followed someone down a path he may not have naturally taken. Who can know for sure? And as a parent, maybe that thought is even more frightening.

The second aspect of *Columbine* that shaped the plot of *Finding Jake* became an even larger influence when I did some research after finishing Cullen's book. He provides some insight into the parenting of Eric Harris and Dylan Klebold. As I read about detachment, implied naïveté, inattention, I couldn't help but think it can never really be that simple. I came across an essay that Dylan Klebold's mother published in *O, The Oprah Magazine*. I wonder if anyone can read it without seeing things in a different light.

Susan Klebold begins her essay: ▶

Just after noon on Tuesday, April 20, 1999, I was preparing to leave my downtown Denver office for a meeting when I noticed the red message light flashing on my phone.

Clearly the beginning of *Finding Jake* mirrors this, because when I read her essay, my heart broke. I saw Susan Klebold as a person, a mother, no different than the rest of us. I saw her normal day be interrupted by a call that would destroy her world, and the world of so many others, in a matter of minutes. As she writes in her essay, she did not see it coming. She makes no apology and expresses no anger. Her thoughts read like the thoughts of any parent, one that faced what, to me, felt like the ultimate nightmare. I am not in any way saying one person's tragedy is more severe or more anything. What I am saying is that anything like what happened at Columbine is a nightmare. Yet when I looked for an example of what, as a parent, I thought I could never survive, I thought of Susan Klebold.

Introversion

Somehow, introversion and school shootings have become linked, whether in reality or by our overzealous need to explain away the unexplainable, to predict the random. I am, in fact, an introvert. There are people in my life who would disagree, but it is true. I am also fascinated with the subject, particularly how it carries such an odd stigma along with it. In fact, my wife used to cringe when I called myself that, like I admitted to being a serial killer or an abuser of small puppies.

The way I see it, it comes down to a simple question. If you have the night free would you most often rather (a) stay home or (b) go out with friends. I would chose (a) about 80 or more percent of the time. I have friends who abhor staying home and would chose (b) 95 percent. They are extroverts. I am an introvert. And we are all okay.

As many parents know, raising an introvert can be challenging. Or more accurately, it can draw out insecurities. It's actually not hard to parent a kid who is reading a book for an hour. What is hard is parenting a kid who is reading a book for an hour while ten other kids are playing outside next door.

In tragic situations, introversion takes on a haunting characteristic. How often do you hear some neighbor of someone suspected in a violent crime say, "Oh, he's very quiet. Never spoke to anyone." Ironically, Albert Einstein's neighbors may have said the same thing.

Stay-at-Home Dad

That brings us to the book I really wanted to write. I read *Columbine* when my kids were young and I was a stay-at-home dad. One day, just after I picked them up from preschool, I decided we'd go to a local playground. For the first hour or so, we had the place to ourselves. I played a little with the kids, following them around, chasing them until I got tired (or bored, depending on how honest I feel), then found a nice bench to sit down on. I watched them, feeling pretty content.

Within a half hour or so, three moms showed up with a bunch of kids in tow. My kids stared, which they tend to do at first, and hovered around, half wanting to join in, half perplexed. My daughter slipped into the group first. She played with them for a few minutes while my son remained on the perimeter. I glanced over at the moms, who had either not seen me or acted like they had not seen me. They were deep into a conversation, barely looking up at all.

Then one of the boys hit my daughter. They had been playing and my daughter was in line for the slide. The kid tried to cut. My daughter, who I wouldn't even cut in front of, stood up to him. And he slugged her. My daughter screamed and I bolted up, ready to do . . . well, I don't know what. The mothers, reacting more to me I think than to their children, stood but didn't move. I went to my daughter and shot a look at them. One of them laughed and said, "Boys will be boys."

I am far from proud of what happened after that. Seeing my daughter get hit brought out the worst in me. In a calm, probably chilly, voice, I said, "Maybe if you watched him he wouldn't go around hitting girls."

I can still feel the awkward silence after that one. I gathered my kids and took them home. If I'm going to continue to be honest, ▸

my hands shook most of the drive. When I got them settled
I called my wife and told her what happened.

"I can't believe I said that. What kind of a role model am I?"

A coworker sat in my wife's office. She heard the story and told
my wife I should write a book. At the time, I figured it would be a
self-serving, spiteful therapy session so I didn't want a piece of it.
Instead, I wanted to slip off to some cabin in the woods and
become a hermit.

Years passed. Before I even considered writing about a school
shooting, I'd changed my mind and decided to write a book from
the point of view of a stay-at-home dad. It was a label I shunned,
hid from, raged against, and finally accepted as I wrote this story.
It was a choice my wife and I made, one that at the time seemed
so simple but proved to be one of the most difficult experiences
in my life.

It's funny how people respond when I say I stayed home with
twins. Often, that gets this amazing look, like how could I figure
out how to change two diapers at the same time. It implies that
the hardest thing about being a stay-at-home parent is caring for
your children. That, to me at least, was the easiest part by far.
That is the part I will always cherish. I am thankful for every
moment I spend with my kids, to this day and hopefully beyond.
I consider myself very lucky.

What did I find so difficult, then? EVERYTHING ELSE! It's
funny how much I changed during the early years. I'd always
been on the artsy side. By the time my kids were two or three,
I'd gotten a crew cut and wore a lot of Champion and Under
Armour. Never over-the-top about sports, I was coaching Little
League baseball, soccer, and basketball. Never on the outgoing
side, I withdrew into a defensive shell, assuming every guy I met
judged me immediately as less of a man. I became even more
awkward among the moms, never knowing what to say or how
to think. Now I freely admit that most of my angst stemmed from
my own insecurities. At the time, though, I blamed everyone
around me.

I would never claim to walk in another person's shoes, but
I can say I know what it is like to be different. Most people would
say that dads staying home is far more common. Oddly, I never

met another one who had a child in my kids' grade. I didn't search out a daddies group, mostly because I couldn't stomach the thought of telling people I was in a daddies group. I tried a playdate. Mostly, though, I felt very alone. I once asked a female work acquaintance what she thought of stay-at-home dads. In a moment of brilliant honesty, she said, "I assume they are losers." Reading that, many may say that they'd never . . . But I bet they have.

It all sounds awful, but that isn't my point. In that experience, I found a voice. I drew from that stranger-in-a-strange-land experience. I've had people, both moms and dads, working or staying home, who have read the book and said they relate to many of the parenting issues touched on in *Finding Jake*. At the same time, I've had readers say they hated the main character and found him whiny, or worse, unrealistic. I can say that while writing the book, I often put myself in Simon's shoes. Most writers wouldn't want to admit that. Neither do I. But it's so darn obvious, really. None of the events in the book happened in real life, at least not exactly. But I imagine that many of Simon's reactions would mirror mine if I faced the same test.

Finding Jake

This all being said, I put the three pieces together. I took a stay-at-home dad with an introverted son and thrust them into the worst nightmare I could imagine. As I told the story, I often felt like I lived the moments with them. I still find it hard to reread the book. I will never claim to understand how tragedies like that can happen. Nor will I even guess at a viable preventative solution. I will never claim I was the best stay-at-home dad. My daughter is still a little mad that I dressed her like a "boy" when she was little, but she swings a bat like nobody's business. My son has come to predict when my patience is at a low and I sometimes find him managing me. I drive my wife crazy when things aren't going great and I often pine for my old office job. But I tried, and survived.

The one thing I hope someone takes from reading *Finding Jake* is that parenting isn't always easy. If I stand at the bus stop and can't think of a word to say, it's nothing personal. If you see ▶

a kid who's hovering around the group, he's not insidious. Most likely we both want to be a part of it. We just don't always know how. But we are people. We have struggles, and so do you. More often than not, they are similar, even at the hardest times.

My Dog Simon

After *Finding Jake* came out, many people assumed that I'd named my main character, Simon Connolly, after my dog, Simon. As my bio ends with a shout-out to our rescue dog, I'm not surprised. Although I am sure it will be hard to believe, I didn't. In fact, *Finding Jake* was half written before we adopted our Simon.

I had wanted a dog for a while. We live in a very country suburb where the nights are dark and the yards are perfect for running in frantic figure eights. My kids, having grown up with only cats, weren't the most relaxed around dogs. So getting one seemed to make sense. I'd decided it was the only way for them to grow comfortable with larger, more slobbery pets.

We hesitated, though. My wife had never had a dog. And we'd just gotten to that point in life when we had some nice things that we didn't want chewed, or worse. At nine, the kids required far less strenuous parenting. The idea of bringing a brand-new fluffball of energy, needs, and destruction had started to sound less and less appealing.

So, I'd pretty much given up. To my surprise, I caught my wife surfing Petfinder.com one night. While I tried to watch a playoff game on the television, she leaned across the couch and handed me her iPad.

"Oh my God, you have to see this," she said, and showed me a picture.

I was shocked. This was a nondog person. Looking at the picture, I couldn't even tell what type of dog this was, but it clearly wasn't a cute little fluffball. My wife kept on about this dog, pointing out the wrinkles and the sad eyes. I wanted to say, "And the ginormous head!" But she was sold. She had to have this dog.

We went to the website for the adoption organization. They had rescued a litter of four, fostering them in a home nearby. The angel who took them in named the four after the judges on *The X-Factor*. I saw a picture of Reid, a big, healthy-looking tuxedoed bruiser and wanted him. Simon, the runt of the litter (pictured on the next page), was described as laid-back.

My wife, unfamiliar with the adoption process, opened the application. When she scrolled through the ten pages, including references and previous vet history, she nearly lost it.

"Are you kidding?" she said.

"They want to make sure we won't hurt him," I said.

"Ten pages! That's crazy. Forget it."

So she closed her browser and forgot about little Simon.

The next day, without my wife knowing, I filled out the application. As I was driving to the beach a few days later, my phone rang. I answered it on speaker so the entire family could hear. The woman on the line told us that we'd been approved to adopt Simon. My wife got very excited. So did my daughter. My son, however, wasn't convinced.

The next week, we went to see Simon and two of his littermates, Britney and Demi. Reid, it seems, got adopted. When the foster mom took Simon out of the pen, he immediately ran, awkwardly, to get a toy and flopped down in a dog bed. As we spoke, the kids checked him out.

I'd read somewhere that you should flip a puppy on its back. If it struggles, then it might be dominant. When it was my turn, I did it, trying to hide the test from the nice woman caring for the pups. Simon remained on his back, unmoving. I think he might have fallen asleep. The foster mom caught me and laughed. She proceeded to take Simon's paws and perform the YMCA dance. He snored and we were totally hooked.

We had every intention of changing his name. What kind of name is Simon for a dog, anyway? I remember driving home with him the next day. He whined but only for about two minutes. My son got upset. He didn't want to take Simon from his family. I explained to him that all the dogs needed to find a home or they might have to go back to the shelter. He felt a little better, but he remained skeptical. In an effort to make him feel better, I told him he could suggest a name. A fan of the Percy Jackson books and Greek mythology in general, he offered Dionysus. This was the first time the thought of keeping Simon's name occurred to me.

When we got home, the decision made itself. A ball of ▶

wrinkles and snorts, our new dog could barely walk without
tripping over himself. He climbed into any available lap and
immediately fell asleep and his snores echoed through our
kitchen. He took immediate ownership of anything placed in
his new toy box and he loved to lie in the sun and chew on sticks.
All in all, he was, plain and simple, a Simon.

Simon has grown into what we like to call our Frankendog. Part
shar-pei, part boxer, part pincher, and part golden retriever (don't
see it but that's what the genetic test I absolutely had to have said),
he grew into his head (slightly) and out of a lot of his wrinkles.
But his back legs are too long and too straight and he still snorts
(although he stopped snoring). He's a great dog, although he acts
more like our third child. The kids now love all dogs and we often
wonder what life was like before he arrived.

Although I did not name Simon after Simon, dogs did start
appearing in *Finding Jake* soon after he arrived. As I continued to
work on the book, he rarely left my side. Often, he sat and stared
at me for long periods of time.

As you can see, it's no wonder a police dog comes to Simon's
rescue near the end of the book. That scene, in fact, is one of my
favorites. And again, a new puppy plays a part in the Connolly's
recovery. Every day, I'm thankful Simon Dionysus Reardon
found his way home. Maybe he didn't inspire the name of
the main character, but there is no doubt he left his mark
on *Finding Jake*. ◠

Reading Group Guide

1. Who is Jake Connolly? Does Simon have a good understanding of his son's personality?

2. Most parents assume they know their children well. How true is that assumption? Should parents know everything about their children? Where is the line between privacy and parenting?

3. Are Simon and Jake introverts? Is *introvert* a bad word? Could Simon have done more to teach Jake to be social?

4. As more fathers stay at home with their children, has it become a socially acceptable family paradigm? How do you think stay-at-home dads are really seen in our society? How do you think stay-at-home dads view their decision to buck social norms? Would you want Simon at a playdate?

5. Why does Simon struggle to fit in with the other stay-at-home parents? Is it his own insecurities, or their discomfort? What could Simon have done to be more approachable and social?

6. Is *Finding Jake* about a school shooting or about the more mundane challenges of modern parenting? How have parenting methods changed from past generations? How might changing parenting methods influence society? Can parents prevent tragedy? ▶

7. Does the media's response to the shooting and to Jake and Doug ring true today? Do you find yourself delving into the lives of those struck by tragedy? Or those responsible for it?

8. Simon experiences a moment of parental pride when he tells Jake he should always be nice to people, even if others are not. Did that advice contribute to the shooting? Should Simon have gone back to that advice and felt responsible? Or was that just one of a myriad of mistakes he thought he made? Can a parent's influence on a child ever truly be predicted?

9. Do Simon and Rachel still love one another? What factors influence the change in their relationship? Can they survive together? In what ways can raising children challenge a marriage/relationship?

10. Could events have been changed if Jake talked openly with his father about his life and school? Do any children tell their parents *everything*? Does a parent really want to know everything? Where is the line between protecting your child and letting him or her grow up?

11. Did the ending surprise you? What, if any, aspects of the story led you to believe it would end differently? What other ways could the story have ended?

12. Which character did you like or relate to the most? Which the least?

Do you have to love a character to enjoy a book?

13. How responsible is a parent for their children's actions? In a tragic situation such as this, is it fair to blame parents for not seeing what was coming?

14. There are certainly challenges that face stay-at-home dads, and the perspective here is Simon's, but how do you imagine that scenario affects the mothers who work? Is there guilt or resentment on the mother's part that she is not home with her children? Is there too much pressure to be the primary income earner? Does she lose her maternal instincts or feel that she has been denied a natural role? What price do these families pay to break the norm? ◠